Not a
Girl Detective

Also by Susan Kandel
in Large Print:

I Dreamed I Married Perry Mason

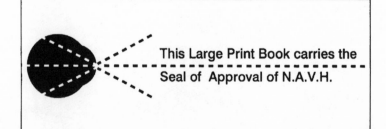

Not a
Girl Detective

Susan Kandel

Thorndike Press • Waterville, Maine

Published in 2005 by arrangement with William Morrow, an imprint of HarperCollins Publishers.

Thorndike Press® Large Print Americana.

The tree indicium is a trademark of Thorndike Press.

The text of this Large Print edition is unabridged.
Other aspects of the book may vary from the original edition.

Set in 16 pt. Plantin by Christina S. Huff.

Printed in the United States on permanent paper.

Library of Congress Cataloging-in-Publication Data

Kandel, Susan, 1961–
    Not a girl detective / by Susan Kandel.
        p. cm. — (Thorndike Press large print Americana)
    ISBN 0-7862-8103-0 (lg. print : hc : alk. paper)
    1. Caruso, Cece (Fictitious character) — Fiction.
2. Women biographers — Fiction. 3. California — Fiction.
4. Large type books. I. Title. II. Thorndike Press large print Americana series.
    PS3611.A53N68 2005
    813'.6—dc22   2005021175

This book is a work of fiction. References to real people, events, establishments, organizations, or locales are intended only to provide a sense of authenticity, and are used fictitiously. All other characters, and all incidents and dialogue, are drawn from the author's imagination and are not to be construed as real.

Library of Congress Cataloging-in-Publication Data
Kandel, Susan, 1961–
Not a girl detective : a Cece Caruso mystery / Susan Kandel.
— 1st ed.
p. cm.
isbn 0-06-058107-7 (alk. paper)
1. Women biographers — Fiction. 2. California — Fiction.
I. Title.
PS3611.A53B55 2005
813'.6 — dc222004055963

As the Founder/CEO of NAVH, the only national health agency solely devoted to those who, although not totally blind, have an eye disease which could lead to serious visual impairment, I am pleased to recognize Thorndike Press★ as one of the leading publishers in the large print field.

Founded in 1954 in San Francisco to prepare large print textbooks for partially seeing children, NAVH became the pioneer and standard setting agency in the preparation of large type.

Today, those publishers who meet our standards carry the prestigious "Seal of Approval" indicating high quality large print. We are delighted that Thorndike Press is one of the publishers whose titles meet these standards. We are also pleased to recognize the significant contribution Thorndike Press is making in this important and growing field.

Lorraine H. Marchi, L.H.D.
Founder/CEO
NAVH

★ Thorndike Press encompasses the following imprints: Thorndike, Wheeler, Walker and Large Print Press.

Acknowledgments

Once again I am grateful to my friends and family, who were always ready with kind words and good ideas. As if I weren't lucky enough on that count, I have Sandra Dijkstra for an agent and Carolyn Marino for an editor. These women know what it means to go the extra mile. Likewise Angela Tedesco of HarperCollins, who has worked tirelessly on my behalf.

The Nancy Drew literature is extensive, but of particular use to me were the collector's bible, *Farah's Guide*, by David Farah, and Betsy Caprio's *Girl Sleuth on the Couch: The Mystery of Nancy Drew*. A special thanks to Jenn Fisher, president of the fan group, Nancy Drew Sleuths, who allowed me to infiltrate the 2003 Sleuths convention and arranged for access to the Stratemeyer Archive at the New York Public Library. Jenn, as well as the other Sleuths I met in New York, impressed me greatly with their knowledge and generosity.

None of this, of course, would be possible

without my husband, Peter Lunenfeld. Unlike Nancy Drew's "special friend," Ned Nickerson, Peter has the patience of a saint — without, thankfully, being one.

1

When I couldn't tell the rain from my tears I knew it was time to pull over. I laid my arms across the steering wheel and choked back a sob. I had gone through the first four stages of grief: denial, anger, bargaining, depression. Now I was stuck on stage five — damning the mechanic. But what good was that going to do? My Toyota Camry was dying. Not peacefully but spectacularly, with great plumes of smoke emanating from the rear and strange wails coming out of the air-conditioning vents.

Yesterday, the tape deck shredded Frank Sinatra's greatest hits. The day before, the cup holder snapped off in my hands, sending Diet Coke all over my favorite beaded sweater. Hell, if I had known it was going to end like this, I would've leased a Jaguar in the first place.

If only I were the cheerful sort, like my best friend Lael. It's unseemly how cheerful Lael is. That's all I'll say. Or conniving, like my second best friend, Bridget, who knows just what to say when, and to whom. Scary. Or better yet, the resourceful type, like teenage supersleuth Nancy Drew. I spent my entire youth idolizing that girl. I'm pushing forty now, but some fantasies die hard.

If only I were Nancy Drew.

I'd pull some Vaseline out of my handbag and fix those windshield wipers lickety-split. I'd solve the mystery of the air-conditioning vents with my superior knowledge of dehumidification, say. And if I couldn't get the car to stop smoking by any other means, I'd ask my daddy to buy me a new one. A pretty blue roadster to match my pretty blue eyes.

Self-recrimination has long been a favorite pastime. I could keep it going forever, but I had someplace to be. I opened the car door and stepped directly into a puddle. Damn. With my raincoat pulled up over my head, I waded around back and stared at the exhaust pipe in wonder. How could it betray me? Vexed, I gave it a kick. It belched, evil thing. Then it occurred to me that it could explode any second — the whole car, I mean. These things do happen. But I was such a sodden mess I probably wasn't combustible. And they say it never rains in Southern California.

I fished my cell phone out of my purse and was about to call for a tow when I realized the bookstore I was heading to was only a few blocks away. I decided to make a run for it. That would be the end of my spike-heeled boots, of course, but they were already halfway to kingdom come. Maybe I could claim them as a business expense. I'd been taking a more aggressive approach to tax deductions lately. My accountant's thinking was that I made so little money they'd never in a million years bother auditing me. I wasn't sure that was sound reasoning, but Mr. Keshigian had managed to keep all his gangster relations out of the hands of the IRS, so I could hardly question his expertise. And god forbid he should fix me up with one of the cousins again.

Dodging the mud puddles, I sprinted down Melrose Avenue. No one sipping organic coffee at the Bodhisattva Café today. What a neighborhood. On sunny days you could drop your car with the Bodhisattva's valet, pick up a soy latte to go, and in the space of a single city block have your palm read, buy a New Age tome, get your colon cleaned, and take a ceramics class — not necessarily in that order. It wasn't my thing. I grew up in New Jersey. I live for synthetics.

11

Frederick A. Dalthorp Rare Books and Bindery was just around the corner, and talk about synthetic. It had fake gothic spires poking into the sky, stained-glass windows, turrets. No serving wenches, however. Too bad. I could've used a tankard of ale right about then. Nope, just the Dalthorp twins. They'd inherited the business from their father, Frederick, a smooth operator who'd sweet-talked the building out of some morticians who'd been there since the thirties. The Dalthorps were cousins of my purported boyfriend, Peter Gambino. A few weekends ago we'd had brunch together and they'd made a big to-do over Gambino's mocha chip pancakes, which I found impossible to stomach myself. But those girls were clearly addicted to sugar. They were eating marzipan at their desks when I pushed open the massive wooden door.

"Heave ho!" I said.

"For god's sake, don't spray the books!" yelled Dena, the older of the two by seventeen minutes and accustomed to milking every one of them.

"What do you think I am, a Saint Bernard?"

"Oh, Cece," murmured Victoria, Dena's more politic sister, "look at your turtleneck!

It shrank in the rain!" She handed me a wad of paper towels.

"It's cropped," I explained, drying off. "It's supposed to be that way. It matches my cropped toreador pants."

"Good god," said Dena. Dena did not appreciate fashion. She was wearing a shapeless woolen sweater, a longish kilt, and brogues. Perfect for stomping through the heather.

Victoria gave me a sympathetic look. "I'm sure you looked lovely."

"Thank you," I said, crushed by her use of the past tense.

"The seventies, right?"

"The fifties, actually. Gina Lollabrigida goes beatnik?"

I was used to being misunderstood. My mother, a rummage-sale diva, never met a pot holder she couldn't love. Or a TV tray table not worth saving. She'd happily plunk down five dollars for a moribund blender, ten dollars for a card table with three legs. Yet she was unable to figure out why I'd want to wear old clothes. Worse yet, somebody else's old clothes.

"So what's this about Nancy Drew?" Dena asked.

The chitchat was over.

"Cece's writing a book about Nancy

Drew!" Victoria exclaimed. "Remember how much we loved Nancy Drew when we were kids? Twisted candles flickering at midnight! Bloodcurdling screams and secret passageways! But we didn't have an attic," she said, sighing. "Nobody in L.A. does. And how could we be detectives without a musty attic to explore?"

"There are plenty of mysteries to solve around this moldering old relic," Dena snapped. "Like why the pipes are always backed up. And where my favorite coffee mug went. Why don't you solve them?"

Thank god I had brothers. They just slugged you.

I slid into a leather club chair. "Actually, my book isn't exactly about Nancy Drew. It's a biography of Carolyn Keene, the author of the series."

"There is no Carolyn Keene," Dena said with a smirk.

"Technically, that's true."

"Dena was the one who told me there was no Santa Claus," Victoria whispered.

"A number of different people wrote the Nancy Drew books," I continued, "based on detailed outlines they were given by the publishing syndicate that originated the character. The Stratemeyer Syndicate was an actual writing mill. They put out the

Hardy Boys, the Bobbsey Twins, dozens of children's series. Anyway, the real identities of the writers they hired were unknown for decades. Everybody took oaths of secrecy. It was pretty cloak-and-dagger. Carolyn Keene was just a made-up name."

"So you're writing a biography of a pseudonym?" Victoria asked.

It did sound perverse when you put it that way.

"Look, why don't we show Cece what we've got, okay?"

"Good idea, Dena. I don't want to keep you." There's your sister's ego to crush and marzipan bananas to finish and it's already four in the afternoon.

She pointed me toward a rickety glass-fronted bookcase in the corner of the room. "We don't usually handle children's books. We had a beautiful first edition of *Robinson Crusoe* that sat here collecting dust for years."

"Well, you did scare off that buyer from Baltimore, remember?"

Dena glared at her twin. "He was a big phony."

"Was not."

"Was too."

As they continued bickering, I opened the cabinet and reached for the white dust jacket. I ran my finger over the familiar emblem on the spine, a tiny silhouette of the blond sleuth from River Heights, looking through a magnifying glass, a scarf thrown jauntily around her neck. The girl could definitely wear clothes.

The Mystery of the Ivory Charm. If I remembered correctly, *The Mystery of the Ivory Charm* featured a strange woman who was trying to deny a rajah his throne. She could go into a hypnotic trance at the drop of a hat, but Nancy saw through her, of course.

I pulled the book off the shelf and turned to the front cover. There she was, Nancy Drew, looking typically surreptitious. She was inside an old shed, sneaking some yellowed documents out of a coffeepot and trying not to get caught. The bad guy was just outside the open door. You knew he was the bad guy because he was going after a mangy hound dog with his leather whip. In Nancy Drew books — as in life, I suppose — you can always identify evildoers because they're the ones who mistreat animals.

Most of the dust jackets I'd seen were tattered, missing bits and pieces. This one was in perfect condition. I ran my fingers over the pages. They felt rough. This was definitely wartime paper, which meant it couldn't be a first edition. The other tip-off was the silhouette, which didn't appear on the spines until 1941, with the second printing of number 18, and subsequent reprintings of numbers 1 to 17.

Dating and assigning valuations to these books was tricky. The first Nancy Drew mystery, *The Secret of the Old Clock*, has been reprinted more than one hundred and fifty times since its original appearance in 1930, with minute variations each time — different paper stocks, boards, endpapers, frontispieces, etc. You'd have to be obsessive-compulsive to keep track of all the details. I'd love to be obsessive-compulsive but I'm too lazy. Still, I was pleased that some of my research had stuck.

"Do you have a buyer already?"

Victoria took the book out of my hands. "Yes, someone local. He wants everything we can get, first edition or not."

"Sticky fingers!" reprimanded Dena.

"You've eaten more candy than I have," Victoria said with a sniff. She turned toward me. "This would be a great thing to own, wouldn't it? A piece of American history! The first role model for teenage girls, ever!"

It seemed churlish to mention Joan of Arc.

"Say, Cece, why don't you deliver it for us?"

"Did you forget to pay the courier service again, Victoria?"

Victoria ignored her sister and started wrapping the book in brown paper. "I bet he'd love to hear about your research. And it would give you a chance to see his collection. It's amazing. I believe he has the only complete set of Nancy Drew first printings in the world!"

How interesting that it would be a man. "I'd be happy to deliver the book."

"Hold your horses," Dena said, squinting at me suspiciously. "Are you bonded?"

This time, it was me who ignored her.

Tucking *The Mystery of the Ivory Charm* under my coat, I stepped out into paradise. Double rainbows streaked across the sky. A soft wind caressed my cheeks. The Bodhisattva Café was packed, the laughter of hemp-clad sybarites filling the air. It was as if the rainstorm had never happened. As if it were a bad dream some colon hydrotherapy had dissolved. This is why people move to Los Angeles. You can live in a permanent state of denial here. Except when it comes to meter maids. They are the hardiest of all urban tribes and one of them was eyeing my Camry. Once her pen touched paper it would be too late. I ran toward her, screaming at the top of my lungs.

"Back off, sweetie," she said, putting her pad back into her pocket. "You made it." Then she shook her tightly coiffed head. "You got enough trouble with those sorry-ass boots."

I was blessed, I think. But there was only one way to know for sure. I held my breath, got in, and turned the key in the ignition. It wheezed and spat and quaked and shook, but my car was alive. Alive! I knew I should probably drive straight to the dealership on Hollywood Boulevard, but I had so much to take care of, and that would be the end of my day. Once those guys get you in their clutches they just keep on talking. No, I'd take the car home and go to the dealer first thing in the morning. They'd probably need a few days to whip it into shape, which was fine. It gave me a perfect excuse to rent a car for the weekend.

A convertible.

I could see it now.

Me and Lael and Bridget, gunning down the 10 toward Palm Springs, the wind whipping through our big hair. We all had big hair. Maybe we'd put the top up if it got too windy. Wind strips the hair of moisture. I guess we could wear scarves.

The three of us were taking a business trip. Well, at least for me it was business. I'd been asked to deliver the keynote address at the annual Nancy Drew fan convention. Some persons in my life had found the very idea amusing. Like my daughter, Annie, and her husband, Vincent, who about choked on their Kombucha mushroom tea when I told them. And a certain Detective Peter Gambino of the LAPD, whom I might have mentioned earlier. But Mr. Keshigian had nodded, pleased. I was to deduct everything.

It was a paycheck, for god's sake. When you write biographies of dead mystery writers for a living, you need as many of those as you can get. And it would be great publicity for the new book, which was almost finished. But I was nervous. Those fans knew a hell of a lot, and they'd probably love to catch me in a mistake, like not knowing that the spine silhouette for number 24 was missing the scarf. Or that early printings of number 18, *The Mystery at the Moss-Covered Mansion*, made reference to the forthcoming volume as *The Quest of the Telltale Map* when it was actually printed as *The Quest of the* Missing *Map*.

Fan is short for fanatic.

Bridget was going to take the opportunity to raid the Palm Springs thrift shops, hoping to find a couple of Bob Hope's wife's discarded Adolfo suits, maybe something with a mink collar and jeweled buttons. Or a Galanos caftan, very Nancy Reagan on holiday. Bridget owned On the Bias, L.A.'s top vintage clothing shop.

Lael was a master pastry chef and oblivious to clothes, vintage or otherwise, but she didn't have any gigs until late next week, and her children's fathers (that would be four for four) were taking the kids for spring break, so she was coming, too.

Not for Nancy Drew. My lusty friend had no patience for professional virgins.

Not for the sunshine. Lael was a Norwegian blonde who freckled like crazy.

I think she wanted an adventure.

Me, too.

We should have remembered that when it rains, it pours.

2

I'm the sort of person who's always looking for signs. And when you're the sort of person who's always looking for signs, you tend to find them. When I was a kid, for example, I had a knothole on the floor of my bedroom that looked exactly like Abraham Lincoln. I was sure this meant I was destined for greatness. Then, one day, my mother announced her intention of installing shag carpeting throughout the house. I begged her not to — or at least to spare this particular spot. I didn't see why the carpet guys couldn't cut a hole around our sixteenth president's head. It was in the corner. Who would notice? After regaling my brothers with the tale, however, she went ahead with her plans for wall-to-wall respectability, thereby dooming me to an ordinary life. But that's another story.

This morning, I had a sign. Several, actually. The first materialized at Hollywood Toyota. A more unlikely spot you could hardly imagine. And things kept getting unlikelier by the minute.

First of all there was the service manager's demeanor, which went from aloof to abashed after one look under my hood. It seemed my crack mechanic had forgotten to put the oil cap back on when he'd serviced my car two weeks ago, which didn't sound like such a big deal until Maynard explained the gravity of the error.

Over the course of the subsequent fourteen days, nearly three quarts of motor oil had bubbled up, coating the outside instead of the inside of my engine and nearly locking up the pistons in the process. Maynard took my hand as he broke the news. My car had had a coronary. But there was no need to panic. He'd get his best guy to fix it up, wash it down, relube everything, and replace the cup holder and tape deck, too. And because this mess was their fault, he'd be providing me with a loaner, free of charge, one from his own collection — a real classic. Before I could say boo, he wheeled me around and pointed toward a baby-blue Cadillac.

A convertible.

My jaw dropped. He beamed. I went starry-eyed. He turned red. There was a dent on the passenger side, a missing rear taillight, and a vanity plate that read

SMUTHE, but I'd still call that car one hell of a sign.

"Maynard, are you sure?" This couldn't be happening.

"Ms. Caruso," he said, "a pretty lady like you shouldn't worry so much."

He was smuthe all right.

"Here's the long and short of it. I'm selling the car. A guy is coming down from Merced the first of next month. You know where Merced is, right?"

"Right." Wrong.

"And, maybe you noticed, I don't know, but there's a little touch-up work I have to take care of. Nineteen sixty-nine wasn't yesterday. But I got time, you're a good customer, what the hey." He ran his thick fingers over a nick on the hood. "That one I'm not touching," he said. "It adds to the patina, right?"

"Right." Wrong.

He tossed me the keys. "Don't do anything I wouldn't do."

I wouldn't have loaned me the car, which I think gave me a lot of leeway.

I had to show somebody. My daughter and son-in-law lived too far away. Lael was probably busy getting the kids' things packed up for their vacations. Gambino was in Buffalo for his parents' fiftieth wedding anniversary. That left Bridget. Her shop was sort of on my way home.

I started up the engine and backed out of the driveway. Maynard gave me an enthusiastic thumbs-up. I reciprocated and narrowly avoided plowing into a Chevy Nova parked at the curb. Good thing I had fast reflexes.

After that, it was smooth sailing. I'd never been so far away from my front bumper. The world felt liquid. Captain Cece Caruso.

New perspectives engender new insights. The farther west I ventured, for example, the thinner the pedestrians and the thicker the foliage. Had to be a money thing. Not that there were many pedestrians. Another money thing. Not that I'm getting into that. It's just that I was heading to Bridget's, where clothes are sold, and I'm addicted to clothes, which cost money, which is a sore spot for me. The money thing. But I'm not getting into that.

Fifteen minutes later, I'd arrived at the brick building on Burton Way in Beverly Hills. There was a space in front, but the jacarandas were in bloom and I was wary of their blossoms. They might stain the tan upholstery. Worse yet, my zebra-striped wrap dress (Diane von Furstenberg, 1977). Also, there really wasn't enough room. I docked by a hydrant. I'd only be a second.

The bell on the celadon-and-gold door jingle-jangled. Bridget's new intern jumped to his feet. He had been sitting on her Louis XIV desk. Even though it was a reproduction and he looked like a rock star, this did not bode well. He said the boss was in back, sorting through some clothes that had just arrived.

Bridget's dachshund, Helmut, led the way. The dog seemed upset.

"What's wrong, boy?" I asked, bending down to pat his head.

"Hi, Cece!" Bridget's Afro poked up out of a clingy mini-cocoon of hot-pink chiffon pleats.

Helmut looked up at me beseechingly.

"Isn't this so *Valley of the Dolls*? I never thought a baby-doll halter dress would work on me. I need hot-pink tights to match and I'm set!"

"For what?"

"That's not the point, as you very well know," she scolded. "Helmut, stop that!" Helmut was trying to bite the wire used to crimp the lettuce-edge hem of the dress. "It's by Travilla, the king of pleats!"

"What does Helmut care?"

"That dog knows more about vintage fashion than most of my clients."

"And he's trying to tell you something."

"Oh, please. Travilla was brilliant. Do you know what he said? He said when he died he didn't want to be cremated, he wanted to be pleated."

"Not to change the subject, but you've got to see the car we're taking this weekend."

"What's wrong with the Camry?"

"It's unwell."

She slipped into a pair of heels and scooped up Helmut, who started licking the ceramic brooch pinned to her dress's peculiarly Elizabethan collar.

"No, baby," she said firmly. "We don't want you to get lead poisoning."

"You look amazing," the intern murmured as we swept by him on our way out.

"Thank you," Bridget said. Her tone was lofty, but she looked like the cat who'd eaten the canary.

"Anything you need to tell me?" I asked once we were outside.

She gave me a wicked grin, the whites of her eyes gleaming against her ebony skin. "Do you want details?"

"You and the intern?"

"His name is Andrew. And he's the only straight man I've ever met who knows how to pronounce *m-a-i-l-l-o-t*."

"My-oh."

"You're a woman."

Bridget walked around the convertible slowly, studying every inch of it with a jaundiced eye. Then she paused significantly.

"Does it have power windows?"

"Why do I bother with you?" I said, climbing back in.

"The same reason I bother with you," she said. "True friends are hard to come by."

"You'd sell me out for a power window."

"Lighten up, honey. What time Friday?"

"Bright and early," I said, waving goodbye.

"Is there enough room for all our clothes?" she shouted after me.

"I am not renting a U-Haul!" Famous last words.

It was a quarter past ten when I got home, home being a 1932 Spanish bungalow in West Hollywood I'd bought with the proceeds from my divorce settlement almost ten years ago. The house, and a Makita power drill. Also Mimi the cat, whom I'd envisioned as a sort of substitute father for my daughter. Mimi was still around. Likewise the drill. The real surprise was that the house hadn't fallen down.

It was a wonderful house, don't get me wrong, but it required near-constant maintenance. A fearless electrician. A plumber who didn't consider emergency calls at three in the morning an imposition. Fungicide for the mushrooms that grew every once in a while out of the cracks in the vintage turquoise tile shower. But it was mine, all twenty-two hundred square feet of it — a good percentage of which were supposedly sinking into the foundation, but I didn't trust that guy. I'd gotten his name from a flyer tucked under my welcome mat. Structural engineers should not have to advertise door-to-door.

The mail had been delivered early. I poured myself a cup of coffee and sat down at the kitchen table. Bills, bills, junk mail, and more bills. Despite my many communiqués, the electric company persisted in addressing me as "Fleece Caruso." I plucked a thick manila envelope from the stack. At least my seeds had arrived. I spilled the brightly colored packages onto the table. This year I'd selected the giant edible sunflowers known as Sunzilla, Baby Ball Dutch beets, Chelsea Prize F-1 cucumbers, tricolor cherry tomatoes, a custom mixture of radishes in rainbow shades of red, white, purple, and pink, some haricots verts, and slow-bolt cilantro. I was cutting back after being overly ambitious last year. No eggplant.

I let Mimi and my teacup poodle Buster

play with the padded envelope while I opened a letter from Clarissa Olsen, the president of the Nancy Drew Society of Chums.

Clarissa Olsen was a stalker. She'd found me after reading an announcement in Publishers Lunch about my upcoming book on Carolyn Keene. You could call her impassioned, I suppose. A fervent believer in the goddess that is Nancy Drew. Other things, too, like plain, old-fashioned correspondence. E-mail was crass and beneath her dignity, but postings on the Nancy Drew Society of Chums Listserv were acceptable. Phone calls were acceptable, too, but only if they dragged me away from *All My Children.* And it was always urgent.

Initially I'd been put off by Clarissa's ferocity. But after a while I'd actually taken a liking to her, despite her proud claim that her daughter had graduated from high school never having eaten a store-bought cookie. I'd had my daughter when I was barely out of high school myself, and had felt less impassioned than imprisoned, but that was all about my ex, not Annie, who'd always seemed perfectly happy with Chips Ahoy.

Anyway, Clarissa wanted to remind me of two last-minute things.

Number one, my speech should run forty-five minutes and not a millisecond longer because the scavenger hunt would follow immediately thereafter.

I stopped right there. Number one alarmed me. It would seem I'd miscalculated. Again.

For weeks I'd been logging onto the Chums' Web site and clicking on the postage stamp–size dust jackets of the "Blue Nancys," the original books published in the thirties. There, in my uninsulated garage office, by the virtual light of my computer screen, I'd ponder the details of Nancy's face. Her bright eyes. Her pert nose. Her blond bob. I've been told I have nice eyes, but my nose is less pert than handsome, and my brown hair — well, on a good day it lacks discipline, and on a bad day it looks like Don King's. Nancy Drew and me: no resemblance whatsoever. So why, then, every time I'd look at her, did I feel so unnerved, like when you catch sight of yourself unexpectedly in a mirror? How, I'd wonder, can *she* be *me?* I suppose a shrink would say I suffer from a pathological overidentification with my subject. It wouldn't be the first time. It's a biographer thing.

To make a long story short, I'd dumped

my assigned topic, "The Changing Demographics of River Heights," and penned an elegy to Grace Horton, the otherwise unknown New York model who'd posed for those covers. I was captivated — not least with the irony of Grace Horton, a working girl, incarnating Nancy Drew, the privileged amateur. And they were going to hate it. Nobody who likes a scavenger hunt could possibly like a Marxist feminist critique.

Well, I wasn't there to wow them. I was there to make a contribution to human knowledge. And to the sleuth-themed gift exchange. That was reminder number two. Bring something simple and preferably homemade. Maybe I could crochet a magnifying glass.

I stuck Clarissa's letter inside a Lillian Vernon catalog and went into the living room. Mimi and Buster had strewn padded envelope stuffing all over the place. Now they were playing with the mohair sweater I'd left on the couch, the object of the game being to shed as many hairs as possible onto it. I pulled it out from under them, checked my watch, grabbed my purse, and headed out the door. What was I doing puttering around? I'd promised Edgar Edwards I'd deliver the Nancy Drew book to him before noon.

I'd forgotten that Wednesday was street-cleaning day. There was a big fat ticket on the windshield of the Caddy.

Speaking of signs, that wasn't one.

I pulled up to Edgar Edwards's house at 1111 Carroll Avenue. It was 11:11 a.m.

All the hallmarks of a sign, but no.

I walked up the steps and reached into my purse for the book. Its brown paper wrapper was shredded to bits.

Definitely a sign.

And not what I'd call a good one.

3

Most people don't find out about Carroll Avenue until they get lost on their way to Dodger Stadium, which means that if you've got a good sense of direction or you don't like baseball, you've probably never heard of it.

Carroll Avenue is the land time forgot. Urban renewal, too. Picture a secret enclave of restored Victorians, painted teal or lilac or midnight blue. Spindly verandas, open belvedere towers, and antique streetlights. Hitching posts at curbside — real ones, not replicas from the Restoration Hardware catalog. People actually navigated this city before they invented the car. By *horse*. It boggled the mind.

Edgar Edwards lived in a rather grand-looking Queen Anne with a third-story porch and a wrought iron railing crowning the roof. I walked up the moss-covered steps. There were no moss-covered steps in L.A. It wasn't humid enough. Those he'd definitely ordered from a catalog. I pushed the buzzer but didn't hear anything, which was why I was somewhat unnerved when a very tall, very bald man opened the door.

I stepped back as he stepped closer. His smile was unctuous, like an undertaker's.

"Yes?"

"I'm Cece Caruso. We spoke on the phone."

"We most certainly did not," he said, still smiling.

"Aren't you Edgar Edwards?"

"Do I look like Edgar Edwards?"

"I have no idea."

"Of course you don't. Let me introduce myself." He put out his hand, which was soft and slightly damp. "I'm Mr. Edwards's curator. My name is Mitchell Honey. Not 'Mitchell, honey,' just plain old Mitchell Honey."

I would be making this fast.

"Nice to meet you. Is Mr. Edwards here? He's expecting me."

"That he is. Follow me."

The interior had a gloomy sort of allure. A small Tiffany lamp in the vestibule shed not enough light onto the gleaming dark wood paneling. Heavy Oriental rugs muffled our footsteps as we walked down the hall and into the living room, where velvet curtains obscured the midday sun. Mitchell Honey sneezed, and a log fell in the fireplace, sending a shower of sparks flying.

"Damn allergies. This way, please."

We entered a hexagonal room stuffed with antique furniture — hulking armoires, narrow cabinets, carved end tables. There were no windows. The air was stale. Everywhere I looked there were ceramic statues of creepy things: eagles with squirrels in their beaks; trolls sticking their fingers into other trolls' mouths; laughing mice. The dark side of Wedgwood, I guess.

"Mr. Edwards has an encyclopedic collection of British art pottery," said Mitchell, who was sandwiched between a pair of three-drawer chests. The ceiling was so low he was stooping, which added to his general air of obsequiousness.

"A lot of pots," I said, studying a satyr hanging off the spout of a teapot.

"A lot of money." The low voice came out of nowhere.

"Jake, please. We have company."

Jake sidled in. He didn't need much room. He was the sort of skinny guy who wore his jeans half falling off his ass because someone had once told him it was sexy.

"Right," he said, rolling his eyes. Ennui became him, but Mitchell, blowing his nose, didn't want to know about it.

"Do you have an extra hundred bucks?" Jake asked, swinging his leg over a small chair with a needlepoint seat.

"Careful!"

"Sorry. Edgar said it'd be okay. I didn't have time to make it to the bank."

Mitchell pulled out his wallet and counted out five crisp twenties.

"Later."

"You're welcome," said another voice, this one deep and sonorous.

"Edgar," Jake said. He hiked up his pants, which promptly slid back down. "I didn't know you were standing there."

Mitchell looked triumphant.

"Don't look so triumphant, Mitchell," the older man said, his gaze going right to Jake's jutting hipbones.

"About what?" Jake asked.

Edgar sighed, tugging at his salt-and-pepper beard. He was heavyset but moved with stealth, a lion intent on dinner. "And you must be Cece. I'm Edgar. Welcome."

"Am I interrupting something?"

"Not at all. What do you think of my babies?"

Mitchell Honey and Jake? They'd go over great on Jerry Springer.

"I started this collection with a single monkey jar in 1978, before the prices went through the roof, and now look at me. Sotheby's calls me for advice!"

"That must be very gratifying."

"Very gratifying!" His laugh came from somewhere deep in his belly. Had I said something funny?

"This, by the way, is for you." I handed him *The Mystery of the Ivory Charm*. The shredded paper remained in my purse. Thank god the book hadn't been damaged. I swear I'd have Mimi declawed if it weren't illegal in West Hollywood. The only city in the country.

"Much obliged."

"Not at all."

"I heard all about you from the twins. You're from New Jersey."

"Asbury Park."

"Teaneck," he said, thumping his barrel chest. "And a beauty queen."

"I could tell."

"Naughty girl. I mean you."

"Strictly small-time."

"Still got the hair."

I sighed. "A genetic curse."

"*The Ghost in the Machine*. Great title."

Jeez, those girls were motormouths. "Thanks. It refers to the ghostwriters hired by the Stratemeyer Syndicate, and also to Edward Stratemeyer himself, who died two weeks after the first Nancy Drew book was published."

"I know something you don't know," he said. "Edward Stratemeyer's daughter Harriet, the one who kept Nancy Drew alive all these years, she had a heart attack, poor dear, while watching *The Wizard of Oz* for the first time on TV."

"I know something *you* don't know," I replied. "Harriet decided to revise all the original Nancy Drew books in 1959, the year Barbie was born."

"When was Ken born? That's what I want to know."

I laughed.

"What do you collect, Cece?"

"Does dust count?"

"No. Little tea sets? Salt and pepper shakers? Navajo baskets?"

"Nothing."

"Nothing?"

"Nothing."

"Funny. You look like the type." He took my arm and steered me back toward the front of the house. Mitchell followed, but Jake was already out the door.

"My Edo fans," Edgar declared proudly, gesturing to a small group of folding paper fans with delicate woodblock prints arrayed on the dining room table. "The one in the middle, with the black and gilt lacquer — that one was carried by a courtesan famous for her exquisite feet."

Corns were another one of my genetic curses.

"In seventeenth-century England, fans were an essential part of one's ensemble. They hid bad teeth. But you have lovely teeth."

"Thank you." Growing up, we had no money, but on the subject of braces, my mother had prevailed: how could I possibly be Miss New Jersey with an overbite? Not that I'd made it even close.

"Let me tell you a story," he said, pulling out a damask-covered chair.

I sat down.

"There was once a rich American collector who believed a certain rare book in his possession was unique. One day a disaster befell him. A disaster!"

I made myself comfortable. Edgar Edwards paced the floor, twirling a fan in his left hand. It was unadorned except for the carved ivory handle, which matched the crisp black-and-white graphics of his shirt.

"The poor fellow," he went on. "He discovered there was another copy of this supposedly one-of-a-kind book, in Paris. So he zipped over on the Concorde. They were screening a Dudley Moore movie, but he didn't even enjoy it, he was so anxious. After the plane landed he went straight to the other collector's house, near the Bois de Boulogne. *Très* ritzy."

It suddenly dawned on me that I'd come across this story someplace, but he'd thrown in Dudley Moore and the Concorde.

"They sipped cognac. They smoked cigars. It took a while to get down to business. When the time was right, the American made the Frenchman a good offer, but the Frenchman didn't want to sell. They went back and forth for a while until finally the American offered the Frenchman a king's ransom. The other gentleman agreed. The American wrote a check, handed it to his rival, took the book, examined it carefully, and then hurled it into the fire." He paused. "Can you tell me why?"

I couldn't resist. "He wanted to own the only copy of the book."

Edgar snapped the fan he'd been holding shut. "Very good."

Bad Cece. I should've confessed prior knowledge, but for some reason I wanted this man's approval.

"Shall we take a look at my antique kitchen knives?"

"You collect those, too?"

41

"My mother was a castrating rhymes-with-witch. It was a no-brainer."

"I think we might have something in common."

"We have a lot in common," he said, studying me intently. "Ever heard of a glitter trap?"

"I don't think so."

"You set it up over a person's desk. You run a string from the back of one of the drawers, up the wall, into an acoustic tile ceiling. You've got to have an acoustic tile ceiling."

I nodded.

"When the person goes to open the drawer, boom!"

Boom! I nodded again.

"It triggers a mousetrap. Snap!"

Snap!

"Up snaps a thin card covering a funnel, releasing a handful of glitter which falls through a hole in the ceiling tile onto the person's head."

"You have a very lyrical sense of humor."

"First, the muffled noise, then the slow, glittery descent of a cloud of brightly colored dust. You get me, Cece, unlike certain persons in my employ. I set a glitter trap for Mitchell yesterday. He was positively kerflummoxed, poor thing."

"I can hear every word you're saying," Mitchell yelled from the other room.

"I used to place strands of hair across my *Charlie's Angels* diary so I'd know if my brothers were trying to read it," I volunteered.

"Were they?"

"They couldn't have cared less."

"Let's nix the knives. I want to show you my Nancy Drews."

At last.

The stairs were covered with a rose-patterned kilim.

"Is it from Turkey?" I asked, following him up. Gambino and his first wife had gone to Turkey on their honeymoon. He'd kept the rug.

"Turkey by way of Pottery Barn," Mitchell interjected snarkily from the bottom of the staircase.

"Be a dear and marinate the chicken," Edgar yelled without turning his head.

We entered a small bedroom decorated all in blue — blue carpeting, blue floral wallpaper, blue checkered bedspread, and three narrow blue bookcases holding Edgar Edwards's world-famous collection of Nancy Drews.

"Blue was my mother's favorite color," he said. "She used to stay in this room when she visited."

"Did she get you started on Nancy Drew?"

"Don't get me started on what that woman got me started on."

He ran his finger across the top row of books, pristine in their blue linen covers and sparkling white dust jackets. The first thirty-eight Nancy Drew titles were released by Grosset & Dunlap between 1930 and 1961. Of these, the first twenty-five are considered the real deal, and all but three of those were written by an intrepid former *Toledo Blade* reporter named Mildred Wirt Benson. (Mildred bolted temporarily when the syndicate wanted to cut her pay from $125 to $75 per book during the height of the Great Depression, but came back at her usual fee for *The Clue of the Broken Locket*.)

"My Blue Nancys," he said. "Never been touched — well, more or less. Like our heroine, come to think of it!"

"May I?"

He handed me some thin white gloves. "Please."

I put on the gloves and pulled out a copy of *The Sign of the Twisted Candles*, which had my favorite cover. Grace Horton/Nancy Drew was wearing a white cloche hat pulled down low over her eyes, a white satin dress with a skinny red patent leather belt and matching clutch purse, plus strappy white stilettos. Russell Tandy, the illustrator, made his career in fashion and it showed. He loved Grace/Nancy in red and white.

"You'd look good in that," said Edgar.

"Actually, I think I'd look better in this," I said, pulling out *The Message in the Hollow Oak*, which featured Grace/Nancy in a honey-colored bias-cut skirt and navy-blue cropped jacket, very foxy-girl-on-the-go.

"Oh, yes. You're absolutely right."

There was also a complete set of "Yellow Nancys," which comprised the revised texts to books 1 through 38, plus 39 through 56. These had no dust jackets and yellow, wraparound covers.

"These are the versions I read as a kid," I said wistfully. "Of course, my mother threw them all out."

Edgar shook his head.

Oh, how I'd loved those stories. Nancy was everything I wasn't. Brave. Forthright. Not Italian. Best of all, she didn't have a mother. Her life was a Freudian fantasy come true. Just a girl, her father, and a housekeeper. You had to love Hannah Gruen. The woman could take phone messages like nobody's business, make a dozen different puddings from scratch, and pack Nancy's bags on a moment's notice. Day dresses, evening gowns, tennis skirts, scuba gear — whatever might be required for a teenager pursuing the truth in such far-flung spots as Hong Kong, Scotland, and darkest Peru. What mother would do that? What about frigging homework?

Back then, of course, I'd had no idea that the Yellow Nancys were considered highly suspect — not by Freudians, but by conspiracy theorists in the Society of Chums. They frothed at the mouth at the mere mention of them. The official, Stratemeyer-sanctioned story was that Mildred's Blue Nancy texts needed to be revised because they were dated — full of forgotten colloquialisms and racist innuendoes. Villains were inevitably dark and swarthy (Jewish) or drunk and mentally deficient (African-American). True enough. But the conspiracy theorists insisted that this was not the only reason for the revisions.

There was also the fact that Harriet Stratemeyer Adams, who'd taken over the syndicate after her father's death, wanted to cut the cost of production by decreasing the number of pages in each book. And that she wanted to transform Nancy into a more passive, traditionally feminine heroine, not unlike Barbie. But the real reason for the revisions, the conspiracy theorists claimed,

46

was so that Harriet, by virtue of these changes, could once and for all lay claim to the mantle of authorship — to the hallowed name of "Carolyn Keene."

The battle between Harriet Stratemeyer Adams and Mildred Wirt Benson over the phantom body of Carolyn Keene was the leitmotif of my chapters two through six.

"Don't you adore memorabilia?" asked Edgar, waving a Madame Alexander Nancy Drew doll in my face. "Limited release! And look!" He handed me a Nancy Drew jigsaw puzzle and a promotional poster from a 1939 Nancy Drew movie starring Bonita Granville. "You gotta love eBay, Cece!"

I was deathly afraid of eBay. God knows what trouble I could get myself into.

"One of Harpo Marx's harps was on there the other day. Did you know someone once gave Harpo a harp with barbed-wire strings? What a present! Look into it, if you don't believe me! Wish I'd thought of it!"

Another blue shelf held Edgar's foreign editions of Nancy Drew.

"In Sweden, Nancy Drew is known as Kitty," I noted, "and in Finland she's Paula."

"In France," he said, pulling out *Alice et la statue qui parle,* "she's Alice Roy. 'Nancy,' as you know, would never fly in

47

France. It's the name of an unsavory port town. Our heroine doesn't walk on the wild side."

"She missed out." Maybe I could log on to eBay just once. Intellectual curiosity.

He raised an eyebrow.

"Well, how can you be an inspiration if you spend your whole life never making a mistake?"

"I am so glad you said that."

I smiled. "I guess you could say I've lived that."

"In which case I think I've got something you'll appreciate."

He opened the door to the closet and pulled out a small oil painting in an elaborate gilt frame.

"Mitchell Honey found this little treasure for me. And I have to say, he's been beside himself ever since it came into this house. Beside himself! It's the jewel in the crown. Look! It's signed *Russell H. Tandy!*"

"Now you've gotten me curious," I said. "I thought all the original cover art burned up in a fire at the Tandy home."

"Oh, this was not a cover, dear," he said with a laugh.

Edgar held the painting up about an inch from my nose. Looking back at me was none other than blond, blue-eyed Grace Horton.

48

But she wasn't wearing red.

And she wasn't wearing white.

Grace Horton — aka the goddess that is Nancy Drew — wasn't wearing anything.

Except a killer smile.

4

"What the hell did you do to him?" The voice on the other end of the cordless phone blared in my ear.

"Who is this?" I sat up in bed and rubbed my eyes, forgetting I had fallen asleep with my contacts in. Mistake. "What time is it?"

"It's nine-thirty in the morning! Wake up! Edgar is missing! Gone! Vanished!"

"Mitchell, honey, is that you?"

"Don't get smart with me, Ms. Caruso. What did you say to him?"

"Nothing," I said, heading toward the bathroom for my robe. I couldn't possibly have a conversation with this guy naked. "What are you, his jailer?" Buster nuzzled my ankle. "I love you," I murmured.

"What?"

"Not you. Listen, he's probably out walking the dog."

"We don't own a dog. We loathe dogs." He started sneezing.

"Then he went to Starbucks for coffee." I needed coffee.

"Edgar drinks green tea."

"Starbucks has green tea."

"I don't think so."

"Maybe he's sick of green tea. Maybe he wants to live dangerously for a change."

"For a change?"

I wasn't touching that one.

"Did Edgar give you anything yesterday?" Mitchell asked abruptly.

Interesting question.

As a matter of fact, Edgar had given me something the day before, which had been kind of strange. It wasn't that he seemed the grudging sort — hardly — just someone who'd value expedience as highly as generosity. But I suppose he and I had bonded over the freakish sight of naked Nancy Drew, because as I was leaving his house, he'd put something in my hand.

It was a brand-new, shiny gold key.

"For you and your girlfriends," he'd explained. "I want you to stay at my house in Palm Springs, for the convention. I want this to be a weekend you'll never forget."

The probability of that was increasing hourly.

"Ms. Caruso, are you there?" Mitchell Honey's dulcet tones interrupted my train of thought. "Are you listening? I asked you if Edgar gave you anything yesterday?"

51

I hesitated for just a minute. "No, nothing."

"Well, you were the last one to see him."

"I left before lunch. How is that possible?"

"I left before you did — after marinating the chicken, which nobody touched, I might add."

"Fresh garlic is a must."

"Garlic is a deterrent to intimacy. Do you have issues in that area, Ms. Caruso?"

Nice. "What do you want with me, Mitchell?"

"When I came back home, sometime around midnight, everybody was out. So I went to bed. When I woke up this morning, I was still alone."

"Looks like I'm not the only one with intimacy issues."

"I have just about had it with you," he yelled. "I am calling the police and I am telling them you were the last one to see Edgar before he disappeared."

"Fine."

"Fine!"

"You do realize they won't do anything for twenty-four hours." Just enough coffee for a full pot. But nothing to eat except jam. "He's not even considered missing until then."

"How do you know that?"

"My boyfriend is a cop." Who claims to be in love with me. But talk is cheap.

"Edgar is a very powerful person. He knows the mayor. That's what I'm going to do. I'm going to call the mayor."

"Don't you think you might be overreacting a little?" I asked, spooning some jam into my mouth with my free hand. "What does Jake say?"

"I don't know where Jake is either."

"Well, there you go. They're probably together."

"You obviously don't get it. Jake often spends the night away."

The coffee would be ready soon. I wanted to drink in peace. I had to feed the pets. I had to go to the market. "Listen, I don't think I can help you with this, so good-bye." I dropped the sticky spoon into the sink. "He's going to turn up any minute. Jake, too. You shouldn't worry."

"Bitch," he muttered as he hung up.

It was way too early for this.

The phone rang again.

"You'd catch more bees with honey than vinegar, you know."

"Cece?"

"Oh, Clarissa, hi. How are you?" It was a little early for Nancy Drew–related matters. *All My Children* wasn't on for hours.

"I'm in a bit of a panic, actually."

"What's wrong?"

"It's my daughter, Nancy."

"The one who lives in L.A.? The singer?"

"Nancy is an artist who sings. And I only have one."

"Sorry."

"Well," she blurted out, "she's missing. My daughter is missing."

What the hell was going on this morning?

"What do you mean, 'missing'?"

"She hasn't answered any of my calls in days."

I sighed in relief. "Daughters are like that. You'd be in trouble if she did answer all your calls."

"We're very close."

"My daughter and I are close, too," I said, bristling, "but she doesn't jump when I call. She's got a life."

"Nancy has a life, too, believe me, but she would never do this. She's supposed to be helping out in Palm Springs this weekend, for one thing, and we needed to work out the details. She knows how important this convention is for me. And I'm supposed to fly out from Phoenix tomorrow. It's just not like her to ignore me when she knows how much I need her."

"Take a breath. It's going to be fine."

"Cece. I wouldn't ask this if it wasn't important."

Warning bells began to sound in my ears.

"Nancy doesn't live too far from where you are, out there in Hollywood."

So easily confused with Sodom.

"If you could just go by her apartment and ring the doorbell, that would be wonderful. And if she answers, that's that. Case closed. My mind would be at rest." She paused. "So you'll do that for me?" It was unclear whether she was asking or telling.

How could I say no? I really wanted to say no. I was going to say no. I said yes.

"Oh, Cece, I knew I could count on you. It's the Holly View on Orange Drive, 1337 Orange Drive."

I jotted down the address on the back of a Thai take-out menu. When I got back home, I'd be ordering mee krob for lunch. And unplugging the phone.

According to the rusted directory posted out front, Nancy Olsen lived in apartment 4B. I pushed the buzzer a couple of times but didn't get an answer. And I'd spent twenty whole minutes finding parking. Such is life. I was ready to pack it in when a middle-aged woman loaded down with shopping bags approached. She fumbled in her purse for her keys.

"Do you need a hand?"

"Oh, thank you."

I held her things while she opened the gate.

"I'm usually not much of a shopper, but they were having a special on recycled envelopes."

"I can never resist a special either," I said, trying to be friendly.

"The cashier didn't know what they were made of, though."

"What what was made of?" I asked, following her in.

"The recycled envelopes," she said impatiently. "I'm going to be licking them, after all. With my tongue."

I had nothing whatsoever to add.

The Holly View was a classic fifties courtyard building, two stories, bougainvillea-draped, the apartments all surrounding a classic kidney-shaped pool. I could imagine Marilyn Monroe before she was Marilyn Monroe holed up in a place like this, waiting for a call from the studio. A starlet living on cottage cheese and vodka.

The woman grabbed her envelopes and took off. I followed the signs up to the second floor. Nancy's apartment was tucked into a corner dominated by a massive clump of dead jasmine. Winter-flowering jasmine has a wonderful, elusive scent (unlike summer's night-blooming jasmine, which, if you ask me, reeks like air freshener). But when it finishes flowering, the vines get choked with dry brown blossoms that don't fall off on their own. You've got to whack 'em off with a pair of hedge shears. I learned that from Javier, my genius gardener.

I knocked hopefully at Nancy's door. No answer. I knocked again. Nothing. I tried to peek into the front window, but the miniblinds were shut tight. Clarissa was not going to be happy. But I'd done what I could do. I went back down the stairs, wondering if I should leave a note with the building manager.

It was quiet by the pool. An older man in a white terry cloth robe was stretched out on a lounge chair, asleep with the morning paper at his feet. A young woman wearing a black tank top and tartan minikilt was seated opposite him, polishing her toenails green. A heartwarming domestic scene.

"Excuse me?"

She looked up.

"Do you happen to be acquainted with Nancy Olsen?"

"Who wants to know?"

"I'm a friend of the family. Her mother is really worried about her. She hasn't answered her phone in days."

"I haven't heard it ringing."

"Why would you?"

"I'm Nancy's neighbor. Three B."

"Nice to meet you. So have you seen Nancy lately?"

"I'm out a lot." She turned to the other foot, bored.

"Do you know what kind of car she drives? Maybe I could check the parking lot."

"What kind of car do *you* drive?"

"Forget it." I started to go.

"That's a very personal question."

"Sorry."

"I don't think Nancy has a car."

"How does she get around, then?"

"Maybe she takes the bus. Some of us actually do. Anyway, in answer to your question, I think I saw her yesterday. In fact, I'm sure of it. She was standing right over there, smoking a cigarette." She pointed to an ashtray underneath the No Lifeguard on Duty sign.

"Well, great. Her mom is going to be really happy to hear that."

"Well, great."

"Not about the cigarette, I mean. About her being here."

"Whatever." The girl moved on to her bitten-up fingernails. The old guy turned onto his side and started to snore.

"I'll be leaving, then," I said to no one in particular. Right after I checked out the parking lot.

I'd taken a wild guess that the Holly View wasn't too big on security. Maintenance either. I made a bit of a spectacle of myself on the way out, tripping over a chipped piece of slate tile. After that, I sneaked back around to the alley running along the side of the building, and down into the underground garage, whose electronic gates were — surprise — on the fritz.

It was dark and musty down there. The trash cans were overflowing. A crumpled McDonald's bag floated idly toward the laundry room. I looked up. There were three or four bulbs hanging from the ceiling, all of which needed changing, and in the corner, by the recycling bin, a single fluorescent light that flickered off and on, off and on.

The parking spaces were marked by apartment. I looked around for 4B, my high heels clicking loudly on the oil-stained concrete. Most of the spaces were empty. It was a Thursday. Everybody was probably hard at work, like I should've been.

Two A drove an old but very nicely maintained Toyota Celica. Maynard would've approved. Six A drove a beat-up yellow van with a bumper sticker that read "I Brake for Spayed and Neutered Pets." Had to be the envelope lady. And what do you know? The girl in the tartan minikilt didn't take the bus. She drove a black VW Bug so new it didn't even have a license plate.

I stopped short in front of a green Honda Prelude. It was parked next to the minikilt's VW. Nancy's car — it had to be. Was that good or bad? I stood there for a minute, bewildered. I think it was bad. But not necessarily. It didn't mean her body was sprawled lifeless on her living-room floor. Or that her head was in the washing machine, clunking around on the spin cycle. It was too quiet for that. The only thing I could hear was the buzz of the broken fluorescent light.

There were many possible explanations. Nancy could be out of town. Or in town and hiding from her mother. Maybe her car was in its parking place because Nancy enjoyed walking. The Holly View was conveniently located. Within a couple of blocks going east or west there were markets, movie theaters, bookstores, restaurants. And night-clubs. The girl was a singer. An artist who sings, rather. Those types are unpredictable.

The driver's-side door was unlocked. I looked to the right, then to the left. No one down here but me. I'd just take a tiny peek and see if anything out of the ordinary jumped out at me. That was it. Then I was going home. Getting back to work. Packing for the weekend. Calling Clarissa. Shit.

I opened the door as quietly as I could and slid in. The car was a mess. There were half-drunk containers of milky coffee in both cup holders, and the floor was covered with supermarket tabloids, the movie section of last Sunday's *L.A. Times*, an army blanket, candy wrappers. A rock-hard bagel down by the emergency brake. Nothing unusual. Except for the green leather Filofax under the blanket.

People don't just leave their Filofaxes in their cars. That was like leaving your baby at a 7-Eleven. Well, not exactly, but you wouldn't do it unless you were in the middle of a nervous breakdown or something.

I picked it up and immediately felt squeamish, as if I were violating this person-I-didn't-even-know's entire being. Which is worse, sins of commission or sins of omission? All those years of catechism and I couldn't remember. Squeezing one eye shut so it didn't really count, I flipped through the pages.

On paper, at least, Nancy Olsen was having an uneventful week. Something with Jeff at nine in the morning on Monday. Something at three-twenty that afternoon. Hip-hop last night, Wednesday. An appointment at Lola's in Silver Lake, also on Wednesday. I'd been to Lola's for a consultation once. I'd wanted to straighten my hair. But the prices were outrageous, and I'd decided against such drastic measures anyway.

What about Nancy? Had she been booked in for highlights? A trim? A mullet cut to spite her mother? Looked like it'd been something. Tucked into a side pocket of the Filofax, along with some receipts and scraps of paper that I'd inadvertently sent flying all over the place, was a parking ticket issued yesterday on Hillhurst Avenue, just around the corner from the salon. Thirty-five bucks for a meter violation. Well, at least that meant she was alive and well and breaking the law. All good things. I could tell Clarissa her daughter was okay. But first I had to stick everything back where it belonged.

I reached between the two front seats to retrieve the stuff that had fallen in there, then bent down to pick up some tiny pieces of cardboard that had gotten stuck inside the movie section.

But they weren't tiny pieces of cardboard. They were slides. I stepped out of the car and held them up to the busted fluorescent light so I could see them more clearly.

Odd.

One was an image of a little girl sitting on a riverbank, lost in thought. It reminded me of Alice before her visit to Wonderland. Another was a photograph of a female nude, curled up into herself, like a seashell. The next was a Japanese print of a geisha girl holding a handful of cherry blossoms. Then a photograph of a headless mannequin draped in fur.

There was one more slide. I leaned my head back and peered at the tiny piece of film. The image was hard to see. It was black-and-white and very grainy. A painting. I looked at it more closely. A painting of a naked woman. A naked woman with pale skin, light eyes, wavy hair, and a knowing look.

And a killer smile.

It was the painting of Grace Horton I had just seen in Edgar Edwards's blue bedroom.

So where was Edgar Edwards?

And where was Nancy Olsen?

And what was Nancy Olsen doing with Edgar Edwards's dirty picture of Nancy Drew?

5

Things can go from bad to worse faster than you might think.

It started when I pulled into my driveway and almost flattened Buster.

Luckily I saw him in time. I slammed on the brakes, tore out of the Caddy, and threw myself upon my entirely unfazed poodle, who endured my ministrations, then squirmed away to perform the life-affirming act of peeing on the grass. I was so discombobulated that I neglected to ask myself why Buster wasn't inside the house where I'd left him. He wasn't the vagabond sort.

It was then that I noticed my front door was wide open.

Now you might think a person would proceed with caution. Especially a person whose father was a cop, whose two brothers are cops, a person who is dating a cop. But you know what they say. Doctors make the worst patients. Trust me, it relates. In any case, Lois, my neighbor from three doors down, carrying a can of cat food, stopped me before I could barrel inside.

"Poor Buster. I saw the whole thing. And good afternoon to you, birthday girl!"

Lois and her twin sister, Marlene, known professionally as Jasmine and Hibiscus, had been showgirls way back around the dawn of time. They amused themselves these days by tottering up and down the block in their scuffed pumps, tending to the neighborhood strays.

"Buster is fine, but what do you mean, 'birthday girl'? It's not my birthday."

"Oh, Cece." She tittered. "Getting old is a blessing."

"Lois," I said, "my birthday is in October. What's going on around here?"

"Your friends came by at one."

"Lael and Bridget?"

"No, no, your gentleman friends," she said excitedly. "They were trying the back gate. They said they wanted to leave the lady of the house a surprise for her birthday. My hands were full" — she wagged a can of Friskies at me — "so I showed them the key you hide in the flowerpot."

"You *what?*"

"Then Marlene called on my cell phone and I had to go. They promised they'd lock up."

I didn't wait for the rest. I scrambled up the steps and straight into the living room. Then I heard Lois hyperventilating behind me.

"Oh, dear. They looked like such nice fellows."

Bad was Buster. This was worse.

The green velvet couch was overturned. The chairs were pushed up against the wall. Tapes and CDs littered the floor. My flokati rug was bunched up in a heap, like a dead polar bear. The dining room was a disaster, too. The armoire had been ransacked and my faded Indian tablecloths from Pioneer Boulevard in Artesia (you take the 10 to the 5 to the 91, and in forty-five minutes you'd swear you were in New Delhi) had been tossed unceremoniously to the ground. At least they'd spared my wedding china — not the pattern I would've chosen, but my ex-mother-in-law was not to be swayed.

The kitchen looked pretty much like I'd left it, which was a total mess, except that the dishwasher door was open. I noted some eggy crust clinging to the frying pan I'd wedged onto the top rack. Damn. That thing still wasn't working. Ilya the repairman had been over three times in the last three weeks.

"This is awful!" Lois wailed.

Then I remembered my computer. I was terrible about backing things up. Things like my nearly completed book on Carolyn Keene. My ex, an English professor and master neurotic, was always after me about that. Heart pounding, I raced out the kitchen door with Lois right behind me, and toward my office. It was still locked, thank god, which made sense since it couldn't be opened with the front-door key. I peered through the French doors and my Bondi Blue iMac peered back at me.

"The research is secure," Lois declared solemnly.

We went back inside and into my bedroom, where things were not as sanguine. My bed had been pulled out into the middle of the room and stripped of the sheets and pillows. My comforter had been tossed on top of the TV. My books had been tossed off the nightstand. But I really didn't care about any of that stuff. Only my computer — and my clothes. I felt my stomach contract into a knot. My precious clothes that I'd been collecting for two decades. They were everywhere, like wrapping paper after you open your presents. *But it wasn't my birthday.*

"Do you have household insurance?" Lois was trying to be helpful, but I wanted to kill her. I knelt down to pick up my metallic knit cocktail dress; 1978 had been a good year for Missoni. And there was my silk chiffon skirt with the scalloped sunburst, one of my first purchases. I had so wanted to be Stevie Nicks when I was fifteen. I plucked my Pucci for Formfit Rogers dressing gown out of the heating vent and clutched it to my chest. You just can't get those anymore, much less for seventeen bucks. Oh, and my Halston silver sequined beret.

"This stuff must be worth a pretty penny," Lois said, fingering a faux leopard bolero.

"Not really. Only to me," I said. But her inane comment got me thinking. I leapt up and yanked open the top drawer of my bureau. My black velvet Lanvin cape from the twenties, with its wide fur collar. At one thousand smackeroos, the single most expensive piece of clothing I'd ever purchased. It was there, safe and sound in its pink tissue paper nest. And that confirmed it.

I'd been robbed and nothing was missing.

My Lanvin cape, inviolate; my TV, still there; my CD player, the microwave in the kitchen, my computer, the god-awful china, all untouched. What was going on here? Had the robbers found religion halfway through the job? I probably needed better stuff. Or maybe my new best friend Mitchell

Honey was behind this. Maybe he wanted to make sure I hadn't tied Edgar Edwards up and hidden him in my closet.

"Are you going to call the police, Cece?" Lois was looking up at me with those hazel eyes, which were still beautiful and clear, unlike her mind.

"Well, I think I have to," I said, exasperated now. "Two strange men broke into my house and are out there wandering around with my key."

"But if nothing is gone, what's the point?"

"What's the point? Lois, a crime has been committed. This is what people do when a crime is committed. They contact the authorities." I started looking for the cordless phone. Hadn't she ever read number 33, *The Witch Tree Symbol*? Never, under any circumstances, let a stranger lock up after you.

Lois sat down on my bare mattress and burst into tears.

I sat down next to her and patted her hand. "Are you worried I'm going to be angry at you? It wasn't entirely your fault."

"I know that. It was your fault for leaving the key in such an obvious place. No, it's the police. They don't like me."

"What are you talking about?"

"What part do you not understand? The

70

police don't like me. They don't like my sister, they don't like our dogs, they hate our landscaping — oh, I could go on and on."

And you will, I thought to myself.

"They've been over here four or five times now," she continued, "trying to get us to chop down that beautiful old tree in our front yard, but I have discovered they can't make us because we simply don't have the money to pay for it. We're penniless. Let them pay for it, I say."

"Lois. You do realize that tree is a hazard to the community." After a particularly windy day, the sidewalk in front of Lois and Marlene's house would be littered with its enormous black pineapplelike pods. Once, when I was walking back from the market, I watched one smash into the roof of an inauspiciously parked sports car with the force of a missile.

"Like I was saying, between the tree and the visits from animal control" — now she was crying again — "they don't need to hear I was involved in something like this. They'll target me for brutality, I just know it. Or they'll take away our parking spot." Lois and her sister had somehow bamboozled the city into giving them their own handicapped spot, though neither seemed to have any problem visible to the naked eye.

"Please, Cece, I don't want to talk to them. Just let me help you get the locks changed, and that'll be the end of it. Marlene's ex-brother-in-law is a locksmith. He can be here in a twinkling."

As it turned out, Marlene's ex-brother-in-law was the best I could do. My unburglary excited little to no emotion in the guy manning the phones at the West Hollywood Sheriff's station. He suggested I come in at my earliest convenience to fill out a report, which I interpreted as a polite way of saying, "You must be kidding, lady." I tried not to take it personally. After Lois left, I gave Lael a quick call and talked her into spending the night. Her kids were already gone, so she agreed. But I should have known the first thing out of her mouth would be something sensible.

"Cece," she said, not even halfway in the door, "I don't care what that guy on the phone said, you have to call Gambino. He would want to know about something like this."

"She didn't mean to step on you," I said to the locksmith, who had arrived a few minutes earlier, and was crouching in front of the doorway. "Listen, can you do something about that knob while you're at it? It comes off in people's hands. And this is for you,

Lael." I handed her a huge pile of laundry. We were washing those sheets before we were sleeping on them.

"Cece, I said you had to call Gambino. Why didn't you answer me? Are you ill? You look pale."

"Peter and I aren't actually speaking right now," I said. "What should we order for dinner? Do you like mee krob?"

"Stop it. Why aren't you and Peter speaking? Again?"

"He told me he loved me."

"And . . ."

"And I don't believe him." I grabbed the laundry out of her hands and headed for the washing machine. She followed me into the kitchen.

"You are one sick cookie."

"Is that an offer?"

"What's that supposed to mean?"

"I have this recurrent fantasy. I'm listening to Mozart. I'm eating your chocolate chip cookies —"

"We have to clean up this mess. It'll take us all night. And your cookie sheets suck, if I remember properly."

"You could spin gold from dross."

"Cece."

"You put Sweet Lady Jane to shame." Sweet Lady Jane was the best bakery in L.A.

73

"All right. You can stop it, Cece. You win. But we are having a long talk about you and Gambino."

"We have all night to talk about my tragedy of a love life."

"Your love life is not a tragedy. You are the tragedy."

"That's a lovely thing to say."

"Where do you keep the brown sugar?"

I opened the door to the pantry and pulled out the box. "There's flour, baking soda, and vanilla in there, too."

"I'll take care of it," she said, pushing me away. She'd found an apron I had no idea I owned, and put it on.

I stared at her, bemused. She had a permanent postcoital glow. She glowed when she was paying bills. When she was scrubbing toilets. "Lael. How come you look like a Stepford wife? When I wear an apron, I look like a fishwife."

"Go tidy," she said distractedly.

I had a couple of phone calls to make first.

Clarissa was semihappy about my semihappy news. Of course, she'd been calling her daughter all day and had left dozens more messages, and now, much to her consternation, Nancy's machine wouldn't accept any more. I encouraged her to give her daughter a little space and assured her that all would be well, that Nancy would be waiting for her at the hotel tomorrow in Palm Springs. Then Clarissa asked about my speech.

"I think it might surprise you."

She detected the hesitation in my voice. "I'm not one for surprises, Cece."

"In a good way, I mean." And who could possibly blame me for jettisoning "The Changing Demographics of River Heights"? I didn't want to put all those good women to sleep. I still had to clarify some details in my own mind, though. How exactly did Edgar's nude portrait of Grace Horton change things? Why had Grace posed in the buff in the first place? Money? Unlikely. A sexy painting by Russell Tandy, a little-known illustrator, would never have fetched much. And would have jeopardized Grace's career as Nancy Drew. For a lark? Perhaps. Because she felt straitjacketed by her role as Saint Nancy? Anyone would have. And what about Grace and Tandy? Were things between them purely business? You know what they say about artists and models.

Clarissa seemed to be feeling a little better by the time we hung up.

Mitchell Honey was another story.

He picked up on the third ring. No, Edgar had not shown up, nor had Jake, but, amazingly, it was no longer my fault. And no longer my business. Mitchell was a very busy man with dozens of things to take care of, and why was I keeping him on the phone? These were private affairs, after all. Edgar and Jake were probably out whooping it up somewhere, and he was no longer doing them the courtesy of freaking out. Fine with me.

I spent the next hour or so doing the laundry, making up the bed, putting things back where they belonged, and finding spots in various closets and drawers for the stuff that was left over. Then I took a long hot shower. By the time I emerged with a towel wrapped around my hair, the locksmith was gone and the kitchen was spotless. There were wildflowers from the garden in a vase, Lael's signature cookies had been arranged on a plate, and there was a carton of mee krob on the counter, along with some spicy chicken coconut soup and pork with mint leaves.

Lael pushed a strand of long blond hair out of her eyes and smiled at me.

It would've been nice to have had a sister, but a best friend was just as good.

6

We couldn't see Bridget. Her entire body was obscured by five antique Louis Vuitton steamer trunks. But we could hear her.

"You ladies said nine o'clock on the nose. You're late. I've been waiting out here for twenty minutes."

"Oh, no," I said. "I warned you about this. You cannot bring those things with you. Who do you think you are, a French *contessa?*"

"If I were French, I'd be a *comtesse.*"

"Morning, Bridget," said Lael.

"Morning, Lael," said Bridget.

Lael pushed the top two trunks aside. "That is a fantastic outfit you've got on, Bridget."

The woman was encased in skintight black leather, the star of a blaxploitation film. I was as pure as the driven snow in a white head scarf, white lace-up minicaftan with long bell sleeves, and white-rimmed Jackie O. sunglasses — not that anyone had taken notice.

"Thank you," Bridget said, pouting. She

scrutinized Lael's stained lavender painter's pants and puffy-sleeved smock.

"Your outfit," she conceded, "has hippie flair."

Lael waited a beat. She had four kids and knew what she was doing.

"I used to be a hippie," Bridget said. "I lived on nuts and didn't want to be burdened with worldly possessions."

Lael waited another beat.

"I guess I *could* leave some of my luggage at home."

Lael shrugged noncommittally.

"People expect me to look fantastic."

Lael clucked sympathetically.

"No time off for good behavior."

Lael nodded sagely.

"I'm exhausted."

Lael smiled victoriously.

We helped Bridget haul three of the trunks back inside and the other two into the backseat.

"Should I sit back here with my luggage?" Bridget asked in a small voice.

"That sounds like a good idea. And I hope you're hungry. Cece and I have packed a hamper with all sorts of goodies — little lobster sandwiches, poached pears, cucumber salad."

"What about Diet Coke? And nacho

cheese Doritos?" Bridget undid the top button of her pants.

"It's a road trip! That's what convenience stores are for! And we love our convenience stores, right, Cece?"

"Right!" I said, getting into the spirit of things. "Right?" I asked Bridget, catching her eye in the rearview mirror.

"Right," she said, peeling off her motorcycle jacket. "No leather! No juice fasts!" And we were off.

We got on the 10 at Overland. Rush hour was pretty much over so it wasn't too bad. Downtown was a blur of skyscrapers and smog. From there we sped through the Chinese suburbs of Alhambra and Monterey Park and a string of towns whose names escaped me but that appeared to consist exclusively of places to buy consumer electronics. Lael used the bathroom at the biggest Toyota dealership in the world. We passed a garbage mountain with a flag flying on top in Ontario. We listened to jazz. We stopped at a 7-Eleven.

"Isn't Riverside somewhere around here?" Lael asked.

"What's in Riverside?" I asked, looking up from my cherry Big Gulp.

"Can we listen to the *Saturday Night Fever* sound track now?" Bridget interrupted.

"Just the most revered fruit tree in the entire United States," Lael said. Then she gave me the look I knew so well, the one that meant business.

We got off the freeway at the next exit and followed the arrows toward the center of town.

"I found out about it researching recipes for orange poppy seed minimuffins on the Internet," Lael said.

"I've never heard of orange poppy seed minimuffins. Don't you mean lemon? We need a map. Can you check the glove compartment?"

"Here." She handed me some crumpled shreds of paper that used to be a map but currently resembled a napkin.

"I can't do this when I'm driving. You figure out where we're going, Bridget," I said, shoving the mess back at her.

"This tree," Lael continued, "is one of two from which all navel oranges in California descended. It came here from Brazil in about 1875 and created an orange empire. The navel is the noblest of all citrus."

"It's marked with an orange," Bridget said after a few minutes. "I think this is it." She handed the map back to me, poking furiously at a small stain somewhere in southern Nevada.

I sighed. "I think we'll stop at the closest gas station to be sure."

The man at the gas station studied us disapprovingly, then directed us to the corner of Arlington and Magnolia. We headed that way.

Bridget was singing, "If I can't have you, I don't want nobody, baby!"

Lael was trying to rip a loose thread off the bottom of her smock.

I was trying my best, but I suspected sabotage. From all quarters.

"Stop, Cece! There it is!" Bridget cried. "Across the street from Donut Tyme!"

"You should trust your friends," Lael said, altogether too smugly.

The most revered fruit tree in the entire United States was located smack in the middle of a commercial district, directly in front of a combination day spa and dental office. Donut Tyme had good parking, so we left the Caddy there and walked across the street.

The tree was surrounded by a dusty, padlocked gate with dangerous-looking spikes running across the top.

"So where's the armed guard?" asked Bridget, who was munching away on a cinnamon cruller.

"It's the honor system," Lael said.

"They look awfully tasty," I said.

Bridget narrowed her eyes. "Stay away from my cruller."

"I mean the oranges. Look at those smooth deep-orange rinds."

"You wouldn't dare," Lael said.

"Seedless, too."

"I can't take you anywhere."

"Bridget, give me a boost."

"But those women are watching."

A couple of day spa clients were lingering out front, gingerly touching each other's freshly peeled face.

"They aren't paying attention. C'mon."

"This is a historic landmark," Lael said, reading the plaque. "We are going to get arrested."

Bridget didn't like that idea. "You really want old fruit, Cece? There are probably worms in there, or fruit flies. You can have the rest of my cruller."

The fence was about six feet high, but there was a leafy branch extending over the top, just within reach. It was dripping with fruit.

"I can stand on this bench. I don't even need your help."

Looking back, I wish someone had warned me about that bench. It must've been there as long as the tree, because the minute I stood up on it the whole damn thing collapsed, propelling me straight toward one of those rusty spikes.

"Omigod!" Bridget shrieked at Lael, who was standing twenty feet away, pretending she didn't know us.

"Cece!" Lael raced over to me.

"I'm fine," I said, picking myself up off the ground. "And I got an orange!"

"You're not fine. You're bleeding."

I looked down at my dress, which was ripped across the front, revealing a scratch on my stomach. And also my oldest underwear. My mother used to warn me about that.

Lael took my arm. "That must hurt. Let's go inside and get you fixed up."

After complimenting me on my teeth, the people in the day spa/dental office cleaned off my cut, which looked worse than it was, bandaged me up, and gave me a couple of safety pins to hold my dress together. I figured I'd change in the bathroom at Donut Tyme.

We walked back across the street, sharing the orange.

"Are you sure you're okay?" Lael asked.

How exactly was I supposed to answer that? The last twenty-four hours had gone by in a fog. Had two strangers really broken into my house, or was that a dream?

"I'm made of strong stuff. You know that." I wiped my sticky fingers on my dress, popped open the trunk, and reached for my suitcase.

"So what's that license plate supposed to say anyway?" Bridget asked. "Smutty or smoothie?"

"Neither," I said. "Smooth, as in 'smooth-talking ladies' man.' "

"Give me a break."

"Lael," I said, looking up, "did you open the hamper?"

"No. Why?"

"It's nothing. The latch must've come undone." I closed it, then opened it again, puzzled. "That's weird. The sandwiches aren't in here. We must have left them on the counter."

"Impossible. I put them in there myself. Let me see that." She rifled through the hamper, frowning. "I guess I didn't. What a lamebrain. I must've left them on the counter."

I opened my suitcase and pulled out an Aerosmith T-shirt and my oldest, softest jeans. "I'll just be a sec."

"Wait," Bridget said loudly.

"What is it?"

"What happened to my Louis Vuitton trunks?"

I looked into the backseat. "They're right where we left them. Both of them. What's the problem?"

"They're there, but not where we left them."

"What are you talking about?" I asked slowly.

"They were behind the passenger seat before. Now they're behind your seat, Cece."

"They must've shifted when we were driving."

"They were the other way around when we went across the street."

"Have they been opened? Check them. Is anything missing?"

She opened the car door and climbed in. "Well, they seem to be locked up, like I left them. And the keys are right here, in my purse." She shrugged. "I'm so spacey."

But Bridget was not spacey. And Lael was not a lamebrain.

And it hadn't been a dream.

We drove off.

"Everything's fine now," Lael said.

Just fine.

The sun was high overhead by the time we saw the first billboard for Hadley Fruit Orchards.

"Do you think hydrogen-powered cars

will ever be a reality?" Lael's eyes were closed. She had exhausted herself searching for a chimerical all-Beatles radio station.

"It's the only thing that will save California," Bridget answered. "What are your thoughts on Indian gaming?"

"How can you think about such things at a time like this?" I asked. "Didn't you see the sign? We're almost at Hadley's!"

"I think we should keep going," Lael said.

The air was hot and dry. How could birds fly through such hot dry air? I looked around. Didn't see any birds. Not many plants either. Just some extraterrestrial-looking Joshua trees poking out of the parched red dirt.

"Hadley's has been an oasis in the high desert since 1931," I said, slowing down to read the next sign.

"I said I think we should keep going."

"You're going to pass on sage honey? Mango-flavored pineapple cones? Apricot-stuffed Medjool dates? Ostrich jerky?"

"I want to take a dip in the pool at Edgar's," she said. "Doesn't that sound nice?"

Bridget piped up. "Perfect."

"I'm thirsty," I said as we drove past Hadley's. I knew what Lael was doing. She was worried about me. She did not approve of my stunts. She feared for my mental health. And she wanted to get me settled in so I could rest up before my speech tomorrow. How little faith she had in me.

"You can have a drink when we arrive," she said. "And a nice hot bubble bath after the pool."

"I have to go to the bathroom," I said stubbornly, pulling off the road and into the Wheel Inn.

Lael sighed. "Just make it quick."

The Wheel Inn in Cabazon was famous for its four-story-tall dinosaurs. Back in the sixties, somebody had planned an entire dinosaur-themed amusement park there, but had never gotten any further than a brontosaurus and a T. rex.

"Looks like there's a gift shop inside the T. rex," said Bridget excitedly. Away from her usual designer boutiques for two hours and she'd lost all perspective.

"We'll get the sodas," Lael said, pushing Bridget inside behind me.

Five minutes later, we walked back out to the car. I pressed the icy can of Diet Coke against my cheek.

Bridget kicked some gravel in the parking lot. "I want one of those pith helmets with a fan attached."

"Edgar must have air-conditioning."

"Are you sure it's fine that we all stay there?"

"He insisted," I said. "I have no idea why, but he insisted."

"Andrew loathes air-conditioning. He doesn't mind sweat."

"Yuck," I said.

"Who's Andrew?" Lael asked.

"Bridget's new intern," I said with a snort.

"Are you jealous?" Bridget asked.

"A little," I confessed. "You seem so happy."

"I am. He's just so . . . worshipful. And all that luscious hair."

"Cece," asked Lael, ever alert, "why should you be jealous? You've got Gambino."

"Why do we always have to talk about men?" I snapped. "Can we please not talk about men for two seconds?"

"Good idea," said Bridget, stopping dead in front of Maynard's Caddy. "I think we've got more pressing concerns."

7

At any hour, in any time zone, by any stretch of the imagination, four slashed tires qualified as a pressing concern.

No one spoke. We just stood around the car like mourners at a funeral.

"How will I explain this to Maynard?" I finally asked.

Bridget shook her head. "Somebody out there doesn't like you, Cece. This is bad mojo."

"Please, would you stop with the mojo?"

Lael smeared some Chapstick on her lips. "Who would do such a thing? This is crazy. Never in my life . . . Cece?" She was yelling at me now. "Cece! What are you doing? You're going to get yourself killed!"

"What does it look like I'm doing?" I was standing half in the road, shouting and waving my arms back and forth like a lunatic. "Hey, hey, stop!" The black-and-white cop car tore past me at full speed. I turned around. "Did you see that? Unbelievable! He didn't even look my way!"

"He was probably pursuing a felon. Come back here this instant."

Bridget studied her fingernails, a practical woman at heart. "Call the auto club, and be done with it."

Fred from Porter's Automotive arrived in less than half an hour. Hot and dusty, we squeezed into the cabin of his truck. Fred was nice enough but his nonstop patter about wore me out. As we drove back to the garage, he complained about the juvenile delinquents who were terrorizing the area, shooting up windows, slashing tires, covering bus stops with graffiti. Then he lamented the good old days, before the gangs came in from Los Angeles. A digression on the nefarious influence of drugs followed. And when I foolishly mentioned the patrolman who'd ignored us earlier, he started in on police corruption, tax fraud, the right to bear arms, and his plans to go off the grid.

All that, plus four new tires, set me back a thousand dollars. I had now officially exceeded my Visa limit. But some months are like that.

We ate sour cream and onion CornNuts from the machine at Porter's while Fred put on the tires.

"You ladies are damn lucky this car didn't

have any of those fancy whitewalls," he said as he was finishing up. "Then you'd really have been in for it."

"We should report this," Lael said.

I crumpled up my empty bag of Corn-Nuts and tossed it into the trash. "I know we should, but we have to get going." I consulted my watch. It was close to three already, and we had to be at the conference hotel by four o'clock for the Chums' wine and cheese party. I'd promised Clarissa we'd be there, and the way her life was going these days, I didn't want to disappoint her.

Lael gave me one of her looks.

"Don't do that. I tried to report it — you saw me. And you also saw how much the cops care about what happens."

"That officer didn't even see you."

"Lael, you heard Fred. This place is crawling with rotten teenage kids. Do you really think anyone on the entire Cabazon police force is going to bother chasing them down for the sake of the three of us? They don't like out-of-towners in the backwoods. Let's just get out of here."

"She's right," Bridget warned. "Remember *Deliverance*."

Lael shrugged. "It's your weekend, Cece."

"And don't you forget it."

★ ★ ★

We pulled up in front of the Wyndham Hotel on Indian Canyon Road at about ten after four. A huge, inflatable bottle of Captain Morgan's Spiced Rum lay inexplicably on the asphalt.

The valet hurried over. He was wearing a red uniform with gold epaulets, and the sweat was pouring down his face.

"Oh, man. Glad you didn't run that thing over. It just fell down. Jesus. The official sponsor. Well, it's crazy around here today."

That was an understatement. People were streaming in and out of the hotel, salsa music was blaring, and the smell of tortilla chips filled the air. A group of women wearing sun visors and tennis shorts brushed past us on their way inside, laughing uproariously.

"So much for cocktail attire," Bridget said.

"Actually, I'm impressed," I said.

Lael smoothed down her windblown hair. "About what?"

"That Nancy Drew can still reel 'em in."

"You here for the party, ladies?" the valet asked, handing me a ticket.

I nodded.

"How long you going to be?"

"I'm not sure. Maybe an hour."

"I'll keep your car out front. It's a beaut," he said, letting out a whistle. "Very cherry."

"Thanks."

The lobby was a mob scene. We made our way back to the reception table where a smiling woman in a cowboy hat handed us each a tiny box of Whitman's chocolates and a golf ball–shaped paperweight embossed with the American Airlines logo. More official sponsors, I supposed.

"Head straight out to the pool," she said. "Things are just getting started."

We followed some people who looked like they knew where they were going down the hall, past a pair of uniformed guards with headsets on.

"Those are the only men we've seen since we set foot in this place," Lael whispered.

"Again with the men!" I said. "Who did you think would be at a Nancy Drew convention? Big, burly truck drivers? Sexy firemen?"

"Calm down," said Lael, right before her mouth fell open.

Females — what seemed like hundreds of them, of every conceivable age, ethnicity, and body type — were packed into the pool area and, from the looks of it, having the time of their lives. The drinks were flowing, the beach balls were flying, the DJ was playing Cyndi Lauper.

"This is not what I expected," Lael said, looking up at the Miller Lite banner silhouetted against the bright blue desert sky.

"Me neither," said Bridget, stepping out of the way of a short Latina with tattoos covering every square inch of exposed flesh, of which there was a lot.

I stared at the swimming pool, dumbfounded. "The Chums are playing Marco Polo."

"That's *Marcia* Polo," said an older woman who came up behind me. She was wearing a tangerine-colored sarong and matching visor. "Do you ladies need beers? There are burgers on the grill."

"We're fine for now, thanks," I said, "but maybe you could help me with something."

"After my last juice fast, the first thing I ate was a hamburger," said Bridget dreamily. "With blue cheese and onions."

"I love women who eat," the woman said, looking Bridget up and down. "Nice outfit."

"As I was saying," I continued, "I'm looking for someone. Clarissa Olsen?"

"If she's hot, I'm looking for her, too," she said, laughing.

"Excuse me, are you here for the Nancy Drew fan convention?"

"Nancy Drew? I *loved* Nancy Drew, are you kidding?" She turned serious. "Nancy Drew was un-fucking-believable. The perfect chameleon. She could fit in anywhere, pretend to be anything or anyone — throw on a wig, join the circus — you never knew who she really was. And her sidekicks, oh, I loved them, too. Bess was always eating, god bless her. And George Fayne — an athletic-looking girl with close-cropped hair and a boy's name. Let's just say been there, done that!"

I turned to Lael and Bridget. "We need to go back to the lobby and find the person in charge."

"What about my hamburger?" Bridget asked.

I took her arm. "Now."

The woman in the cowboy hat was too busy passing out freebies to pay much attention to our queries, but the soft-spoken clerk behind the reservations desk sent us up to the third floor.

The elevator doors opened onto thick pile carpet and the oily tones of Barry Manilow. This was more like it. We followed the arrows around a couple of corners to the Oak Salon, which must've made a great setting for a bar mitzvah back in the seventies, assuming the bar mitzvah boy's mother was into mauve and crystal chandeliers.

I looked around the room. The walls were covered from floor to ceiling in mirrored tiles, which created the chilling effect of an infinitely regressing gallery of Chums. I wiped my sweaty hands on my jeans. To my horror, I realized I was nervous. But that was insane. Why should I be nervous? There were no more than sixty women in the Oak Salon. Sixty sensibly dressed women, not a sarong in the bunch. And they were out to have a good time, not to torment me. I had to get over myself.

The welcome table had been abandoned, but I spied a red marker with a stubbed tip and a pile of blank name tags. I scrawled my name on one and slapped it onto my T-shirt.

"I'm going to find Clarissa. Get yourselves something to eat."

Bridget and Lael headed toward a towering mountain of minibagels. I wandered over to the book display, then to a long table covered with Nancy Drew Christmas ornaments and Nancy Drew slumber party kits. *The Mystery of the Fire Dragon* kit included fortune cookies and a paper cheongsam. *The Bungalow Mystery* kit included two sets of handcuffs and a blindfold. Pretty kinky, if you asked me. As I left the table a tall, very pregnant woman wearing a Chums 1997 Convention sweatshirt and a blue wraparound skirt snapped my picture and handed me a book.

"Will you sign it?" she asked, peering at my chest. "Ms. Caruso, is it?"

"Call me Cece."

"I'm Tabitha."

"You really want me to autograph your book?"

"I do it at every convention. I buy a Nancy Drew book that's missing pages or something and get everybody to sign it. Then I have a record of who was there."

"That's so sweet," I said, writing my name across the ripped title page of a 1944 edition of *The Whispering Statue.* "I never actually read this one. How is it?"

"Togo, Nancy's little terrier, appears for the first time in this book, so it's a favorite of mine," she replied. "I can't have animals because I'm a flight attendant and I'm always traveling, but I love them like crazy! I'm sort of an expert on them," she added, blushing a deep shade of crimson.

"Animals in general?"

"No, in Nancy Drew. Snowball the cat, Nancy's white Persian, appears for the first time in *The Mystery of the Brass-Bound*

Trunk, original text, not revised text, I mean. And Nancy has a horse named Black Prince in one of the spin-off series, number sixty-six, *Race Against Time*. But that's about it. I think Hannah must've been allergic. Or didn't need the extra aggravation."

"Hannah Gruen, Nancy Drew's housekeeper?" I asked.

"Uh-huh," she said, taking back her book.

"Who's allergic?" demanded a potbellied woman standing behind us. "Because I've got a shitload of antihistamines if anybody needs them."

"We were just talking about Hannah."

"Oh, Hannah," she said.

"How're you doing, Rita?" asked Tabitha.

"Fair, Tabby Cat."

"My online persona," Tabitha explained.

I recognized the name from her postings on the Listserv.

"Sleuth or Virgin Sleuth?" Rita demanded of me.

"I beg your pardon?"

"It's Clarissa's concoction. Fresca with or without gin. Over by the minibagels."

"Don't forget the maraschino cherry," Tabby Cat said shyly.

"I'm not thirsty right now," I replied. "But thanks."

"So it's official," said Rita. "I'm getting divorced."

"Oh, no! What about your collection?" Tabitha turned to me. "Rita and her husband — ex-husband-to-be, I guess — have an amazing Stratemeyer collection: Bomba the Jungle Boy, the Motor Boys, the Campfire Girls, Honey Bunch. Who wrote the Honey Bunch books again?"

"Mildred Wirt Benson wrote the Honey Bunch books as Helen Louise Thorndyke," I answered. What a pedant.

" 'Honey Bunch is a dainty, thoughtful little girl, and to know her is to take her to your heart at once,' " Rita recited.

I had to concede defeat.

"You know," said Rita, patting Tabby Cat's tummy, "you could name your baby Honey Bunch."

"What if it's a boy?"

I turned to Rita. "Why don't you collect Nancy Drew?"

"I hate Nancy Drew," she said in a low voice. "But don't rat me out."

"How can you hate Nancy Drew?"

"Haven't you ever noticed how selfish that girl is? She's helpful, but what a control freak! She's always got to have her own way, and to hell with everybody else."

"Now that you mention it —"

"Excuse me, I'm not finished. To hell with everybody else's legitimate concerns. They're supposed to stuff them just like she does. And danger? So what if she puts everybody around her in danger? One inappropriate response after another." She shook her head. "Nancy Drew is a bundle of defense mechanisms wrapped up in a pretty package." Then she looked right at me. "Sound familiar?"

I didn't answer. I got away by pretending I wanted to look at the Nancy Drew sunglass cases.

Lael and Bridget were about done. "Let's go check out our new vacation home!" said Bridget. "The cream cheese is gone."

"Almost," I said. "I love you guys."

"Big smooch," said Bridget.

"Cece Caruso! You're here!" said a voice I recognized.

"Clarissa!" I replied, turning around.

So this was Clarissa Olsen.

"You are not what I envisioned," I said without thinking.

"Neither are you."

"What were you expecting?" I asked, sweeping my index fingers under my eyes and trying to rub off the mascara that had melted somewhere around Cabazon.

"Certainly not someone so young and so gorgeous."

This woman had absolutely missed her calling. With those lines and that sleek blond bob she was meant to be a network news anchor. I half expected her to shove a microphone in my face and ask me for a comment.

"Clarissa, these are my friends Lael and Bridget," I said.

"So nice to meet you. And this," she said, gesturing to a girl whose back was toward us, "is my daughter, Nancy Olsen."

Nancy turned around.

Life can be so strange.

Because the girl I was looking at — Clarissa Olsen's daughter, Nancy — was the same girl I'd talked to at the Holly View Apartments, the one who'd claimed to be Nancy Olsen's next-door neighbor.

"Nice to meet you, Cece," she said, sweet as pie.

"Love the tartan minikilt," I said. "You're some kind of original."

Her mother beamed.

8

"And speaking of Nancy Drew's long-suffering beau, Ned, why do you think his last name is Nickerson? Nickers-on, get it? The poor sap."

A man wearing a name tag that read Big Bad Sebastien was putting the moves on Lael. She took it with her usual good cheer, smiling graciously as he droned on.

"One more minute," I promised, squeezing her arm.

"Cece," Lael said, "Sebastien here is a charter member of the Chums."

"Sebastien-with-an-*e* Kister. Pleased to know you. I publish a newsletter out of Detroit." He handed me a somewhat grimy copy of *Big Bad Sebastien's Super Dicks and Bloodhound Babes.* "Only nineteen ninety-nine a year. I write the whole thing and I'm witty as hell."

"Sebastien has also explained what was going on downstairs."

"Lesbians!" he cried. "Twenty thousand of them! Headquartered here! The Dinah

Shore Classic! One weekend a year the girls take over the city!"

Lael and I looked at each other and cracked up.

"Clarissa about wet her pants when she realized what was happening, but I say, bring it on! I'm crashing the grand ballroom tomorrow night if you ladies want to join me. They're turning the place into Emerald City. There's going to be a yellow brick road that'll start at the entrance and go all the way through to the party. I've seen them setting up. Green lights everywhere! The Munchkins are an erotic belly-dancing troupe from Des Moines!"

"Cece, don't we have that thing we have to get to? Isn't it starting right now? That thing?"

"Give me one more minute, Lael," I said. "Please."

I knew I was pushing it, but I had a couple of questions that needed answering.

"What, are you worried I can't handle the both of you?" I heard Sebastien saying as I stepped into the hall.

Nancy Olsen was standing out there, puffing on a cigarette.

"That's against the law," I said. "And it'll kill you."

She took a long drag. "I've already got a mother."

"I'm well aware of that."

"She makes her presence felt, doesn't she?"

"Listen, I don't know what's going on between you two. That's for you to work out. But I don't appreciate being made a fool of."

Nancy dropped her cigarette into a cup of cranberry juice someone had left behind. "Sorry."

"That's it? Sorry?"

"That's it."

"Well, that's not good enough."

"You were in the way."

"Of what?"

"My fucking life," she said, shoving her chopped-off red hair out of her eyes. "Do you think it's easy having Clarissa for a mother?"

"Do you think it's easy having you for a daughter?"

She looked up at me with tear-filled eyes. "I suppose not."

Well, shoot. I hadn't meant to make her cry. The girl was decked out in full punk regalia but still had her baby fat.

"My mother had all sorts of plans for me, too," I said, leaning against the wall. "I was supposed to become Miss New Jersey, maybe even Miss America. But then I sort of rushed into marriage. I blew it for her."

"Were you pregnant?"

I nodded. "I had a daughter, Annie. She's a little older than you are now."

"Where does she live?"

"In L.A."

"Do you see her much?"

"I do."

"Did you name her after a fictional character?"

I laughed. "No, though I will admit to being obsessed with Annie Oakley. But I never mentioned it to her father. He would've been horrified. He wanted to name her after one of the Brontë sisters."

"Emily was an anorexic."

"I didn't know that."

"Charlotte was a masochist."

"Good thing we stuck with Annie."

"There was an Anne Brontë."

"Bet nobody called her Annie."

"Probably not." She smiled and I saw her tongue piercing glisten. She stuffed her cigarettes into a tiny fringed purse.

"I've got to go help my mother. She'll go ballistic if everything's not perfect. I'll see you tomorrow."

"See you tomorrow."

I went back inside, too, to rescue Lael and find Bridget. Clarissa was furiously scooping up conference programs from the chairs she'd laid them on earlier. She beckoned me over with a long red fingernail. I thought of her daughter's green ones, bitten to the quick.

"Cece, I have news I forgot to mention. We're switching things around a bit. The scavenger hunt will now begin at eleven, and we're going to start your speech a little later than planned because we have a surprise guest coming."

Oh, great. I'd been preempted. "Who is it?"

"Edgar Edwards, the collector from L.A."

"Edgar Edwards?"

"I talked to him this morning. I wouldn't have let him horn in on our event, but he says he's got something to show us that'll knock our socks off. Sounds pretty thrilling. Anyway, I'm thrilled," she said, tucking the now-defunct programs under her arm. "I'll have to redo these tonight, of course."

I knew the man couldn't have vanished into thin air. So much for Mitchell Honey's hysterics. But what was Edgar's big surprise?

Oh, no.

The painting of naked Nancy Drew. What

else could it be? And it was all my fault. I shouldn't have looked so interested. Man, oh, man. That painting was not going to fly with this group — except maybe for Big Bad Sebastien, who'd be licking his chops. Poor Clarissa. Between the lesbians and the painting she was going to commit hara-kiri right here in the Oak Salon. Not to mention the fact that Edgar's bombshell was guaranteed to scoop my keynote address.

Which reminded me of something. I'd forgotten to ask Nancy what she was doing with a slide of Edgar's painting. Actually, I think I forgot on purpose because I didn't want to have to mention the fact that I only knew about the slide because I'd broken into her car and pawed through her things. But there was no way around it now.

I scanned the room, rehearsing my mea culpas. I didn't mean to sneak into your car. I *did* mean to sneak into your car, but I only did it out of concern for you, a person I'd never met. I did mean to sneak into your car, but I did it out of concern for your *mother,* another person I'd never met. I snuck into your car because I'm a sucker. Because I suffer from Catholic guilt. Because I've got a savior complex. Because I'm easily bored.

I was making myself dizzy and it looked like Nancy had already left anyway. I poured myself some cranberry juice and downed it in a single gulp. It was just as well. Soon enough everything was going to come out in the wash. Maybe even the juice I'd just dribbled onto my Aerosmith T-shirt.

The moon was out, though the sun hadn't set. We drove straight toward snowcapped Mount San Jacinto, a jagged wall of gray stone that seemed to have crashed down on the center of town, like a gargantuan space rock.

At least we knew where we were going. The valet at the hotel, Norman, had sketched us a map on a cocktail napkin. It was pretty simple. To the west was the neighborhood of Las Palmas with its Spanish-style houses, the epitome of old money luxe. To the north was the Movie Colony, named for the influx of Hollywood stars in the 1920s and 1930s who'd come to get away from it all. (So said Norman, who'd also informed us that when he was five years old, he'd seen all four Gabor sisters slurping down oysters at a well-known French restaurant in town.) Farther north was Little Tuscany, where famous, once-isolated modernist houses were being crowded out by newer subdivisions. Edgar Edwards's desert hideaway was somewhere in there.

The shadows shifted. The date palms swayed. The breeze caressed my cheeks. This was paradise. Apparently, I was not alone in this opinion. I turned up a steep hill thronged with houses. Many of the newer places had a watered-down, generically Mediterranean feel indistinguishable from that of your average So-Cal upscale chain restaurant. Elsewhere, kitsch abounded. There were several statues of impudent cupids peeing in plaster fountains. A lone cactus stood guard over a house with a golf ball–shaped mailbox. We passed another place with a butterfly roof so exaggerated it looked ready for liftoff. Another had a mirrored front door and a Rolls-Royce golf cart parked out front.

Edgar Edwards's glass and steel house was impossible to miss. Perched on a jagged outcropping, it was pure drama — just the way the man liked things. Why else would he keep a loon like Mitchell Honey around? I drove to the end of the long pebbled drive, then cut the engine. It was dark now, and I should have been exhausted, but I've always been something of a contrarian.

Lael got out of the car and stretched like a cat after a marathon nap. "I feel amazing!"

"Me, too," I said, taking a deep breath. "There must be something in the air."

"My armpits," said Bridget. "So who's going to help me with all this shit?"

We hauled everything out of the car. I put up the top and locked the doors. For a moment I was surprised to see lights on inside. Then I remembered our host was in town. Given the change in circumstances, I had no idea what to expect. After all, I barely knew him. Probably more drama. Would he slam the door in our faces? If he'd decided upon an impromptu tryst with skinny Jake, that was a good possibility. Still, the place looked huge, and I was broke — both mitigating factors.

We'd stay out of their way. We weren't going to be home all that much anyway. And in the evenings, we could all hang out around the pool doing cannonballs while Lael made s'mores and Bridget mooned over her boyfriend. It'd be just like summer camp.

Bridget started to drag the first of her steamer trunks up the narrow flagstone path, which was flanked by huge boulders, the kind you couldn't haul up a hill just for atmosphere. "I like this place. It's unyielding, but tranquil."

Lael looked dubious.

"Talk about unyielding, what did you put in this thing?" I asked, kicking the other trunk up the walk. "A body?"

"What do they say about people who live in glass houses?" Lael asked.

"They should shower in their swimsuits," I replied.

"You're such a prude," said Bridget, smiling.

"At least my boyfriend's of age."

"Oh, are we going there again, honey?"

"Cut it out, you two," said Lael.

I rang the bell.

"Didn't he give you a key?" she asked.

I pulled it out of my purse. "But I think he's in there. I don't want to walk in unannounced."

I rang again, but there was no answer.

"Let's get this show on the road," said Bridget.

"Good idea." I opened the door, hoping we weren't intruding on anything.

"Holy smoking Josephine!" Bridget exclaimed.

She did have a way of putting things. The place was right out of the pages of *Architectural Digest*: textbook midcentury modern, with a Barcelona lounger and Eames chairs and birch built-ins and sleek aluminum shutters and thick walls of glass. So unlike Edgar's sepulchral mansion on Carroll Avenue. But I had the same feeling of not being able to breathe.

"Hello," I called out. "Is anybody here?"

"Nobody here but us freeloaders," said Bridget.

"Then why are the lights on?"

"We are not freeloaders," Lael said briskly. "We are going to leave a carrot cake as thanks. And some perfumed soaps." She frowned at Bridget disapprovingly, then went to nose around. Bridget and I plopped down on a long, low black leather sofa, which offered little in the way of comfort.

"Hmm," said Bridget.

"Beverages might help matters," I said.

"I can fix that." She grabbed a bag and headed into the kitchen. We'd picked up provisions at the liquor store at the bottom of the hill.

"You should see these towels," called Lael from the bathroom. "They're folded like origami flowers."

I heard the sound of glass breaking in the kitchen. "Sorry," called Bridget. "It's slippery in here. I like my floors to have a little grit on 'em."

It *was* kind of eerie how pristine the house was. I got up to look around, thinking about the white gloves Edgar had asked me to put on before touching his books. The man obviously had a hygiene fetish. A lily pond ran the length of the breezeway

leading from the living room to the bedrooms. The water was smooth and glassy. I
couldn't resist sticking my finger in it, and
immediately felt like a criminal. Crimes
against hygiene. Guilty as charged.

The door to the master bedroom was
open. The bed looked like it had been
carved out of rock. Everything else was glass
and mirrors. There wasn't a fingerprint, a
smudge, or a speck of dust anywhere. Not
an item out of place — not a book, a newspaper, an ashtray, sunglasses, keys, nothing.
I looked inside the closet. Empty. Hmm.
Maybe Edgar was still on the road.

I slid open the glass doors. The elliptical
pool was pushed right up to the edge of the
house. Again with the drama. I hoped Edgar
didn't walk in his sleep.

Outside, the full moon looked like a
glowing beach ball. I heard the popping of a
cork. Bridget and Lael appeared, holding
crystal glasses and champagne. There was
no place to sit so we propped the bottle
against a bush and stretched out on the
grass, which was clipped low, like carpeting.
We lay there for hours, talking, until Bridget
and Lael staggered off to bed. I hugged
them good night, then grabbed a blanket
from the hall closet and went back outside
with the romantic idea of finding the Big

Dipper. I'd never been much of a stargazer. I was always too busy. But that night I felt like I had all the time in the world.

The next thing I remembered was the sun coming up and the sprinklers going on.

I decided to skip my shower.

9

We spent the morning at a number of thrift stores, trying on various abominations (including a purple python–print caftan and an orange-and-white polka-dot jumpsuit with rhinestone trim) and convincing ourselves they would make fabulous conversation pieces, until we came to our senses and remembered that no one actually wants to look like a conversation piece. Bridget declared the whole morning a bust, though we did earn the undying friendship of one fellow shopper, a biker sporting Doc Martens and a handlebar mustache, who was set on a well-priced peach mother-of-the-bride dress until we convinced him it was just too short in the torso. We found him a lovely striped shift instead.

It was about eleven-thirty when I headed over to the hotel. I wasn't on for another couple of hours, but Edgar — wherever he might be — was scheduled for noon and I didn't want to miss a minute. The girls had finally decided on seaweed body wraps and video poker (Bridget's idea) at the Spa Hotel and Casino down the street. They'd promised to be back at the Oak Salon by two.

Norman was out front parking cars. "Let's hear it for SaturDaze! Today's event needs a warning tag — not for the faint of heart!"

I looked at him. "I wasn't born yesterday."

"They told me to say that," he said, embarrassed. "Don't forget your validation."

The crowd in the lobby had reached epic proportions. It looked like the set of an all-girl Cecil B. DeMille movie. Somebody stepped on my little toe, an errant margarita almost ended up in my handbag, and I got stuck for a while between two shrieking women in Mardi Gras beads who hadn't seen each other since 1973, but I finally made it across the room. It was too early for the hard stuff, so I decided on a cup of coffee. I needed to stall anyway. The last thing I wanted to do was interrupt the scavenger hunt in progress.

The Bugle Bar was tucked into a dark alcove. The music was silky R&B, but the decor was colonial raj, lots of rattan.

The bartender was polishing glasses.

"Excuse me?" No answer. "Excuse me, barkeep?"

" 'Barkeep!' " echoed a woman sipping

116

something blue. She was wearing a Stars-and-Stripes visor. "I love that!" She turned to the woman sitting next to her. "Did you hear what she said? 'Barkeep'! That is so cute."

"You're so cute," the second woman murmured.

I caught a glimpse of her. "Victoria? Is that you?"

"Cece Caruso!" she said, leaning over her friend to grab my hand. "How delightful to find you here!"

"How delightful to find *you* here! And without your twin sister."

"How are you?"

"Good. You?"

"I'm wonderful." She paused for a second. "And you are here for . . . ?"

"The convention, of course."

"Which convention?"

"The Nancy Drew fan convention."

"I am so relieved to hear you say that," she said. "I mean, you and my cousin Peter and everything."

"Isn't that what you're here for?"

"Oh, no," she said, wrinkling her freckled nose. "I'm on holiday."

"Oh." I did a little drumroll on the bar. "That's great."

"What's great?"

"That you're out — I mean out and about, not *out* out, because that's none of my business, of course." I felt my cheeks getting hot.

"But I am out. And it's totally fine."

"I'm just happy to see you so happy."

She smiled. "Thanks. This is my partner, Celeste, by the way."

"Pleased to meet you, Celeste."

"You, too. 'Barkeep,' I love that," she said, chuckling. "What are you having, Cece?"

"Just coffee."

This time the bartender heard me. A steaming mug materialized as if by magic.

"So," asked Victoria, "have you talked to Peter lately?"

I tore open a packet of sugar and spilled the white crystals into my cup. Then I poured in some cream and watched it swirl into nothingness. "Not since he left for Buffalo, no."

"Is everything okay with you two?"

I looked up into her kind eyes. They ran in the family. "Not really."

"What is it?"

I sighed. "I've made so many mistakes with men that I'm not sure I can trust my own instincts anymore. And I'm ruining everything."

"You're not ruining anything."

"I should say not," added Celeste.

"Peter is crazy about you," Victoria continued. "He told me so himself. And he's a straight arrow."

"Do you mean straight shooter, hon?" asked Celeste.

"That, too. I mean, someone a person can count on. When we were kids he used to beat up anybody who was mean to me."

"Even Dena?" I asked.

"I see you know Victoria's evil twin," said Celeste.

Victoria laughed. "Peter did once steal all of Dena's Halloween candy, which about killed her. He ate all the Sweet Tarts and gave me everything else."

"He still likes Sweet Tarts," I said. "The candy."

"I know. Listen, we've got to go." She took my hand and gave it a squeeze.

Celeste finished her drink and the two of them walked away, arm in arm. Some people seemed to have things all figured out. Then again, I'd always been a late bloomer. Maybe there was still hope.

Upstairs, it should have been business as usual. But Clarissa, an ice bucket in each hand, accosted me as I got off the elevator.

"You're riding down with me," she said, pushing me back in.

"I am?"

"The ice machine on this floor is broken and we need to talk."

"That sounds ominous," I said, pressing the button for the lobby.

She shoved the ice buckets at me, then bent down and pulled off a red high-heeled pump.

"Blisters?"

"Pebbles." Once her shoe was back on her foot, she directed the full intensity of her gaze on me. "So. Cece. If I have learned anything I have learned that one must be flexible. The winning individual must be able to turn on a dime, roll with the punches, sway with the breeze, do you read me?"

"I read you."

"You are on in five minutes. Edgar Edwards is history."

"What do you mean, 'Edgar Edwards is history'?"

"That's precisely what I mean. I trust you speak English?"

"Clarissa, take it easy."

"I'm getting upset. Don't get me upset, Cece. That's a very bad idea."

I could see that. So. The ladies weren't going to see the nude portrait of Grace Horton after all. Did that mean I was supposed to go back to my previous comments? Or was I going to plow ahead and tell them

120

about a painting they weren't going to see and that was likely to make them crazy if and when they did see it? Probably not a great idea. I'd save it for a less squeamish audience. It'd be perfect for my book. I was sure I could get Edgar to give me permission to reproduce the painting. I could give it a whole chapter, even. I took a deep breath. That was settled. As for today, well, the winning individual rolls with the punches and sways with the breeze. If Nancy Drew — while bound and gagged by villains — could tap out HELP in Morse code, I could handle Clarissa and the Chums.

"You will be speaking directly after the scavenger hunt, and the ladies should be on their last clue by now." She pulled a piece of paper out of the pocket of her red blazer. "This last one is from *The Mystery of the Fire Dragon*. 'Aunt Eloise treats everyone to dinner at a Chinese restaurant,'" Clarissa read, "'but ends up taking the food to go after a flowerpot falls from a balcony and knocks Nancy Drew unconscious.'"

"Are they looking for doggy bags in the kitchen?" I asked.

"No." The elevator doors opened and I followed her out. "Aunt Eloise ordered Peking duck. They've got to find the pond in the West Garden." She pointed toward an exit sign. "There are ducks out there. In this heat, can you imagine?"

"That's pretty obscure, don't you think?"

"It's supposed to be a challenge." She stopped in front of the ice machine. "Most of us here are experts, Cece."

"Well, I'm sorry about Edgar, but I'm ready." I'd disappointed her. She'd actually been looking forward to catching me off guard, the sadist. "Yes," I said, patting my purse, "I have my notes and even a change of underwear right here."

"Be prepared. It's not just the Boy Scout motto. It's a life lesson."

She looked at me and I looked at her. Then she snatched the ice buckets out of my hands and filled them up.

I think I won that round, but I'm not exactly sure.

The lights went down. I began with the bland stuff — the Stratemeyer Syndicate and the multiple Nancy Drew ghostwriters and half-ghosts, so called because they worked from such detailed outlines. Then, on the theory that pandering never hurts, I talked about the role of fans in series fiction. Tabby Cat nodded like crazy during that part. (She'd recently written a twelve-page account of Nancy's wedding and posted it on the Chums' Listserv. Her vision of the Drew-Nickerson nuptials had Nancy wearing a simple white sheath, no sequins or beads, and the bridesmaids, Bess Marvin and George Fayne, in pale yellow pantsuits. The hors d'oeuvres were likewise pale yellow: deviled eggs and curried chicken salad on endive spears.)

From there, I hashed over Nancy as gothic heroine, virgin goddess, feminist icon, and WASP legend. Finally it was time for my personal obsession: Grace Horton.

Grace Horton. She was the black hole at the center of my research, inescapable and invisible. I knew she had been a model with the Harry Conover agency in New York, where the idea of the celebrity model had supposedly originated. Other than the Nancy Drew covers, however, and a single newspaper advertisement from 1942, in which Grace, dressed in a red bathing suit and polka-dot slingbacks, professed to staying slim on the Ry-Krisp plan, I could find no images and no information whatsoever about her.

The Stratemeyer archive at the New York Public Library yielded nothing. Databases at various societies of illustrators and institutes of pop culture, also nothing. The Internet, zilch. And still, Grace haunted me, another one of the Stratemeyer ghosts — or maybe just a half-ghost.

The cool blonde. The good girl. She was both at the same time. That much I could fathom. What I just couldn't wrap my head around, however, was the fact that Grace Horton used her beauty to become Nancy Drew, a young woman who only ever had to use her brain.

Nancy was beautiful, of course, but her beauty was beside the point. Poor Ned Nickerson. He never quite got it. He was the kind of guy who was always underfoot, a puppy waiting to be stroked — or kicked. There were others, too: Dick Larrabee, Dirk Jackson, Don Cameron, Jack Kingdom, as all-American as their names. But Nancy was indifferent. With her adoring father and unlimited bank account she could afford to be. Everything about her was inspirational: her bravery, her loyalty, her spirit of adventure. But it was this obliviousness to money and sex that made her an icon, especially to readers too young to have developed much of a taste for either. Then again, maybe that was me, a two-bit beauty queen from the working class who got pregnant and blew her one shot at a serious life.

The lights went up. All eyes were on me. I felt naked. I was clearly some kind of exhibitionist, because I liked it. And everyone seemed to be clapping.

Lael and Bridget arrived just as Clarissa opened the floor to questions and comments from the audience.

"Sorry," Lael mouthed as they crawled into the back row, but I think she could tell from my face that things had gone well.

Rita was waving her arm with grim determination.

"Yes, Rita?"

"You've inspired me to come out of the closet. As I said yesterday, I think Nancy Drew sucks."

After a chorus of horrified clucks, the audience turned en masse from Rita to me. Somebody had to be the source of this perfidy.

"Perhaps I didn't make myself clear," I said. "I do not think Nancy Drew sucks. I am a huge Nancy Drew fan. She made it possible for me to dream of doing things I never even could have imagined. She was fearless. And nothing could sway her."

"Absolutely," Rita said, cutting me off. "That's a sign of psychosis."

"Why don't we move on?" I looked around the room for a friendly face. Nancy Olsen's hand went up. Oh, great.

"Nancy?"

She looked at her mother for a minute, then back at me.

"What would a Nancy Drew book be without a happy ending?"

"Real life," I answered without thinking.

Clarissa stood up abruptly.

"Do you have something to add?" I asked her.

She glowered at me by way of response, then walked slowly up to the front of the room. With the lights up I could see that her face was red, almost as red as her suit.

She turned to face me. "Thank you, Cece, on behalf of the Chums. That was very interesting. Of course" — and here she paused dramatically — "if you had bothered to inform me that you would be speaking on a topic other than the one we had agreed upon, 'The Changing Demographics of River Heights,' I might have been able to provide you with some pertinent information." She addressed the Chums. "What I mean to say is, had I been better informed, I might have saved Ms. Caruso from making such egregious errors."

What errors? Little beads of sweat began trickling down my sides.

Clarissa strolled around the room, up and down the aisles, her hands clasped behind her back. The Chums were mesmerized, heads swiveling in unison, pens poised over their pads. This was way more excitement than they'd bargained for when they'd sent in their registration forms.

"It would seem that Ms. Caruso finds our Nancy Drew to be some sort of elitist ideal." Clarissa paused next to the sleep-over kits. "Fine. I don't agree, but one could certainly argue the point."

I scanned the crowd. Big Bad Sebastien, sensing a catfight, looked happier than a pig in shit.

"However, I find it *reprehensible* to use an actual individual to make such a point. I'm speaking about Grace Horton. Let me tell you a thing or two about Grace Horton, the original Nancy Drew. First of all, she was not a sociological cliché — some poor exploited girl from a humble background forced to use her beauty to rise in the world."

I didn't say she was, I wanted to scream. But I remained calm.

"Grace was a highly moral, highly principled individual. And more to the point," Clarissa continued, walking back up to the front of the room, "she came from a wealthy and accomplished family — my family, to be precise."

At this, the Chums went crazy.

Tabby Cat leapt up from her seat.

"Careful — the baby!" Rita warned.

"I need to know how Clarissa is related to Grace," said Tabby Cat urgently.

"Grace Horton was my ex-husband's mother, my daughter Nancy's grand-mother."

I looked over at Nancy, whose head was buried in a book.

A dark-haired woman wearing glasses raised her hand.

"Yes?"

"Who chose Grace as the cover model? Was it Edward Stratemeyer or the illus-trator, Russell Tandy?"

Before Clarissa could answer, another woman shouted out, "What was she really like? Was Grace anything like Nancy Drew?"

Then another: "Did your ex-mother-in-law get to keep any original cover art, any-thing like that?"

"Ladies, ladies. These are all fine ques-tions. Indeed, on the subject of Grace's re-lationship with Russell Tandy and her impact on the creation of Nancy Drew, I have much to say. But you will have to be patient."

They didn't much like that idea.

"Now, now." She smiled. "What I mean to

say is, I will be addressing all of these questions in my forthcoming book."

The Chums were beside themselves yet again. What forthcoming book?

"It will be chock-full of surprises, I promise you that. All sorts of secrets will be revealed." She smiled again, showing all of her thirty-two teeth.

Lael sounded like she was choking. She was a good friend.

"And now, Chums, we will adjourn for lunch. When we return, Allie Nemeroff from Shreveport, Louisiana, will give her talk, 'Boullion with a Speck of Nutmeg: Savories in Nancy Drew.' Finally," she said, looking right at me, "something we can all enjoy!"

In the world of boxing, they call that a technical knockout.

10

Edgar Edwards's pool turned out to be an excellent place to recuperate. The water was a crystalline blue, the temperature a balmy eighty. The three of us floated along on rafts we'd bought on sale at Target, soaking up the healing rays of the sun. All negative thoughts were banished. They were like the tiny leaves floating on the surface of the water. If you didn't get rid of them, they'd eventually clog your filter.

So Lael and Bridget had lost three hundred dollars at video poker. They had their health, didn't they? Bridget had a boyfriend who adored her. Lael had amazing children. As for me, well, I could hardly complain. I let my hand dangle in the water and tried to feel contentment wash over me. It took a minute. I had a happy daughter. Wonderful friends. My book was almost finished. I was done with Clarissa's games. Her bad attitude was not my problem. Her daughter was not my problem. Her quote-unquote book was not my problem. My romance with Gambino, however — that was definitely my problem. I'd derailed it, and only I could set it right. I pulled my hand out of the water and shook the droplets off.

"You woke me up," Lael said groggily.

"Go back to sleep," I whispered.

I grabbed my cell phone from the raft's cup holder and punched in his number. He'd be back from Buffalo by now. And if I knew him at all he would've gone straight from the airport to his office in the Hollywood Division.

He picked up on the first ring.

"Gambino."

"Hi. It's me."

I thought I could hear him smiling. He'd be rumpled. The blue eyes behind his wire-rimmed glasses would be red. He couldn't sleep on planes. And he'd be on his fourth cup of coffee by now, heavy on the cream and sugar.

"I missed you."

"Me, too," I answered.

Lael was wide awake now. She and Bridget drifted over, so they could hear our conversation better. "I want to hear all about your trip, but first I have something I need to tell you." My stomach was doing flip-flops. "It can't wait."

Lael squealed. Bridget reached over to clutch her hand but inadvertently bumped her raft into mine. That's when the phone flew out of my hand and fell down to the bottom of the pool.

"Shit!"

"Were you going to tell him you loved him?" asked Lael, positively deranged with anticipation. She was sitting up now, and clutching the sides of her raft. "What was he saying?"

"Now we'll never know," I said.

"Your love has plunged into the bottom of a watery abyss," said Bridget. "Just like *Titanic*."

I climbed out of the pool and adjusted my black bikini, which set off to perfection the wound I'd gotten stealing the orange in Riverside. "I'm calling him back from inside. You two can wait here."

I probably needed a new cell phone anyway.

We had, of course, forgotten to bring out towels. Dripping wet, I traipsed across the velvety green grass to where I'd left my Diet Coke, took a swig, then walked through the sliding glass doors into the living room. The air conditioner was blasting. Shivering, I turned it off and tiptoed through the breezeway toward the bedrooms. The linen closet was located just opposite the room I'd been using.

"Love is in the air," I hummed to myself, da-da-da-da-da-da-da-da. Halfway through the next chorus, something caught my eye.

The door to the master bedroom was ajar.

Strange. I'd walked through the master bedroom earlier this morning, when I'd come in after getting soaked by the sprinklers. I distinctly remembered closing the door behind me before I walked across the hall to my room. Why would Lael or Bridget have opened it in the interim? They wouldn't have. Maybe Edgar had finally arrived.

"Hello!" I called out, suddenly conscious of the fact that I was for all intents and purposes naked as a jaybird. "Who's in there?" There was no response. I walked slowly toward the door. "Who's in there?" I asked more insistently. "Edgar, is that you?" I wondered if I should knock. I hesitated for a minute, then tapped gently. No one answered. I pressed my ear to the door and thought I could hear soft music playing.

I stepped back for a moment, then knocked harder. The door swung open and banged against the wall. The noise startled me. Not to mention the unmade bed. There were sheets and blankets everywhere. A pair of faded blue jeans was lying in front of the fireplace.

Jake.

But where was he? And where was Edgar? They'd obviously been here. And now they were gone.

I backed away from the room and headed to the kitchen. I remembered seeing a typed list posted by the phone with emergency contact information. This didn't seem like an emergency, not exactly, but something wasn't right. I wanted to talk to Edgar. The first number on the list was the Carroll Avenue house. I dialed and waited. The machine picked up. I hung up, frustrated. The next number was Mitchell Honey's cell phone. It rang and rang. No answer. I started pacing back and forth.

"Ow!" Jesus H. Christ. Perfect. I'd stepped on some broken glass. Bridget had dropped something in here yesterday. Of course, it was too much to ask that she clean up her messes properly. I bent down and rubbed my hand across the bottom of my foot. Damn it. This was a monster piece. How could she have missed it? And now I'd cut my hand, too, and there was blood all over the place.

I grabbed some paper towels and started blotting up the drops of blood, then wrapped the last few sheets on the roll around my hand and foot. I peeled the list off the wall and studied it. Jake's cell phone was next. I limped across the living room, trying not to stain the beautiful wood floors, and back out to the pool.

"Did you talk to him?" asked Lael. "What happened to you?"

"I never realized you were so accident-prone," said Bridget.

"I cut myself," I said, glaring at Bridget, "that's what happened to me. And something strange is going on. Someone's been in there. Edgar's bedroom is a mess."

"How can that be?" asked Lael.

My hands were trembling as I dialed Jake's cell. "I'm sorry, you have reached a number that is no longer in service."

Of course, he didn't pay his bills. The next number was Edgar's cell. Time to get to the bottom of this.

It rang several times.

"What's that?" asked Bridget.

"What's what?" I asked, thoroughly confused. I hung up. Who else could I call? Edgar's was the last number on the list.

"That noise I just heard."

I hadn't heard a thing.

"It was probably nothing." Or it was them. Somewhere out here.

"Edgar? Jake? Are you in the backyard?" I cried. "Please come out." I stepped around an enormous palm tree embedded in some cement, and toward a sea of boulders leading to the mountains beyond.

"Where are you going, Cece? You don't have any shoes on," Lael said.

"Only bloody paper towels," added Bridget. "And they're going to get bloodier if you keep heading out there."

"I'm coming to help you. C'mon, Bridget."

They got out of the pool and huddled next to me.

"I'm going to try Edgar's cell again. I didn't let it ring long enough."

"There's that noise again," said Bridget.

This time I heard it, too. Coming from beyond the boulders.

I hung up. The noise stopped. I dialed Edgar's number again. The noise started again.

It sounded like a phone ringing.

Like when you're home, but you don't want to get the phone, and you're waiting for the answering machine to pick up, to release you from some obligation you don't want. But the ringing goes on and on, insistent, like a reproach.

I headed toward the edge of the property, my heart in my mouth. I went past the boulders, through the cactus, and deep into the brush. And that was where I found him, Edgar Edwards, with a small hole in the middle of his forehead.

His cell phone was lying next to him, still ringing, still insisting.

11

The Eames chairs in Edgar's living room were unrelenting. I guess that was the theme of the day.

"Let's go over it just one more time." Detective Mindy Lasarow tucked a strand of prematurely gray hair behind one ear and smiled grimly at me.

"No problem," I said.

"Why are you ladies here, in this house?" She looked at me as if she were hoping for a different answer, if only to relieve the monotony.

"We were invited here," I recited. It was the fourth, maybe the fifth, time I'd explained it.

"By whom?"

"Edgar Edwards."

Her partner, Detective Dunphy, scribbled madly, as if this were brand-new information.

I turned to Detective Dunphy. Cindy. She didn't look like a Cindy. Cindys have dimples. This one had a single furrowed brow.

"I'm talking about the dead man."

"Uh-huh."

She wasn't exactly the conversationalist Detective Lasarow was.

"Okay. The dead man invited you here, to stay at his house."

"Right."

"And your friends, too."

"We have every right to be here," exclaimed Lael. "We were planning to leave a carrot cake."

Detective Dunphy spoke up. "If you just answer the questions, ma'am, we'll all get out of here sooner."

"Don't you ma'am me." Lael outraged was a thing to behold, but now was probably not the time.

"Should we be contacting our lawyers?" asked Bridget, who was sweating profusely, as if she were already locked up in a Third World prison. "Don't we get a phone call?"

"Don't be silly, Bridget," I said. "We aren't suspects. Right, Detective Lasarow?"

She glanced at her partner.

"Not yet, Ms. Caruso."

They were so cool, these two. But Edgar was dead, and they were wasting precious time. Surely we didn't look like the type of lowlifes they usually dealt with. My bikini was by Dolce and Gabbana.

"Okay. You were invited here by Mr. Edwards. But he wasn't planning to be in town."

"That's right."

"But he showed up unexpectedly."

"According to Clarissa Olsen, yes."

"Spell it."

Come on. *"O-L-S-E-N."*

"And she said what?"

"She told me Edgar was here, in Palm Springs. He was planning to give a talk at her conference at the hotel. But I never saw him. He canceled his talk. Or she axed him, I don't know." Bad choice of words. But she was pretty riled up about something.

"So back when he didn't think he was coming he gave you a key."

"Yes."

"You and your girlfriends were supposed to let yourselves in."

"Correct."

"And you did. Last night."

"Correct."

"And where is that key?"

Here was the sticky part. "I lost it."

Detective Lasarow sent a meaningful glance to Detective Dunphy, who promptly started a new page in her notepad.

"I think the key fell out of her purse at the Wyndham," volunteered Lael. "We had it this morning when we left. I remember seeing Cece lock up. But we didn't have it when we came back this afternoon. We had to go around the back. The gate was open."

"Did you leave the gate open when you left?"

"I'm not sure. I don't even think it locks."

"Why are you all cut up, Ms. Caruso?"

I looked down guiltily at my hand. She didn't know about the foot, of course. "I told you. Bridget broke a glass yesterday in the kitchen."

"By accident," Bridget insisted.

"Of course it was by accident," I said. "Anyway, I went inside to make some calls after noticing the bedroom door open, and I cut myself."

"Must've been a pretty big piece of glass."

"I can't sweep to save my life," said Bridget.

"Actually, you did a great job. The crime scene guys didn't find so much as a splinter."

Bridget looked pleased until she realized what Detective Lasarow was implying. I was fed up. We hadn't done anything and these glorified meter maids had nothing — not a shred of evidence — to suggest otherwise.

"Just stop this," I said, my voice trembling. "Forget about us and find Edgar's boyfriend, for god's sake! What are his jeans doing in the bedroom without him in them?"

Everyone turned to look at me.

"How do you know whose jeans those are in the bedroom?"

How embarrassing. "He was wearing them when we met, on Wednesday, I guess it was."

Detective Dunphy could barely contain her excitement. With some color in her cheeks, she looked more like a Cindy. Her partner took over with the pen and pad.

"And you recognized them, glancing through a half-open door, crumpled in a heap on the floor?"

"Cece is very good with clothes," said Bridget.

"That means a lot, coming from you," I said.

"Okay, okay," said Detective Dunphy. "You girls can save that stuff for the Wyndham."

"Excuse me?" Lael said. "Excuse me? Did you say what I think you did? That's sexual harassment. We could report you for that."

"Sorry. I just assumed."

"That was totally inappropriate," Lael said. She loved this sort of thing. A righteous cause. "How dare you?"

Mindy Lasarow took back the reins. Cindy Dunphy looked chagrined. "So, was Wednesday the day you were given the key?"

"Yes. Look, just call the boyfriend, curator, whatever. His name is Mitchell Honey. He was there that day. He'll vouch for me."

"The boyfriend whose pants you saw? How can I call him? You said he's missing."

"Those are Jake's pants. I'm talking about the other boyfriend. Mitchell Honey would never fit into those pants."

And Mitchell Honey would never vouch for me. He hated me, plus he hadn't actually been there when Edgar had pressed the key into my hands. He probably knew nothing about it. I thought back to my conversation with him on the phone Thursday morning. He'd been really concerned about Edgar giving me something. Maybe he *had* known about the key. Why would he care? For that matter, why had Edgar given it to me if he was planning to use the house himself? I guessed I'd never know. One thing was for sure. Mitchell was going to believe the absolute worst of me. That I'd broken into the house with my desperado girlfriends. That I'd shot Edgar. That I'd done something equally horrific to Jake, but only after stealing his pants. I hoped Jake was all right.

Where could he be? Maybe back in L.A., with Mitchell. The two of them would really be stuck with each other now.

The detectives consulted their notepads one last time, then stood up. They were finished with us. We shook hands without meaning it. They gave us permission to return home but advised us, in the strongest language possible, to stay in touch. To be available for further questioning. And not to be foolish. A serious crime had been committed, and we were to conduct ourselves accordingly. I found that last part a bit obscure. I wondered if they were trying to tell us that we were no longer suspects. Or maybe it was routine procedure for homicide detectives to remind people to watch their backs.

Two uniformed cops took over from there. They helped us pack up our things, fished my apparently waterproof cell phone out of the bottom of the pool with a net they'd found in the storage shed (three messages from Gambino), then escorted us out to Maynard's car. What a road trip this had turned out to be. Lael switched on the radio so we didn't have to talk to one another, which would've been a good idea except that I was distracted by the sudden blast of rockabilly and ran over the yellow crime scene tape on the way down the pebbled drive.

I was a little offended that nobody believed I'd done it by accident.

12

The next few days Gambino and I were all about crossed signals. I finally caught up with him Wednesday morning at his desk. But we'd barely said hello when his partner showed up, champing at the bit. They were working a double homicide, two men found dead in a burning car. It had taken them out to Yucaipa three times since Saturday night, and they were on their way out there again. He knew I had something important to tell him, and asked me to be patient. I wanted to be patient, but I was afraid that if much more time passed I'd lose my nerve.

Looked like it'd been a good week for the grim reaper. Besides the twosome Gambino had told me about, the newspaper was full of inventors, mathematicians, retired army lieutenant generals, prizewinning horticulturists, and theatrical producers all winging their way to the hereafter. Poor Edgar's obituary didn't make it into the *L.A. Times* until Thursday.

I read it with my morning coffee.

Edgar Edwards was born in Teaneck, New Jersey, the only child of a machinist and a homemaker. As a teenager, he played sax. After graduating from high school, he moved to Chicago and worked as a hospital orderly during the day while fronting a local band at night. He was good. But it was in the early seventies that his lucky streak began. He won $15,000 in the state lottery and within ten years had parlayed it into a fortune in real estate, buying up buildings in Chicago's warehouse district when they were cheap and riding the gentrification wave all the way to the bank.

I dropped an English muffin into the toaster and read on.

Edgar brought his sax with him to California, a retiree at forty. He took a crash course in art history at UCLA, then threw himself into collecting. He was catholic in his tastes: plein air painting, Mayan carvings, documentary photography. I'd seen only a fraction of what he'd amassed.

Several works from his British art pottery collection were considered masterpieces, promised gifts to the Metropolitan Museum of Art in New York. "Edgar had a voracious appetite," said a prominent dealer from San Francisco. "Once he believed in something, he wouldn't let it go." The director of a small *Kunsthalle* in Cologne claimed that "he could see through to the insides of things, not merely on their outsides," which had to have lost something in the translation. A curator of Japanese art and antiquities at the L.A. County Museum commented that Edgar had "that rarest of talents, the ability to recognize true quality." Probably true, but I'll bet she was after those Edo fans, the ghoul.

My muffin popped up, a little burnt around the edges. I scraped the black parts into the sink. I hadn't known this, but Edgar was on the board of JazzFest L.A. and the Children's Museum, and was active in several AIDS charities. It didn't seem fair. He was a good guy whose luck had run out too soon.

Services were to be held Thursday afternoon at Hollywood Forever Memorial Park, with a private reception to follow at the home of the deceased. The executor of the estate, Mitchell Honey, asked that in lieu of flowers, donations in Edgar's memory be sent to the charity of one's choice. That didn't sound like the Mitchell Honey I knew. Then again, he had all those allergies. Probably didn't want any more pollen around him than necessary.

There were no immediate survivors.

I made quick work of my muffin, washed my plate and cup, and placed them on the dish rack to dry. Then I went to the hall closet and pulled Buster's leash from its hook. The little guy raced to the door, leaping and yapping with excitement. I think we both needed some air.

It was a beautiful day, which contrary to popular opinion not all of them are around here. August and September are too hot; June is known for its gloom; January, February, and March bring the rain; but April can be as perfect as early July, and today was one of those perfect days.

I sucked in the air, greedy for oxygen. Ever since getting back from Palm Springs I'd been having a hard time sleeping. I was so tired. The phone never stopped ringing. Who did I think murdered Edgar? Could I speculate on the missing Jake Waite? Too bad about his solicitation arrest. It was several years back, but it still didn't look good. Unlike Jake's mug shot, which I have to say did him justice. Still, rough sex gone bad seemed to be a prospect no news reporter could resist.

Then there was everyone I'd ever met, wanting to bring me a casserole. Annie and Vincent beat them all to the punch. Dinner had been waiting on my doorstep every night this week: I had no idea tofu could be so versatile. My mother took a different tack. She called several times, then FedExed me a two-pound box of dark chocolate turtles with a note reading something to the effect of, did I not care that my shenanigans were sending her blood pressure through the roof? I suppose it was comforting to know that solipsism was alive and well in Asbury Park, New Jersey.

Buster started pulling me across the street. He'd spied Scarlett, an attractive standard poodle from around the corner. She towered over him, but Buster liked a challenge.

"Hello, Buster!" said Melanie, Scarlett's owner. She was carrying a fistful of plastic bags and a half-gallon jug of water. "How are you today? You're looking very frisky."

In West Hollywood you address the dog, not the human. I didn't dare break protocol with Melanie, who was unnaturally attached to her pet.

"Hello, Scarlett," I said. "You look like you've just been groomed."

"I have," said Melanie. "And Mommy and I are exercising this morning so we can't chat for long."

I was about to throw up when Pushkin, the sex-crazed Siberian husky from down the street, showed up. After the requisite greetings, Buster and I beat a hasty retreat.

We were headed for Book Soup. The new edition of *The Chicago Manual of Style* was hot off the presses, and I'd special-ordered a copy. What can I say? Strange things excite me. Like the fact that the comma is omitted after short introductory adverbial phrases unless misreading is likely. And that *cross-country* gets a hyphen and *crossover* does not. But maybe everybody's interested in such things.

I was partial to the scenic route so we took the steep detour up La Cienega to Sunset Plaza, a Eurotrash oasis smack-dab in the middle of the Sunset Strip. The Strip was the fabled home of rock clubs and run-aways; Sunset Plaza was more moneyed if equally sleazy. It attracted, among other colorful types, a sizable contingent of tanned Italian sexpots with dachshunds in their purses, along with the ne'er-do-well younger sons of deposed dictators trying to get into said sexpots' Versace jeans.

Buster enjoyed the ambience.

I'd planned on stopping for a chocolate croissant, but there was a middle-aged man with a ponytail sitting out front at Clafoutis who gave me the kind of grin that kills appe-tites. Maybe I should go there more often, I thought, tugging at the waistband of my skirt. Today I'd gone Andalusian retro, with my hair pulled back into a bun, an off-the-shoulder blouse, and a matching silk chiffon skirt with tiered ruffles. The skirt was a size too small, but beggars can't be choosers when you're talking marked-down Prada. I passed on the pastry and flounced down Sunset past Holloway to the bookstore, one of the best in the area.

While I waited at the back counter for my book, I wondered about Edgar. There were no immediate survivors, the paper had said. So who was going to get it all? The houses. The art. The Blue Nancys. The painting of Grace Horton. Shoot, I'd never had a chance to speak to Edgar about reproducing it in my book. I wondered if Mitchell could give me permission. Right. I'm sure he'd bend over backward to help me out.

"Excuse me?" I asked, my patience wearing thin. "Did you find that book yet?" The clerk had taken several phone calls since I'd been standing there, and was now engaged in a spirited debate with a coworker about the year Francis Ford Coppola's *Rumble Fish* had been released. He held up his index finger. What did that mean? One minute? I walked over to the fashion section to wait. Some leisurely pace they kept around there.

"Cece?" The voice came from behind a top-heavy rack of paperbacks. "I'm over here."

I peered around a pile of books on animal prints.

"Andrew?" It was Bridget's intern, bearing little resemblance to the sexy layabout of the other day. There were beads of perspiration on his upper lip and his clothes were wrinkled. "What are you doing, scaring me like that? Don't tell me you're playing hooky?"

"It's my day off, and I followed you."

"Excuse me?"

"I followed you, from your house. I wish you hadn't taken the long way. I'm in a hurry."

"Does Bridget know you're crazy?"

"I'm not crazy. I need you to come home with me."

He had a lot of cojones. "Hold it right there. Bridget is one of my best friends, as you very well know, not to mention the fact that I have a boyfriend. A policeman!" Buster started barking. He knew when I was upset. Not that he was much of a Gambino fan.

"Calm down. It's not what you think. But we didn't know who else to turn to."

"We? Who's we?"

"Jake and I." He paused, waiting for it to sink in.

"Andrew," I whispered, stealing a glance in either direction. "Are you talking about Jake Waite?"

"Yes," he said. "Jake's in trouble, and you have to help him."

"Me? You've got to be kidding."

"I'm not."

I felt a tap on my shoulder. It was a tall man in a Burberry raincoat. "Can you point me to Sylvia Plath?"

"Bugger off," I said rudely. We waited for him to move on, which took forever.

"I am dead serious, Andrew," I said, turning back to him. "Do you know where Jake is? Because if you do, you have to tell him he's got to go to the police. He's got to turn himself in. Throw himself on their mercy. He's making this much worse for himself."

"He's innocent, Cece. He didn't kill Edgar. I've known Jake for years, and believe me, he doesn't have it in him. But he's scared. He's got a record. You know what the papers are saying."

"All the more reason he should come forward."

"You must be kidding. Do you really believe that's how it works?" He started plucking at the buttons on his shirt. "I told Jake this was a bad idea," he said, shaking his head. "Regardless of what Edgar thought."

"Edgar?"

"Jake says Edgar spoke very highly of you. He thought you were a decent person, which was high praise coming from him."

Even though I barely knew Edgar, I felt the same way about him.

"What does Jake want me to do?" I asked in a low voice.

"He wants to talk to you, face-to-face."

"Where is he?"

"At my apartment. Are you coming?"

Consorting with a known criminal. Aiding and abetting a fugitive from justice. Accessorizing (or whatever) after the fact. My rap sheet was getting longer by the minute.

"Let's go," I said.

For someone with the face of an angel, Andrew drove like a bat out of hell. We must've hit every red light between West Hollywood and Echo Park, which might have slowed down the average person, but not this guy. He glanced right and left, and if no one was coming he just kept right on going, fifty miles an hour down Sunset Boulevard, which I truly didn't think was possible. By the time we got to his place, I was totally discombobulated. But it was less the driving pyrotechnics than the prospect of seeing Jake. Actually, of being alone in an apartment with a suspected killer and someone who knew him from the good old days — the good old hustling days, that would be.

Andrew lived above a mom-and-pop grocery store at the top of a terraced complex facing Echo Park Lake. Anywhere but L.A., Echo Park Lake would have qualified as a mirage — a shimmering body of water right in the middle of a working-class community. On sunny days you could find families picnicking along the shore, vendors selling blow-up toys and shaved ice, and lovers paddling among the lotuses. After dusk, however, the gangs owned the place. It had one of those stratospheric murder rates, which wasn't exactly soothing my frayed nerves.

We parked the car in the garage around the side, walked back to the front, which was decrepit by anybody's standards, and up four short flights of stairs. We didn't say a word to each other until we were at his front door. We looked at the peeling paint, beneath which was more peeling paint. Finally, Andrew turned to me.

"Please don't tell Bridget about this."

"Andrew, I can't promise you anything."

"This has nothing to do with her. But I couldn't turn my back on a friend."

"Let's talk about it later, okay?"

"Okay."

We went inside.

"Hey." Jake was sitting on the couch, his hands folded in his lap. He looked suspiciously like a choirboy, except for the shirt unbuttoned to his waist. Force of habit, I guess. A liar, I'd have no trouble believing; a murderer, I didn't know. I didn't think so.

"So I'm here," I said, crossing my arms. "What did you want to say to me?"

"Andrew, shouldn't we offer Cece something to drink?"

"This isn't a party."

"What about your dog?"

"He's fine, too." Buster was uncharacteristically quiet. I picked him up. "Why haven't you gone to the police?"

"I haven't been a model citizen. But everybody's entitled to a past."

"True enough." What exactly did Bridget know about Andrew's past?

"Please. Sit down."

I took a seat next to him and held Buster in my lap. "If you're innocent, you shouldn't have anything to hide."

157

"Don't you have anything you want to hide?"

"This isn't about me, Jake."

"Tell her about Mitchell," prompted Andrew.

"I know he's a hothead," I interrupted. "I've been on the receiving end, and I've only met him once."

"He hates me," Jake said. "He's jealous of what I had with Edgar."

"Which was?"

"A relationship, not that Mitchell would know anything about relationships. Also, Edgar was my patron, I guess you'd call it. I'm really a sculptor. I've been in two group shows. I'm trying to arrange another one. My work is really taking off." Jake chewed on his lower lip. "We'd been fighting a lot."

"Who? You and Mitchell?"

"That, too, but I meant me and Edgar."

"About what?"

"Nothing. I don't even remember what."

"Did Mitchell know?"

"Mitchell thinks he knows everything."

That had the ring of truth.

"I'm sorry, but I still don't get it."

"Sleazy hustler kills older lover before gravy train runs out. I know that's what he's been telling the police."

"But that doesn't make sense. Why would you kill him if he was your meal ticket?"

"He wasn't my meal ticket. We loved each other."

"Well, can't you just explain that to the police? Why should they believe the dirt Mitchell's spewing?"

"Mitchell doesn't know this, but Edgar and I saw a lawyer together."

"So?"

"The guy specializes in estate planning."

Then I got it.

He let out a sigh. "I realize it looks bad."

"Did he leave you *everything?*"

Jake was handsome all right, but Edgar was no fool. Still, love can mess you up.

"I don't know what he ultimately decided. But I know what everybody's going to think."

What was I doing here? "Let's say you didn't kill him."

"I didn't."

"Then who did?"

He shrugged.

"You must have seen something. You were there that night. I saw your pants."

"What?"

"Never mind."

"Look, I was there earlier that morning. But like I said, Edgar and I were arguing, so

I left. I went to see a friend. By the time I came back, the police were all over the house. I didn't think. I just ran."

"Well, where's your friend? He's your alibi."

"I don't know." He looked sheepish. "We're not all that well acquainted."

Oh, god. "So what can I do?"

"You can figure it out."

I shook my head.

"For Edgar, Cece."

I turned to Andrew, who had pretty much said nothing since bringing me here. "I don't have the slightest idea how to figure it out, Andrew. I'm sorry."

"Cece," said Jake, "listen to me. There was something going on these last couple of weeks. Something Edgar was worried about. And it had to do with Nancy Drew."

I laughed. "Please."

"I know it sounds stupid, but it's true. Nancy Drew has something to do with what happened to him. And who knows more about Nancy Drew than you?"

About a million people. Clarissa. Tabby Cat. Rita. Big Bad Sebastien, probably.

Andrew knelt in front of me and took my hands. "Bad shit happens to good people every day. Most of us keep our heads down, or run the other way. We're too busy trying to keep our own lives from falling apart. But there are some people, maybe you'll meet one in a lifetime, who don't cut and run. There are some people who stay."

"The ones who can't keep their noses out of other people's business."

"Bullshit. Edgar knew right away what kind of person you were. Jake told me."

"A person in over her head. A person who should know better. A person who should get a grip."

"Stop." He reached out to touch my cheek. "I can't believe you don't get it, that you don't see who you are. Look in the mirror sometime, Cece. Everybody sees it but you."

No wonder Bridget was smitten. This guy barely talked, but when he did, he knew exactly what to say.

13

Andrew was persuasive, but no match for me. I was too smart. I could see a snow job from fifty paces. I was going to leave it to the police. They were experts. Trained professionals. They knew what they were doing. Forensics, ballistics, profiling, they had their methods. And I would have stuck to my guns, I swear I would have, if the mailman hadn't chosen that afternoon to bring me a letter from 1111 Carroll Avenue.

My hands started to tremble when I saw the return address. Mitchell could have sent me something, or Jake. But even before I ripped the envelope open and pulled out the note, scrawled in felt-tip pen on a sheet of lined paper, I knew exactly who had written it.

Dear Cece,

Every girl should have a collection. Especially girls like us, who made it out of Jersey unscathed. So consider this a start. I'll see you in Palm Springs. Oh, yes! Surprise!

Love, Edgar

Surprise.

Inside the envelope was a small black-and-white photograph of a woman wearing some kind of white shift dress. The image was faded, bent at the top, and utterly indistinctive. A dark-haired woman in a dark, old room. I didn't understand. I looked inside the envelope again. There was nothing else there. I looked at the picture again. What kind of a collection? Who was this? What was this?

It was Edgar, trying to tell me that he and I weren't through.

I believe in signs, like I said. So I took the photograph into my bedroom and tucked it safe and sound between the folds of my Lanvin cape. Then I pulled out the scrap of paper Andrew had given me with his phone number on it, and I called him. Jake got on the phone, too. This time I talked and they listened. I said I'd see what I could do. End of story. I'd see.

Which is how I found myself, three hours later, wading through wet grass in search of Jayne Mansfield's grave.

Edgar's memorial service. It had seemed the logical place to start. But I was too early and too morbid for my own good. Still, who could possibly resist the annotated maps to the stars' graves on sale in the Hollywood Forever gift shop?

The woman behind the counter, dressed for success in a maroon gabardine suit and floppy tie, gave me the hard sell.

In the twenties and thirties Hollywood Memorial Park, as it was then known, was the premier burial spot for the showbiz elite: Cecil B. DeMille, Rudolf Valentino, Marion Davies, Douglas Fairbanks Jr., Tyrone Power, Nelson Eddy. By the forties, however, as Forest Lawn in nearby Glendale grew in popularity, it had already slipped into decline. Weeds crawled over the tombstones, graffiti covered the crypts, and the reflecting pools were dull and murky. The family of legendary makeup artist Max Factor even had his remains moved elsewhere. In the nineties the cemetery hit the auction block and things looked dire until a last-minute reprieve by somebody from St. Louis with big money and big ideas.

Today, the woman in the suit concluded, they were industry leaders. Did I know they were building a brand-new 60,000-square-foot mausoleum, and that I could have my funeral simulcast live on the Web, and might I be ready to pick out my plot, with a view of the Hollywood sign perhaps?

I was not.

Back to Jayne Mansfield. I wandered around for half an hour with my map until I found Lot 218 by the edge of a large pond with a mini Greek temple floating in the middle of it. Only it turned out she wasn't in Lot 218. She was buried in Pen Argyl, Pennsylvania, though I suppose this was as nice a place as any for her fans to pay their respects. I wished I'd brought flowers. I consulted the official directory. She'd hit it big in *Will Success Spoil Rock Hunter?* and lived in a pink mansion with Mr. Universe before biting the dust outside Biloxi. I'd always liked Jayne Mansfield.

From the pond I made my way over to the freshly dug mound of dirt. It was pretty conspicuous. With a big hole right next to it. Some white folding chairs lined up in neat rows. Still nobody around but me. And Edgar, of course. He was somewhere in the vicinity. In a back room of the Court of the Apostles? Propped up in the Abbey of the Psalms? Cruising around in a hearse?

Stop. This was not productive.

I decided to check on Edgar's new neighbors.

Lady Sylvia Ashley to the left. I checked the directory. She was a regal dark-haired beauty whose first marriage to Lord Anthony Ashley ended when Douglas Fairbanks Jr. divorced America's Sweetheart, Mary Pickford, for her. Another titled marriage came and went before she married Clark Gable, whom she left for a Russian, Prince Djorjadze.

I think Edgar would've liked Lady Ashley. She was a true femme fatale.

Virginia Rappe to the right. She was the young actress who'd had the misfortune to catch the attention of former Keystone comedian Fatty Arbuckle, who'd invited her to a party at the St. Francis Hotel in San Francisco in 1921 to celebrate the signing of his new contract with Paramount Pictures. What happened to her in Fatty's three-room suite on the twelfth floor of the hotel will never be known, but within a few days she was dead, and he was charged with her murder. Though he was acquitted, Paramount canceled his contract and the Hays Office banned him from making films.

According to the directory, Virginia Rappe's grave was one of two at Hollywood Forever said to be haunted.

I wrapped my sweater tighter around me. The sun was about to set and it was getting cold. Finally, the others were arriving. They had that slow gait mourners do. Mitchell Honey stepped out of a small white car, on the arm of a tall man in dark glasses. He looked shaken. When I'd pictured this moment, I'd imagined I'd sort of blend into the crowd. No such luck. Mitchell looked past dozens of people straight at me. I thought I saw something like regret in his eyes. But maybe it was the light. I nodded at him and to my surprise he came over and gave me a hug. His face was wet.

"Thanks for coming. Edgar was genuinely taken with you."

"I'm sorry, Mitchell," I said, my voice cracking.

"Thank you," he said. "Please join us afterward at the house."

He shook some hands and exchanged some hugs. Then he sat down in the front row of seats, next to the tall man in dark glasses. I stood in the back. The minister started talking. My mind wandered. I remembered the flag that had been draped around my father's casket. My brothers had carried it home, all folded up into a neat triangle. My mother wouldn't let me attend the funeral. She thought I couldn't handle it. I'd always held it against her. But deep down I knew she was right.

Edgar's service lasted about thirty minutes. I don't remember anything anybody said. I only remember thinking about my father — that, and a strange feeling of foreboding.

I hoped Edgar's grave wouldn't be the third haunted one at Hollywood Forever.

Detectives Lasarow and Dunphy intercepted me on my way out.

"Fancy meeting you here," I said.

"Ms. Caruso, how are you?" Lasarow asked courteously, a stretch for her.

"I've been better, thanks."

"Thought you barely knew the man," she said.

"Do you have a specific question for me, or may I go?"

"A couple of things. Do you own a gun?"

"Of course I don't own a gun."

"We're looking for a twenty-two. Edgar Edwards was killed with a twenty-two."

"I do not own a twenty-two, nor have I ever owned a twenty-two. Or any other kind of firearm."

"No, I didn't much think you were the type. But I had to try. Another thing."

"Yes?"

"We're looking for Jake Waite. We have reason to believe he's in town. Somebody tried to get some of Edgar Edwards's money out of an ATM on Wilshire and Vermont last night."

Idiots.

"Have you seen him, Ms. Caruso?"

They couldn't possibly know where I'd been. "No, of course not. I told you, I don't even know him."

She looked at me through that shock of gray hair. "And you don't know Edgar Edwards. And you don't know Mitchell Honey. And you don't know anything. You just happened to find the body."

"That's the way it is," I said, throwing up my hands. "I'm sorry I can't make it any easier for you."

"Don't worry about making it easier for us," Dunphy said, jumping in. "Just call if you see Jake, all right?"

"Yes, of course."

"Good-bye."

"Wait." Something had occurred to me.

"What is it?" Dunphy asked.

"When you went through Edgar's house, in Palm Springs, did you happen to find a painting?"

"What kind of painting?" Dunphy glanced at her partner.

"A small painting of a nude woman."

Dunphy cleared her throat. She had put on lipstick today and looked almost fetching.

"We didn't see anything like that hanging on the wall, Ms. Caruso," she said, carefully choosing her words.

"How about in a closet, or the garage, or under the bed, or someplace like that?"

"No," said Dunphy.

"Is there something you want to tell us, Ms. Caruso?" Lasarow asked. "About that painting or anything else?"

"No. Nothing. It just relates to some work I'm doing. I'm sorry to bother you with something so silly." Maybe Edgar hadn't brought the painting with him to Palm Springs, after all. Or maybe the surprise he'd planned for Clarissa was something else entirely.

I got into my Camry — which, by the way, Maynard had successfully resuscitated, cup holder and all — and sped through the wrought iron gates.

It felt better leaving than arriving.

14

The gathering on Carroll Avenue was under way by the time I got there. A pretty young Latina opened the door and directed me to a guest book. I signed my name but didn't feel right about sharing a memory. My last memory of Edgar wasn't exactly the kind of thing you wanted to share.

In the living room a jazz combo was playing and waitresses were passing hors d'oeuvres. It should've been lovely but the house smelled like rot. I had the overwhelming desire to throw open the curtains and steam-clean the rugs, not that I'd ever steam-cleaned anything. How could Edgar have tolerated it? Maybe he'd had a split personality: dark Edgar lived in the shadows and dust, while light Edgar craved the desert sun and Fantastik.

I hung out for a while in the library with a tubby friend of Edgar's from the Chicago days, who shared a heartfelt memory about the time they'd wired an ex-lover's bed so he'd receive an electric shock every time he lay down.

Then I joined a group of Edgar's neighbors, who were complaining about the difficulties of owning a home in a designated historic preservation zone. One man spent an entire year trying to get a permit to install a built-in dishwasher, and Edgar, apparently, had spent two years trying to get permission to turn his attic into a third-floor bedroom only to give up entirely. Emboldened, I launched into a defense of illegal garage conversions, but when they realized I lived in unprotected West Hollywood, they tuned me out like yesterday's news.

From there, I headed into the dining room, where I hung out with a petite lawyer who consumed a prodigious amount of cheese. She told me she had once done some real estate work for Edgar and had found him to be an excellent negotiator. He was someone who always got exactly what he wanted, without you even realizing it. I nodded. I could believe it. But what had Edgar wanted from me?

After that, I was party to a failed seduction.

"I'm a Sagittarius," said a pear-shaped man, sidling over to a short woman stationed by the table. She was carrying a *New York Times* crossword puzzle tote bag. "That's the sign of the hunter. I am spiritual and sensual. I don't hold grudges and I'm disarmingly happy. What sign were you born under?"

The woman popped a soda cracker into her mouth and, hefting her bag in my direction, asked, "What sign is she?"

"Scorpio," I answered. Scorpios are fiery, intense, and creative.

"Ah, the scorpion," he said. "You are secretive, controlling, and manipulative."

I suppose it's all in how you spin it. I turned to the woman. "I believe this man asked you a question."

She wiped the crumbs from her mouth. "I was born under the sign of the schlep."

It seemed like a good time to get a glass of wine. Better yet, to go upstairs. There was a closet I needed to check.

The second-floor landing was dark. There was a stained-glass skylight overhead covered with wet leaves, which meant that even in the daytime it would've felt like the middle of the night. I stood still for a moment, listening for signs of life. Dead calm. Everyone was downstairs. Good. Except that unfortunately, I couldn't remember which way the blue bedroom was.

I stared down the long hallway at a series of closed doors. It seemed like a sign. Turn back. You are not dressed for success. You do not own a maroon gabardine suit and floppy tie.

Then I thought of Clarissa. The winning individual must be able to turn on a dime, roll with the punches, sway with the breeze.

I tried the first door on the left. It was full of gym equipment. The second door on the left seemed to be Edgar's bedroom. No, thank you. The third door opened onto an office of some kind. I flicked on the light. There was a big oak desk pushed up against the wall, underneath a painting of a crusty old fisherman. There were books everywhere. Looking at people's books is even better than looking in their medicine cabinets. I tiptoed in.

French Symbolism. The Warhol Look. Dada, Surrealism, and Their Heritage. The latter was propped up against a tower of Kleenex boxes. This had to be Mitchell Honey's office. Every family needs a curator.

The surrealism book was opened to a section on Salvador Dalí. I'd come across something else about Salvador Dalí recently, but I couldn't remember what. Oh, well. I sat down. Then I looked up at the ceiling. No glitter trap in evidence. Still, I wasn't opening any drawers.

I started reading. In 1939 Dalí designed a window display at Bonwit Teller in New York featuring a fur-lined bathtub. The store was unhappy with it, and in the ensuing agitation the artist crashed through the display window's plate glass. I read on. Dalí's famous painting of melting watches was inspired by a very ripe Camembert: ". . . one of the strangest statements in art of man's obsession with the nature of time." I looked up at the clock, chastened. Time waits for no man. I turned off the light and went back into the hall. I tried the next door.

This was it.

I took one quick look around, just to make sure I was still alone, then went in, closing the door behind me.

The Shrine.

Everything looked the same as it had the other day: the blue wallpaper, the blue bed, the blue shelves lined with the Nancy Drew books. And unlike the rest of the house, the air smelled fresh, like Ivory soap.

Last time I was here I hadn't noticed a shelf filled with scripts from the Nancy Drew TV series. It had aired briefly in the late seventies, with Pamela Sue Martin (a brunette) playing the lead. The premiere episode outranked other detective shows like *Kojak*, *Barnaby Jones*, and *Starsky and Hutch*, but the series lasted only a season. Then Pamela Sue Martin made an appearance on the cover of *Playboy*, wearing a seductively draped trench coat. When asked how she could do such a thing to the fans, she answered, "What the hell do you think? You think I'm Nancy Drew?"

Sounded like she and Grace Horton would've had a lot to talk about.

Grace Horton. The reason I was here. Well, one of the reasons.

I walked past the bookshelves to the closet, my pulse racing. This was where Edgar had kept the painting. But when I opened the door and looked inside, it wasn't there. There were a couple of wire hangers on the rod, a water-stained box of envelopes on the floor, and that was about it unless you count the dust.

So where the hell was the painting?

Just then I heard footsteps out in the hall. Damn it, I didn't want to get caught. If I'd had any sense whatsoever, I'd have marched right out the door and pretended I'd been looking for the bathroom. But no, I had to panic. I had to go and hide inside the closet.

Maybe it was someone who really was looking for the bathroom. I'd wait for the flush, give it a few minutes, and then come out. But time passed awfully slowly in that tiny, stuffy closet. I stared at the four walls. I studied the hangers, which are actually ingenious devices. I was done. It couldn't have been more than three minutes and I was going mad. Feeling claustrophobic. Then I heard the door to the blue bedroom open. Shit. I was done for. My foot started to itch. Oh, hell, let the chips fall where they may. I threw open the door.

"Cece Caruso?"

"Nancy Olsen?"

What was she doing here?

"What are you doing here?"

"I'm looking for something," I said. Honesty is the best policy, not that this mini-kilted minx would know anything about that. "How about you?"

"I knew Edgar. The jazz world."

"I thought you were into punk."

"I'm into whatever."

"Obviously."

"I'm paying my respects to Edgar."

"In his bedroom? That's a little strange."

"This *isn't* his bedroom. And what did you say *you* were doing here? In his closet?"

"This *isn't* his closet. And I said I was looking for something."

"For what?"

"A nude portrait of your grandmother, Grace Horton."

That shut her up.

"Grace Horton *was* your grandmother, right?" I walked over to the blue bed.

"That's right," she said, fiddling with her purse, which was shaped like a crescent moon. She pulled out her cigarettes, then put them back. She didn't want to look me in the eye.

"Amazing," I said, smoothing out a wrinkle in the spread.

"Not really. Everybody's got a grandmother."

"My grandmother's claim to fame was her baked ziti."

"Lucky you."

"What was Grace like?"

"She died before I was born. I never knew her."

"But your mother knew her. She's writing a book about her."

"Looks that way." The mother is always the sore spot.

"So, Nancy, what do you know about the painting?" I wanted to know why she had that slide in her car.

"So, Cece, what do you know about it?"

"I know that Edgar was planning to show it at your mother's Nancy Drew party, but that didn't happen. Somehow, it's disappeared."

"What are you implying?"

"Me? Absolutely nothing. But I do suggest you lock up your car in the future. You don't want to lose anything valuable." I turned on my heel. Let her stew for a change.

Another night of tossing and turning.

The phone stopped ringing around eleven. I thought about Edgar. I looked up *fan* in the encyclopedia and learned many things. That in ancient Greece palm-leaf fans were sacred instruments used to tend the fire of the virgin goddess Hestia. That in China peacock-feather fans kept the wheels of the empress's chariot free from dust. That in eighteenth-century France fans had a language all their own. Twirling a fan in the left hand, for example, meant that you were being watched.

I went through all three hundred channels two times. There was nothing to watch. I filed my nails. I turned off the light. I turned on the light. I reread *The Moonstone Castle Mystery*. I ate a bag of Milano cookies. Then the doorbell rang.

It was Gambino. Unshaven and bleary-eyed, he looked beautiful to me.

I didn't lose my nerve.

And I didn't get any sleep.

Given the circumstances, however, that was fine with me.

15

Gambino and I looked at each other across the breakfast table.

"Great toast," I said.

"Great coffee."

"Want some jam?" I asked.

"Want some insulin?"

"You're not suggesting I'm laying it on too thick, are you?" I wagged my spoon at him. A dollop of raspberry jam landed on the sports section.

" 'I love you' was the easy part, Cece."

"Not for me."

"Come here." He pulled me onto his lap.

"The thing about domesticity . . ."

"Yes?" He kissed my neck.

"It's an art form."

"I know."

"We've blown it before."

"This time it's different."

"Why?"

"We're different. Things are different." He gave me a little push. "Get up. I've got to take a shower."

"Wait for me," I said.

Afterward I lay on the bed while Gambino stood at the sink, shaving. I could see his reflection in the mirror, but the frame of the doorway cut off the top of his head. He was very tall. Tall people take up a lot of room. But I had a lot of room. That, come to think of it, was one of the things that was different.

"I'll try to call you later, Cece, but I don't know exactly where I'll be."

"I understand."

"The double homicide. We've finally got something."

"That's great."

"Yeah. We needed a break. Things have been really slow otherwise. Did I tell you about this idiot who called us yesterday from under his bed? Somebody was in his house stealing his marijuana plants."

"That's good," I said, laughing.

"What about you? What are you up to today?"

I sat up. "Absolutely nothing."

He came out of the bathroom with shaving cream all over his face.

"You said that too fast."

"I talk too fast."

"You think too fast."

"Thanks, Santa."

He rinsed off his face and came back out holding a wet towel.

"Careful, you're dripping."

He looked at me sternly. "Is there anything I should know, Cece? Anything at all you need to tell me?"

Oh, god, where to begin?

"I need to finish what I start," I blurted out.

"Finish what?"

No, I couldn't get into it. He'd be furious. And what was there to tell, really? That I'd found Edgar's body? He knew that part already. That Andrew had taken me to see Jake? That I was looking for an obscure painting of an obscure woman by an obscure artist? And trespassing on private property to do so?

"Finish what, Cece?"

I paused. "My book. I'm so close, but I can't quite finish. It's a classic problem."

He looked skeptical, but he was in a hurry. If you have to lie, lie to people who are rushing. They will not pursue it. They may not even be listening to you. Except if they're detectives. Then they're always listening.

He pulled on his pants and buckled his belt.

"Anyway," I said, throwing my legs over

the side of the bed, "I have all day today, and the only thing I'm going to do is sit at my computer and work."

"Sounds like a plan."

That it did. But even the best-laid plans — well, we all know the rest.

The first problem was the fact that my office was located in the garage behind my house. It had seemed like a good idea at the time. But its location had proven a serious hindrance to productivity. Your work should be in your face at all times. This is what compels you to do it. Out of sight, out of mind. The problem was exacerbated in the winter months, when I was actually compelled to put on footwear to make the ten-yard journey across the grass.

The next issue was my desk. Once, in despair over something, I had swept the thousands of apparently useless pieces of paper covering its surface directly into the trash, a gesture I was to deeply regret. One of them was my property-tax bill. Another was Annie's birth certificate, which had the effect of delaying her wedding by a week. But merely to clear a space large enough to accommodate a yellow pad and a cup of coffee was an hour-long ordeal. And I wanted to make Gambino a risotto.

He loved risotto. Porcini mushroom and

asparagus. I had everything I needed. I flung open the refrigerator door. Except for the mushrooms and the asparagus. I walked over to the cupboard and peered inside. And the rice and the chicken stock. I did have white wine and an onion. Maybe I could just slice the onion and drown my sorrows in the Pinot Grigio. Or maybe I could stop procrastinating. Maybe if I were actually working on my book I'd be ordering out more. And less tempted to solve the problems of the world. The problem of Carolyn Keene was more than enough.

The problem of Carolyn Keene.

I needed a conclusion.

Half an hour later I was seated at my desk. An hour after that and I'd cleared a spot. Then I had to call Lael and fill her in on the latest developments in my exciting life, which should have taken under a minute, but all of a sudden it was lunchtime. *All My Children* and an avocado and fontina sandwich later, I was back at my desk, determined to wrap this thing up for real. My editor, Sally, was not known for her patience.

Who was Carolyn Keene?

That was the sixty-four-thousand-dollar question.

Edward Stratemeyer had come up with

185

the name. He'd had a gift for pseudonyms. One of his first was Arthur M. Winfield, under which he wrote and published the Rover Boys and Putnam Hall series. Stratemeyer explained it by saying that Arthur sounded like author; *M* was for the million books he'd sell; and Winfield referred to the success he would achieve in his profession. Other examples of his genius at work included Laura Lee Hope, Margaret Penrose, Victor Appleton, and Roy Rockwood. Roy Rockwood I particularly loved. If I were trapped in a burning building, I'd want Roy Rockwood to save me.

Carolyn Keene was another killer combination: Carolyn sounded vaguely patrician; Keene conjured someone razor-sharp yet ingenuous. The name proved Stratemeyer's most enduring. Carolyn Keene may not have existed, but that didn't stop her from writing hundreds of books about a girl detective from River Heights. Seventy years later she's still writing them. And still does not exist.

Walter Karig, Margaret Scherf, Harriet Stratemeyer Adams, Wilhelmina Rankin, Mildred Wirt Benson — they all existed. And each of these ghosts was, at one time or another, the author who didn't exist — Carolyn Keene. But that was hardly the end of it. Take Mildred Wirt Benson. She was also, at one time or another, the following authors who likewise didn't exist — Frank Bell, Joan Clark, Julia K. Duncan, Alice B. Emerson, Don Palmer, Dottie West. Ditto Harriet Stratemeyer Adams, who, when she wasn't busy being Carolyn Keene, was the author of the Kay Tracy mysteries, Frances K. Judd.

That was another good one. Frances K. Judd made you think of Francis Scott Key, the flag, civic pride. And Kmart.

The names kept multiplying. The supply was inexhaustible. An endless family tree of ghostwriters and their progeny: the Bobbsey Twins, the Dana Girls, the Outdoor Chums, the Motor Boys, the Four Little Blossoms, the Six Little Bunkers. I was being stalked by Edward Stratemeyer's apple-cheeked army of the undead. Maybe that was why I couldn't think straight. My biography of Carolyn Keene was supposed to be a ghost story, but it had turned into a full-fledged horror show.

I logged on to the Chums' Listserv for comic relief. But all I got was a tale of someone's father's botched knee replacement and the good wishes of half a dozen sympathetic souls. There was a semitragic exchange between Lana S., who'd posted pictures of her daughter, wanting to know if she could play Nancy Drew in a movie, and Bill 45, who responded that her hair seemed more red-brown than red-blond, but not to fret because it could always be dyed before shooting. Clarissa had posted an announcement about her book, which I skipped out of pique. And then there was a lengthy digression on how to keep from being cheated on eBay posted by a woman who'd bought an autographed first edition of *The Clue of the Tapping Heels* only to learn that Mildred Wirt Benson never signed autographs as "Millie."

I wandered back inside to pour myself a fresh cup of coffee. But there was none left from breakfast so I decided to brew another pot. I'd drink all twelve cups if it would help me arrive at anything resembling a coherent thought, which you'd think I'd have by this point, one month before my delivery date. Oh, please, let Sally not hate me. While I waited for the coffee I turned on the TV. I flipped past a talk show featuring dysfunctional teens, the local news, an animal psychic in touch with a dead Pekinese, and Boris Karloff hamming it up as Frankenstein.

I spent the rest of the afternoon at my desk, brooding over Frankenstein. It seemed relevant to my book — the mad scientist, the larger-than-life creation. The only problem was I couldn't decide which larger-than-life creation was the more troublesome: Carolyn Keene or Nancy Drew.

I clicked the Save key nonetheless.

It wasn't the theory of relativity, but it was something to chew on.

Later that evening I was reminded that dogs prefer more tangible snacks. Within seconds of walking into Bridget's shop, Helmut had gone straight for my snakeskin granny boots.

"I told you he knows vintage," Bridget said.

"Will you get him off?" The dog was sucking away at my feet like a tiny demented lover.

After separating us with some difficulty, Bridget grabbed some Kleenex off her desk and was about to wipe Helmut's mouth when I snatched the box out of her hands.

"I guess I'll just clean this slobber off now," I said.

"Sorry."

"So do you like the boots at least?" I asked. "Annie found them for me at that shop in Topanga Canyon."

"Let's just say I could leave out a pair of Charles Jourdan sandals with amber Lucite heels from the seventies and Helmut wouldn't go near them. He has respect for the good stuff."

"Do you edit your thoughts at all, Bridget? I was just wondering."

"Well, you can do better. On the vintage food chain, the only thing lower than snakeskin granny boots is zippered housedresses."

I had at least two of those.

Bridget went into the back and came out with a white box trimmed in blue.

"Change into these."

"Excuse me, I am not an employee."

"Very funny."

"Have you ever read *Frankenstein*?"

"I've seen the movie."

"Never mind, then." I opened the box. Inside was a pair of burgundy suede peep-toed platforms.

"They're gorgeous, but aren't we just about to go shoe shopping?"

She sighed. "You can't go shoe shopping in bad shoes. It's not done."

The platforms did go better with my outfit.

While I tested out their pain quotient by jogging in place, Bridget walked to the back of the shop to activate the alarm system.

"Cece," she called, "while you're up there, can you turn off the lights? And grab my wallet from Andrew's desk? Watch the drawer. It sticks."

"Sure," I said, bending over to rub my hand across the back of my ankle. No incipient blisters. That was good news. I hit the switch and watched the lights in the display window go down, plunging a tiny teal ruched mini by Giorgio di Sant'Angelo into darkness. The discotheque was now closed.

"Where's Andrew, by the way?"

"Poor thing is out sick. Some flu that's going around."

Nice excuse. I guess the flu sounded better than babysitting a fugitive.

I sat down at Andrew's desk. What a fastidious fellow. There were piles of small papers and piles of large papers and piles of medium-size papers with no overlap whatsoever. Paper clips in a magnetized paper-clip holder. Pencils as sharp as daggers. But it was when I opened the drawer that I was really surprised, and not because it was a mess. I already knew that appearances could be deceiving.

I was surprised because there, in Andrew's desk, right under Bridget's wallet, was a shiny gold key — the same shiny gold key I thought I'd lost, the one that opened the door to Edgar Edwards's Palm Springs death house.

16

"What took you guys so long?" asked Lael, studying her feet. She had a chocolate brown T-strap on the left one and an apple green T-strap on the right. "After two drinks," she said, waving a martini at me, "these shoes seem downright cheap. I do believe I need both colors."

"That's the spirit!" exclaimed Bridget, raising her pink lady aloft. She pushed me into the red leather booth with her spare hand and slid in after me. "I'd given up on you, Lael, but this place gets 'em every time."

Star Shoes on Hollywood and Ivar was one of those hybrid spots that shoot up in this town as fast as weeds by the side of the freeway: Laundromat/Internet cafés, wig shop/travel agencies, UPS drop spot/piñata outlets. I suppose it makes good sense, parking being at such a premium in Los Angeles. And with its inventory of 100,000 pairs of inverted wedgies, buckled boots, and faux crocodile pumps, designed by the late, legendary Joseph LaRose of Florida, who'd numbered Joan Crawford and Betty Grable among his clients, Star Shoes was a better place than most to park your vehicle, at least for some of us. And now even Lael — levelheaded Lael — had crossed over to the dark side.

"Those are awful," she proclaimed, pointing to a pair of two-toned Mary Janes in the display case opposite us. "And these are my rejects," she said, indicating the mess on the floor.

"Fine work," said Bridget.

I tore my attention away from the Jetsonsesque light fixtures, which reminded me of the ones in our dining room in Asbury Park. "Speaking of work, exactly how long has Andrew been out sick?"

"I don't remember," said Bridget, turning back to her tipsy protégée. "What's your opinion of those over there?" She pointed to a pair of suede elf boots with fur trim that someone had left at the table next to ours. Lael recoiled in horror. "Correct," said Bridget, elated. "Do you want another Diet Coke, Cece? I'm getting another." She started to get up.

I'd decided to keep my wits about me, given my unfortunate Visa situation. "No, I'm fine, thanks. Has it been a couple of days, or more?"

"I *said* I don't know."

I reached out for her hand. "Bridget. Do you think he was sick last weekend, when we were in Palm Springs? Stuck in bed, maybe?"

"What's your problem with Andrew?" Bridget said, snatching her hand back. "Why don't you just spit it out, Cece? If you really want to know, it's insulting just how negative you've been about the whole thing. So what if Andrew's younger than I am? Am I such a hag that a younger man couldn't find me attractive?"

Lael was looking at me like I was Adolf Hitler.

"That's not what I'm implying. Not at all. You know me. I'm just nosy."

"That's for sure," she said, barely mollified.

How could I explain to her that I had to know where Andrew had been last weekend? Had he followed us to Palm Springs? And messed up Maynard's car? And eaten our lobster sandwiches? (Which were *not* waiting on my counter when we came home, by the way, but Buster could have been responsible, I suppose.) Had he actually stolen that gold key out of my purse? I'd meant to take it back, but Bridget had suddenly materialized at my side, and I'd gotten all flustered and shut the drawer, missing my chance. Dumb. Very dumb. But even if I could be absolutely certain Andrew had taken it, did that necessarily mean he was a murderer?

No. I refused to believe it was possible. But what were Andrew and Jake up to? They certainly weren't the brightest bulbs, trying to get money out of Edgar's ATM. Then something else came to me. Could they have been the ones who'd broken into my house before we even left for Palm Springs? Lois had said two men, carrying a birthday present. Andrew and Jake were two men.

"Cece."

Bridget was waiting for an explanation.

"Maybe," I said, stalling for time, "well, maybe I'm asking all these questions because I have a crush on Andrew." I looked down bashfully.

Lael studied me with narrowed eyes.

"Of course you have a crush on him," said Bridget. One could never go wrong appealing to this woman's vanity. "He's very attractive. But hands off. You've got one of your own."

"I know," I said. "And he's very attractive, too."

"I'll say," said Lael.

I studied her this time.

"Oh, Cece. You know I like them less beefy."

"Gambino's not beefy."

"You've got to admit he's big," Bridget said.

"Herculean."

"Ah, yes, herculean."

"Can we leave now?" I asked.

"I'm hungry." Bridget picked up her purse.

"I vote for In N Out," said Lael. There was one close by, across the street from Hollywood High. Five minutes tops.

We walked out into the brisk night air. A crowd had gathered in front of the club next door, where they were doing a makeup promotion. There were posters of disembodied pink lips plastered to the brick wall. A model in purple latex twirled on a makeshift stage, smacking her own surgically enhanced lips for the cameras. As we passed by, someone handed each of us a goody bag with a small pot of lip gloss at the bottom.

Lael unscrewed the top of hers. "It's scented," she said, sniffing. "Spearmint . . . and strawberry, I think."

"Chuck it immediately," said Bridget, pointing to a trash can.

Indeed. In number 23, *The Mystery of the Tolling Bell*, one learns that complimentary makeup never looks good, especially when applied by a gypsy pushing a cart.

"Let's take my car, since it's right here," I said, pulling my keys out of my bag. "We'll drive you back to your car afterward, Lael."

"Okay."

And then I saw Mitchell Honey emerge from the crowd, swinging a goody bag of his own.

"It's Mitchell! Duck!" I yelped, dragging Lael and Bridget behind a white van parked next to my car. Mitchell crossed the street, heading west, away from the bondage shops. He was easy to track. His bald head glowed like a beacon in the night.

"Why are we ducking?" asked Bridget.

"I don't want him to see us," I said.

"Why?" asked Lael.

"I don't know yet."

"I'm hungry," Bridget repeated. "This is stupid."

"C'mon," I said, pushing them into my car while keeping one eye glued to Mitchell. "Hurry up. He's leaving. We're going to lose him."

Mitchell climbed into an old blue Jaguar and attempted to pull out into traffic. It was Friday night and Hollywood Boulevard was mobbed. The city had recently passed an anticruising ordinance, obviously to no avail. But that was a good thing. There was no way Mitchell would be able to get away.

"Whoa! What are you doing?" Bridget asked, clutching at the passenger-side door.

"I'm making a U-turn, of course."

"In this traffic?"

Drivers in Los Angeles are, generally speaking, a courteous lot. And uncannily attuned to their fellow drivers. They know to back off when a nut job is in the vicinity.

They backed off.

There was only one car between us now. I could see Mitchell perfectly when I craned my neck outside my window, which only worked at stoplights for obvious reasons. I think he was fiddling with the stereo. Everybody's window was open and everybody's stereo was blaring. Hip-hop, Christian rock, Tejano ballads. I was getting a headache.

"You've just passed In N Out."

"You're obsessed with food, Bridget. We're on a mission now. There's no time."

"What mission exactly are we talking about?"

Lael said, "Perhaps if you explained yourself a little better, Cece."

"Edgar is dead! Isn't that enough?"

"It's enough," they said in unison.

Mitchell's car crawled along Hollywood

until La Brea, where he pulled a quick right. I was stuck on red, behind the same Chevy truck that had been between us since Ivar, and I was getting pretty darned tired of looking at the decal in the rear window of that little cartoon guy, Calvin, peeing on a Ford. I tapped my fingers on the wheel. Finally, the light changed and I zoomed up and over to La Brea, scanning the street for Mitchell, whom I caught sight of a few cars ahead. He'd been stuck on red, too. I zigzagged into position, and slumped a little in my seat.

"Slump, you guys."

"He doesn't know us," Bridget said.

"Fine. Don't slump."

"All right. We're slumping." Bridget turned around to look at Lael. "Get with the program."

Now Mitchell was heading deep into the hills. Great. The hills. Isolated houses. No sidewalks. Hairpin turns. Maybe I should see someone, but I feel trapped if I can't see down the full length of a block to the cross traffic beyond.

"Cece, pay attention," Lael said. "He's gone down that narrow, windy street."

"Of course he has." Mitchell had turned onto a narrow, windy street that would surely lead onto many other narrow, windy streets. Like I said, the hills were loathsome. But so far so good. I hung back some so as not to be conspicuous, and I knew that if he happened to take a good look in his rearview mirror we were goners, but luck was on our side. He drove like an old lady, nice and slow and oblivious.

And then I made my first big mistake of the evening. The last narrow, windy street Mitchell turned down was not a narrow, windy street at all. It was somebody's very long driveway. Somebody who lived in a big white mansion with tall white columns. Somebody with a Rottweiler, probably. And there was no way out.

The motor court was full of expensive cars. Mitchell parked behind a silver Bentley. I cut the motor, turned off the lights, and assessed the situation.

"It looks like Tara," said Bridget.

"Or a government auction," Lael offered.

"Down, down!" I whispered. Mitchell was getting out of his car. He walked up to the front door, then turned around.

"What's he doing?" asked Lael.

"I don't know."

He walked back to his car, opened his trunk, and pulled out a smallish, squarish package.

"Hostess gift?" Bridget asked.

"Mail-order smoked salmon," Lael answered.

He headed back to the front door.

I turned around. "Okay, when he goes inside, we back down the driveway and get out of here." We had accomplished nothing, of course.

"Cece, he's not going in," Lael said.

"He's walking this way!" Bridget was clutching at the door again. "You better switch into reverse!"

But it was too late for that. One minute I was stealth incarnate, the next minute Mitchell Honey was knocking on my window.

"Ms. Caruso, is that you?"

I rolled the window down. "Mitchell! What a surprise!"

"What are you doing here?"

"We're looking for the . . . Ellerbee house," I said calmly.

"Ellis Ellerbee," Bridget said, "the famous record producer."

"Never heard of him."

"He's a mogul, a cigar-puffer. He lives right around here," Lael said. "Right around here somewhere." She produced a map. "On . . . Ellington Street."

I grabbed the map from her. "We've been looking for the place for an hour, and then I think . . . I think we must've fallen asleep."

Bridget stretched her arms over her head and yawned. "Time change."

"We just flew in from Norway," Lael said.

"Visiting relatives," Bridget said.

"Mine, not hers," Lael explained.

"You know those circadian rhythms," I said. "Once they're out of sync, you're sunk."

Mitchell picked some lint off his jacket. "I thought I recognized your car from the other day."

Now how was that possible? When I'd first visited the house on Carroll Avenue I'd been driving Maynard's Caddy. Maybe he meant the memorial service. But I was sure he hadn't seen me arrive.

"Why don't you come in and have a drink? To revive yourselves. A friend is having a little party."

"Great," said Bridget, practically leaping out of the car. She loved a party.

"What about Elliott Ellerbee?" I protested, fighting the inevitable.

"Ellis. It was a cocktail thing. It's over now."

"Right."

I opened my door and a rush of wind blew my skirt up around my waist. Would this evening never end? I yanked it back down, not that Mitchell was barking up that alley. He introduced himself to Bridget and Lael, and we followed him to the front door.

He pushed the buzzer.

Bridget yawned energetically.

"Just tell me one thing." Mitchell was staring straight ahead. His voice was soft. "How the hell did you find out about Asher Farrell?"

17

Asher Farrell did not have a Rottweiler. What he did have was a prison record, not that I discriminate against ex-cons. But it's a good thing to know what you're up against.

A big-time contemporary art dealer, Asher Farrell had started out peddling Lladró figurines, only to discover he had a gift for catering to rich people's insecurities. And an "eye," which I think meant he could see dollar signs where the rest of us could only see, say, collages made of cut-up Wonder bread bags. He'd been married half a dozen times, to increasingly beautiful actresses, several of whom went into early retirement when he was done with them. As for the prison record, it was a short stay in a minimum-security facility. Farrell blamed an overzealous accountant, but tax fraud, it would seem to me, was tax fraud. The thing is, the man was a looker, and people will forgive a looker anything.

I'd read that in a profile in *People* magazine.

The inside of Asher Farrell's house did not match the outside. It had been hollowed out like a pumpkin, painstakingly scraped down to the drywall. Must've been an aesthetic statement. We went down a couple of steps to the living room, which had been consecrated to two very large abstract paintings. There was a tufted white leather chaise in the middle of the room, but otherwise it was unfurnished.

Mitchell went to disengage our host from a woman wrapped in a formfitting white dress. It might've been sterile gauze. Hard to tell. He gestured in our direction. Farrell took Mitchell's package, looked over at us, and grinned. That's when Lael began radiating pheromones. I was getting hot and twitchy just standing next to her. This wouldn't do at all. I tried to pull her toward the bar cart in the next room, but the damage had been done. Farrell was heading our way.

"He's trouble," I whispered in her ear.

She was breathing so hard she couldn't hear me.

He walked straight up to Lael and looked at her, his eyes translucent, glittering even. Oh, please. She wasn't going to fall for that. His longish dark hair was slicked back and he was wearing a black suit that fit him like a glove. His white shirt was unbuttoned one button too many, a ploy obviously designed to put his chest hair on display. I would have recommended a depilatory, if asked.

He tore his gaze away from Lael and addressed yours truly. "I think we saw each other at Edgar's memorial service." He put out his hand.

"Did we?" I shook it. Of course. He'd been the one wearing dark glasses, the one who'd arrived with Mitchell. "Yes, you're right. It's so nice to see you again."

"I'm so pleased you could be here."

I wondered if he said that to all his trespassers. Farrell shook hands with Bridget, too, and they chatted for a moment. It turned out that they knew some people in common, and he was familiar with her store. I looked over at Mitchell, who was standing at his right elbow. Poor guy. Born to be the toady of a powerful man.

"Mitchell," said Farrell, shaking him off expertly, "get Cece and Bridget something to drink." He took Lael by the hand. "I want this one all to myself."

Mitchell watched them go, then fabricated an excuse to get away from us. Bridget and I found ourselves marooned under a massive color photograph of the interior of a 99 Cent store.

We stood there for a while not talking. Every snort of laughter and clinking ice cube echoed loudly, making conversation between us somehow redundant. The party had come with its own sound track.

Finally, I said, "I think there's some connection. We're getting close. I can tell. It's good we're here. Very good. Except for Lael. That part's very bad."

Bridget shook her head. "You don't know the half of it. A girl who used to shop with me once went with him for a weekend to the Hamptons. He picked her up from the airport and when they got to the car he announced that she couldn't put her bags in the trunk because there was something already in there. About an hour into the drive, she was feeling kind of cramped with her things on her lap. When she asked him what was so special in the trunk, he pulled over and told her the weekend was over. He left her standing by the side of the road."

"Omigod."

"He's cold-blooded," she said, "like a snake."

I scanned the room for them. They were nowhere in sight.

"Why are we here again?" Bridget asked.

"You were the one racing out of the car."

"I had no idea who lived here."

"I think Mitchell thinks we know something. Now I'm wondering if it was Mitchell and Asher Farrell who were the ones who let themselves into my house. What did they want?"

"What do you mean, 'now you're wondering'? Who did you think it was before?"

I didn't answer her.

"Since we're here, let's just see if anybody knows anything about anything."

Bridget put her hands on her hips. "It's not like we can just ask around."

"I don't see why not," I said, turning on my heel. "Follow me."

We joined a couple standing in front of a fireplace in the dining room. They looked old and dignified.

"So he fucked you over, too?" asked the white-haired matron.

The grandfatherly type in gray flannel nodded. "He fucked me over, too."

"I gather we're talking about Asher Farrell," I said.

"Run, young lady," Grandpa said. "Run, don't walk."

"Why are you here, then?"

"I'm going to drink up all his scotch." The woman banged her cane on the floor for emphasis.

"The good stuff," the man added.

Bridget cut to the chase. "How did he really make all his money?"

"Selling nudie pictures to the Japanese," said the old man. "He's got inventory like you wouldn't believe. Tits and ass. That's his bread and butter."

"He doesn't pay his artists," the woman noted.

"He says, 'It's a Canadian bank holiday, so the check's delayed.' "

"He borrows your Rauschenberg for a show, then sells it to someone else."

"Or uses it as collateral for a loan, then defaults on the loan, and the bank gets it."

"He screws with your head."

"He doesn't call you back."

"He's morally dyslexic."

"He's a mad monk, like Rasputin."

"But what an interesting mind."

They both nodded.

"He loves art."

They nodded again.

"To art," the woman said.

"And twelve-year-old single malt," the man chortled.

Bridget pulled me aside. "He ought to start a cult."

"Let's get Lael and go."

"Fine."

Bridget went in one direction and I headed in another. I bumped into Farrell at the bottom of the stairs.

"We're going to be leaving now," I said. "It was very kind of you to have us. Thank Mitchell for me, too."

"I will." He smoothed back his already smooth hair. "Mitchell tells me you're a scholar of mystery writers."

"Yes."

"And that you're an expert on Nancy Drew."

"I'm working on it."

"Don't be modest. Mitchell's a fool about some things but smart about others."

"Can you tell me where Lael is?"

"She's in the powder room," he replied, indicating a closed door behind us.

We waited in silence.

"I hear you like tasteful nudes," I said finally.

"I prefer tasty ones."

I banged on the powder-room door. "Lael, hurry up."

He rubbed his hands across his lips. "So who's been talking to you about me, Ms. Caruso?"

"No one."

"No one?"

"Actually, it was Edgar."

"Too bad about Edgar. He was a wonderful man."

"Yes, he was." Nudie pictures. That's how Asher Farrell had gotten rich. Of course. He must've been the one who'd found the portrait of Grace Horton and sold it to Edgar. That put him smack in the middle of whatever it was that was going on.

"Edgar showed me the painting you found for him."

"A beauty. I bid on it at auction."

He pondered my face as if it were a work of art he was considering. Then he said, "Edgar was proud of his things. He liked to show them off. Did you see the knives and fans?"

I nodded.

"He was generous, too. With his time. His money. He was always giving things away. Perhaps he gave you a small token?"

"Nope. No token. No token I can think of."

Lael opened the door, looking flushed.

"There you are," I said. "We have to go. Early day tomorrow."

"You don't have to worry," she said. "Asher's going to drive me home later."

He gave me a smile. "Good night. Sleep tight." He smiled again, then steered Lael away from me.

18

"He won't be in until eleven," explained the girl with the twitch seated at the front desk of Asher Farrell Fine Art.

"I guess that gives me fifteen minutes to look around."

Oh, Lael.

Last night I'd called her every hour on the hour until around three, when I'd given up and gone to bed. I'd tried her again this morning, after my shower. She still wasn't picking up, but at least her machine had been turned on, which I was hoping meant she'd gotten home safely.

"Do you have an appointment? I don't remember seeing anything in the book. . . ." The girl wrinkled her forehead, like it was something she'd recently learned. What to do when confronting an unexpected visitor. She opened an expensive leather folio.

"Oh, I'm not in there," I said with a smile. "Asher told me no appointments were necessary."

"Of course not," she said quickly. One

wouldn't want to alienate the boss's potential bedmates. "Please, have a look around. The show opened last night. It's already sold out."

"Great."

She cleared her throat. "The artist is thrilled. First big solo show. Mr. Farrell's discovery. He has such an eye." Her chest was heaving with the effort.

I glanced up at the name stenciled onto the wall by the door. Lari Uklanski. "I'm a big fan of Lari's. Her work is amazing."

"His work."

"That's what I said."

"Of course." She smoothed down her black skirt. "Can I offer you a catalog?"

"No, thank you. I'm dyslexic."

She blinked a few times, then returned to her seat.

The gallery was large and cavernous, like Farrell's house. But the art was more modest in scale: maybe two dozen black-and-white snapshots pushpinned to the wall.

I wandered around, looking at the images. They showed models in various stages of undress — yanking up their panty hose, scooping their boobs into their bras, scratching their pointy knees. Lari Uklanski was really going out on a limb. Gorgeous girls in their underwear. Very daring.

I stopped in front of a photograph of a girl of about sixteen applying false eyelashes. It had been shot at an oblique angle so that she seemed to be falling out of her chair. I looked at her face more closely. She had the faintest trace of a black eye.

"Posing is a profession," said a voice behind me. "Sometimes the mask slips and the pose is revealed."

"You're very cryptic this morning," I said, turning around. Farrell's hair was slick even in daylight. He had a cup of coffee in one hand and his briefcase in the other.

"You keep surprising me, Ms. Caruso. To what do I owe this pleasure?"

"I'm very interested in photography."

"Oh, really?"

"Yes."

"And what do you think of the show?"

"I think it's exploitative."

"That's not what the *L.A. Times* says." I followed him over to the front desk. He put his things down and picked up the arts section. He riffled through the pages. "Ah. Here we go. It says, and I quote, 'Uklanski offers a poetic rumination on the vampirism of the fashion industry.' "

"Let me guess, a man wrote that."

"Actually, it was a woman." He gave the newspaper back to the twitchy girl, who traded it for a stack of phone messages. It was like choreography. He flipped through the little pink pages. "I have a lot to take care of this morning."

"Maybe you should get up earlier."

"What can I do for you?"

I pulled a manila envelope out of my purse. "I've started a photography collection. I'd like to show you my first acquisition. I need a professional opinion."

"I'm afraid I don't do appraisals."

"It's something Edgar gave me." That earned me his undivided attention. "Turns out I'd forgotten all about it."

He stared at the envelope in my hand. He may have had an eye, but he didn't have x-ray vision.

"I've got a few minutes, I suppose. Why don't we go into my office? It's more private."

"Good idea."

"Will you be taking calls, Mr. Farrell?" the girl asked.

"No."

We walked down a short hallway, past a large open space lined with wooden racks holding paintings of all sizes, tightly wrapped in plastic.

"Bet you wouldn't want to let a dirty old man in a mackintosh near that room," I said.

"I have everything in there from Roman dynastic busts to the first issue of *Spider Man*."

"I didn't know your taste was so eclectic."

"I like what I like. But I have whatever you need."

He shut his office door behind me.

The room had a glass desk in the middle, with a big leather swivel chair on his side and a small wooden chair on mine. That ploy was about as subtle as a whoopee cushion.

He could barely contain himself. "Let's see what you've got."

I pulled the black-and-white photograph out of the envelope and placed it on his desk.

It was a strange picture, I saw that now. A dark-haired woman wearing a slim white dress was posed midstride. She didn't look frightened, not exactly — watchful, perhaps. Her left hand reached beyond the edge of the picture; her right hand dissolved into a circle of white light. Behind her was a gray wall, with a chest of drawers pushed up against it, and toward the right-hand side of the frame, the barest hint of a painting hanging on the wall. The print itself was scratched and bent a little on the upper right side. On the back there was something written in black crayon: "L. Sands #3."

216

Farrell studied the photograph intently, turning it over several times.

"She looks like you," he said finally. "In some odd sixties incarnation."

"Maybe that's why Edgar gave it to me."

"Did he say anything about it?"

"Just that he was starting me on a collection. I'd told him I didn't collect anything, which wasn't exactly true. I do collect something."

He displayed not the slightest curiosity about what that might be.

"This is worthless."

"Are you sure about that?"

"It looks like a stock photograph. It was probably used in an advertisement. Or for some kind of commercial work."

"Who's L. Sands? The photographer?"

"Never heard of him."

"It could be a her."

"Never heard of her."

"Maybe this woman's not posing. Maybe somebody was following her." And maybe Edgar was warning me about something.

Farrell rolled his eyes. "You have an active imagination, Cece. She's a model. She's acting. Can't you tell?"

You can't always tell. But someone like him wouldn't want to hear that.

He stood up. "Listen. Why don't I keep it

for a while, ask around, give you a more specific answer?"

"I don't think that's necessary." I took the photograph out of his hand, slipped it back into the envelope, and tucked it into my purse. It wasn't what he'd expected, that much was obvious. But he wasn't entirely satisfied that it was unimportant, and neither was I.

He walked me back up to the front.

"Excuse me, Mr. Farrell," the girl said.

"Yes?"

"They called from Book Soup. The books you ordered are ready."

"That's fine, Melinda," he said sharply. "You can get them after lunch."

"My neighborhood bookstore," I said.

"I thought you were dyslexic," Melinda said.

"I buy cookbooks. I like the pictures. Fancy canapés. Ganaches."

"Please show Ms. Caruso out," Farrell said, picking up his mail. With that, he was gone.

"This must be a fun place to work," I said. She blinked again.

"So long, Melinda."

"Please, Ms. Caruso, won't you take a catalog? You can give it to a friend."

"Okay. Sure." I didn't want to get her into

trouble. God knows what he'd do to her if she were stuck with leftover catalogs at the end of the week.

"I'll get you a fresh one from the back."

She was gone only a minute or two, but that was enough time for me to go through her drawers. I had no idea what I was looking for, but, like I said before, if you want to find something, you usually will. Only this time I didn't find much of anything — not in the drawers, at least. But right on top of the desk, near Melinda's voluminous to-do list, was definitely something.

It was a color postcard, announcing a one-night-only cabaret show on Sunday the eighteenth at a nightclub in Silver Lake. I picked it up. I wasn't all that interested in cabaret, but I was extremely interested in the headliner. She had chopped-off red hair, thick black eyeliner, and green fingernails.

Nancy Olsen.

Another person with a talent for posing.

And for turning up in the strangest places.

I had to go to Book Soup anyway. What with the whole Andrew commotion last time I was there, I hadn't had a chance to pick up my *Chicago Manual of Style.*

It was less frenzied today. A different clerk

was on duty. She went over to the *C*'s and pulled my book from the stack.

"Would you mind checking the *F*'s? The name is Farrell. I'm picking up some stuff for my boss, too."

"Sure."

I looked away guiltily.

She heaved a thick stack of books, wrapped in a white piece of paper, onto the counter.

"Here you go."

"Great."

"These are going to cost your boss a pretty penny. Some were ordered from Europe. He speaks French?"

"You wouldn't believe what he's capable of."

I unwrapped the white paper and took a look.

La Double Vie de Salvador Dalí.

Dalí in the Nude.

Conversations with Dalí.

The Unspeakable Confessions of Salvador Dalí.

Salvador Dalí: A Panorama of His Art.

Homage à Salvador Dalí.

Six big fat books on Salvador Dalí. What was going on here?

The clerk cracked open the one on top.

"What a freak! Look at this!"

It was a sculpture of the Venus de Milo as a chest of drawers. Her nipples were the drawer pulls, and she had eight of them. Underneath the sculpture was a small painting of a woman whose face was being consumed by ants. Freaky indeed. But I needed to get out of there if I didn't want to cross paths with Melinda. I made a show of searching frantically through my purse.

"Look at that. I must've forgotten my corporate credit card. I'll have to come back for these tomorrow. But I'll take my *Chicago Manual.*"

"Sure. Have a nice day."

"You, too!"

I paid for my book, then walked out to my car.

A nice day.

I didn't think that was in the cards.

There was way too much to think about.

19

I came home loaded down with supplies. Post-it notes in four sizes. A three-pack of index cards in pink, blue, and classic white. Yellow legal pads. A package of pointy No. 2 pencils, which can be used for self-defense in a pinch. A Pink Pearl eraser. And last but not least, a whiteboard — three by three feet, as unblemished as a baby's bottom.

I set up shop in the dining room.

"Edgar is dead," I wrote on the top of the whiteboard. I took a bite of a Milano cookie and chewed thoughtfully.

Then I wrote "Who killed Edgar?" directly underneath.

This was hard. But I'd spent so much money on supplies.

There was Mitchell. I wrote "Mitchell" in red capitals, and drew an arrow from Edgar's name to his. Why would Mitchell have killed Edgar? I ate another cookie, then went into the kitchen to pour myself a glass of milk. Horizon Organic. It didn't taste as good, but the last thing I needed was more hormones. Back to Mitchell. There were many reasons he might've wanted to kill Edgar. Because he was jealous of Edgar's relationship with Jake, for one thing. A crime of passion. Mitchell comes upon Edgar and Jake in flagrante delicto. He's wild with rage. He can't think straight. He storms into his bedroom and pulls out his twenty-two. Does he own a twenty-two? It doesn't really matter. Someone who's determined can get a gun, though that would rule out the crime-of-passion theory and point directly to premeditated murder.

I walked back into the dining room and stuck a Post-it note onto the whiteboard. It read "Premeditated murder: a whole different ball of wax."

Moving on to Nancy Drew.

Jake said that Edgar had been worried and that it had something to do with Nancy Drew. Now that I gave it some thought I realized it was probably just a line, something to reel me in with. But it was worth considering for a moment.

For Nancy Drew, I needed a yellow pad.

Edgar was obsessed with Nancy Drew. Mitchell was privy to the details. Did he share the obsession? Did he want to get his hands on Edgar's books? That was ridiculous. The whole lot couldn't be valued at more than, say — I started scribbling numbers on the yellow pad — $50,000, maybe. That wasn't worth killing for. Unless, of course, you were a member of the Nancy Drew Society of Chums. I'd get to them later. Which led me to the matter of the missing portrait of naked Nancy, if it was indeed missing, which I was willing to bet it was. I drew a red arrow on the whiteboard from Mitchell's name to the words "Blue Nancy Drew."

Where was that painting? All of Edward's things were exactly where they belonged. The fans were still in the dining room, the kitchen knives in the kitchen, the books in the blue bedroom. But the painting wasn't in the closet where I'd last seen it. And it hadn't been found anywhere in the Palm Springs house. And Mitchell and Asher Farrell kept asking me if Edgar had given me anything, which tended to suggest that they were looking for something that wasn't where they thought it was supposed to be. Which begged the question of why either of them should know. Or care.

Asher Farrell. He merited a big piece of whiteboard real estate. He was already a convicted felon, for starters. You learn all sorts of things in prison, and I don't mean the finer points of tax fraud. He sold Edgar the aforementioned painting of Grace Horton, and though he was acting blasé about it, there was more to the story. That was a given.

Asher Farrell was a bad guy. And he knew I knew. Maybe Edgar knew, too, and he (Asher) knew it (that Edgar knew). And maybe what Edgar knew was that Farrell was up to no good once again. One of his signature scams was selling multimillion-dollar artworks using invoices with fraudulent out-of-state corporate delivery addresses, to avoid sales tax. He'd been caught once, but you know what they say about old dogs and new tricks. Well, reverse it. Of course, you need the cooperation of your client to get away with this one. And your gallery staff. Maybe Melinda wasn't so innocent. Maybe Edgar, good citizen that he was, was ready to blow the whistle on everybody.

And what did Salvador Dalí have to do with it? Was it mere coincidence that Mitchell and Asher Farrell were both interested in Salvador Dalí? Why had his name rung a bell? Salvador Dalí was now a pink index card.

Suddenly I remembered Lael. I'd left her another message on my way to Book Soup, but she still hadn't called me back. I'd try her one more time.

Lael's fifteen-year-old son, Tommy, answered the phone. That couldn't be good.

"What are you doing home? Is everything okay over there?"

"Sure. Why wouldn't it be?"

"Well, aren't you kids supposed to be at the dads' houses for the weekend?"

"Yeah, but my dad's ulcer was acting up. He wasn't that into having me around, so I came home."

"I'm sorry to hear that."

"He eats for shit, that's why."

Tommy and his eleven-year-old half sister, Nina, had recently become vegans, much to Lael's distress.

"Do you want to talk to Mom?"

"Yes."

"She's out."

"Where'd she go?"

"I don't know."

"But everything's fine with her?"

"Sure."

"Have you actually seen her?"

"I just said so."

"No, you said she was out."

"I saw her."

Thank goodness.

"Yeah and she looked like shit, too. All that refined sugar. The body can't process it."

"Your mother is gorgeous. Show some respect, young man."

He laughed. "Yes, ma'am."

" 'Ma'am.' I like it. Don't forget to tell your mom I called."

Speaking of parents and children, you wouldn't want to forget the Olsens, mother and daughter, Big Psycho and Little Psycho. I hung up the phone and wrote their names beneath Asher Farrell's, then drew red arrows back up to Edgar. My flow chart was starting to get very congested.

The daughter was a practiced liar, somebody who for the hell of it would pretend to be her own neighbor. Well, maybe not for the hell of it, but to stick it to her mother via me. What else would she do to hurt Clarissa? Would she kill Edgar to ruin her mother's Nancy Drew convention? That seemed a bit far-fetched. But I'd still never gotten a straight answer about what she was doing with a slide of Edgar's painting — a painting that would undoubtedly unhinge the woman in question, not to mention compromise the book she was working on, the bona fide, true-life, G-rated story of Grace Horton, patron saint of nude models.

What exactly is an artist who sings?

I dialed Gambino at work.

He'd called me last night while I was at Asher Farrell's party, then again this morning while I was at the gallery. That art-dealing scumbag was ruining my social life. I walked back into the kitchen for another glass of milk. There was no answer, of course, but I left him a long and rambling message asking if he'd like to go see a cabaret show tomorrow night in Silver Lake. He was probably going to be stuck out in Yucaipa again. I couldn't wait until that murder investigation came to a close so we could get back to the more pleasant business of being in love.

Let me try that one more time.

I am in love with Peter Gambino.

Hmm.

I am in love with Peter Gambino.

Interesting.

So what about Clarissa? Maybe she'd found out about the painting somehow and done the dirty deed herself, to prevent the truth about Grace Horton from ever coming out. She'd said it herself, the winning individual must turn on a dime, roll with the punches, and sway with the breeze. And be able to handle a twenty-two, I suppose. Stranger things have happened. And maybe she'd taken the painting on her way out and hidden it somewhere. Or burned it,

228

more likely, so it could never again see the light of day.

Last but not least, there was the crime duo of Andrew and Jake. Jake the hustler, currently running from the police, the erstwhile boyfriend of the deceased, the one (maybe) with the most to gain from Edgar's death; and Andrew, the erstwhile boyfriend of my second best friend in the world, in whose desk I found a shiny gold key that had been stolen out of my purse and possibly used to get into the house of the dead man. The two of them were old friends. How old? How good? Andrew had followed me once. Maybe he'd followed me twice. Maybe he'd tossed my house with Jake's help. But could a man who loves vintage clothing have found it in himself to have thrown my Missoni cocktail dress on the floor? And the two of them had been the ones who'd asked me — begged me — to look into this whole thing to begin with. Were they sincere? Or was it a ruse to throw me off the track?

My stomach started rumbling. I needed more Milano cookies.

And a bigger whiteboard.

20

"Say cheese!" The flash went off in Mitchell's face.

"Ms. Caruso? Is that you? What are you doing?" He stood in the doorway of the Carroll Avenue house, rubbing his eyes. He was still in his bathrobe at three in the afternoon.

"What am I doing?"

"That's what I asked. What are you doing?"

"I'm taking pictures of the house is what I'm doing. Were you asleep?" I stuck the camera in my purse and started backing down the steps.

"Stop right there."

"It's nice to see you, too, Mitchell. I hope you've been well."

"You just saw me last night."

"You could've taken ill."

"This is ridiculous. Hold on a minute." He grabbed his slippers from the foyer, put them on, unlatched the door, and shut it behind him.

"Okay, but I'm in a hurry. I've got to get these developed."

"You are too much."

"Listen, are you sure you want to be seen outside in that robe, not that brocade isn't elegant, but given the hour . . ."

"I was out doing yoga. It's part of my routine. Thursday and Saturday mornings with Guru Chakravorty. I haven't had a chance to change since I came home."

I could just see him in the lotus position. "I'm sure it's very good for your allergies."

"Exactly why are you taking pictures of my house?"

"It's your house now?"

"Edgar's house, that's what I meant." He was livid.

"I'm thinking about covers for my Carolyn Keene biography. This place is so evocative. It reminds me of the house in number 18, *Mystery at the Moss-Covered Mansion*. I think it would make a great cover. You know, Edgar's big old haunted house, the title of the book, *Ghost in the Machine*, spelled out in some spooky font, and then, of course, my name, in huge gothic letters. What do you think?"

He swatted at his bald scalp. It looked to be his version of knocking his head against the wall. "You need legal permission. Surely even you realize that."

"Then we should get our people together soon."

Speechless at that point, he watched me go.

And off I went, to the one-hour photo kiosk at Sav-On, to my dentist's office (conveniently open on Saturdays), and then to extend an invitation to my trusty neighbor, Lois.

I tapped my foot impatiently.

Lois smiled at me and reached for another biscuit.

I paced a bit.

Marlene, her twin, took a lingering sip of coffee.

"Are you done yet, Lois?" I asked. "Marlene?" The ladies were clearly unacquainted with the usual social clues.

Lois tossed back the rest of her coffee and handed me her lipstick-smeared cup.

"And here's mine, Cece," said Marlene. "Aren't you a sweetheart to have us over?"

I walked over to the kitchen and dumped the cups into the sink. "This isn't a social call, remember. We're trying to ascertain who broke into my house, and why."

For some reason I'd dropped that ball entirely, and between my whiteboard and a second bag of Milanos, it had finally occurred to me that you couldn't go wrong proceeding in chronological order. I met Edgar last Wednesday, my house was broken into Thursday, my car was vandalized Friday, and Edgar was killed Saturday — exactly one week ago today. Maybe it was time to go back to the beginning and retrace my steps.

"This is so exciting! Isn't this exciting, Marlene?"

"It's one for the memoirs."

"All right, ladies," I said, clearing off the coffee table. "Let's get down to business. And, Marlene, please don't distract your sister."

"Oh, no," she said, shaking her head. "I'm here for moral support." She gave her sister's hand a squeeze. They exchanged looks of pure glee, like five-year-olds with double-dip ice-cream cones.

I laid the pictures of the suspects out.

"So here they are," I said, reddening a little. Well, I'd done my best. I had the photograph of Mitchell I'd just taken. He was not a photogenic person, plus there was a lot of haze. I had Jake's mug shot from the newspaper. As for Asher Farrell, I'd stopped at Dr. Fabbiani's and taken the copy of *People* magazine I'd read there maybe a year ago, in which Farrell had been featured as one of the fifty sexiest bachelors. Andrew was a bit more complicated. I didn't exactly want to go over there and deal with him and Jake just to get a picture. So I'd found the closest approximation I could inside a box of old records I'd been storing in my basement.

"What is this?" Marlene asked.

"*Frampton Comes Alive!*" her sister read.

"Was he reincarnated?"

"No, silly," Lois replied. "It's a metaphor."

"Would you look at that gorgeous head of hair! What I could do with hair like that," Marlene murmured, fingering her own thinning locks.

They say everybody's got a twin. Andrew's was definitely Peter Frampton.

Lois scrunched up her face. She put her hands on Jake's mug shot and nodded.

"Does he look familiar?" I asked.

"I don't know . . ." She moved her hands over it, like it was a Ouija board. Then she picked up Mitchell's photograph.

"Yes. Yes. He has very cold eyes. And you can't trust men with no hair."

"Are you saying you recognize him?"

"He's definitely a type, but I don't think it was him at your house that day, no."

"What about this one?" I asked, handing her *People* magazine, opened to the page with Asher Farrell's picture on it.

She peered at the page. "Let me get my glasses." Great. She needed glasses. Some witness. She pulled a pair of bifocals out of her handbag and put them on.

" 'His eyes closed, his Hugo Boss jacket askew, Asher Farrell leaned back in his chair and contentedly puffed on a Cuban cigar. Like the difficult art he champions, this smoldering man-about-town has never played by the rules — ' "

"Lois. I don't want you to read the article. Just look at the picture."

She took her glasses off. "Well, I don't need these, then, do I?" She looked offended.

"Where's your cat?" Marlene asked.

"Probably napping on my keyboard," I said.

"That's not good for the computer."

"I realize that, Marlene. Please. Let your sister concentrate."

"All right. I think I'm sure. It was him," she said, grabbing *Frampton Comes Alive!* with her left hand, "and him." She pointed to the picture of Mitchell.

Andrew and Mitchell? "That's impossible, Lois. I don't even think those two know each other. Are you positive?"

"Well, let me look again. Okay. I think I have it now. Yes, yes. The singer and the jail-bird. Those were the two. There's no doubt in my mind."

Andrew and Jake. Not what I wanted to hear.

"No," she exclaimed suddenly, patting Peter Frampton's leonine head. "I'm mistaken. They weren't this handsome, those two. I would've been far more suspicious if two such handsome men wanted to leave you a present."

"Thanks a lot, Lois."

"For what, dear?"

Annoyed, I stomped into my bedroom, got my childhood photo album from a shelf near the window, and pulled out pictures of my two older brothers, Richie and James Jr., in their prom clothes. I went back into the living room and slapped them on the table.

"What about these two, Lois?"

She pondered them.

"Italian, am I right? Look at those eyebrows. Those ruffled shirts." She nodded. "That's them all right. But they were dressed differently, of course. Why have you been holding out on me?"

"Sheer perversity, Lois."

"Tsk, tsk," said Marlene.

21

Maybe it was better to do things in *reverse* chronological order. Look at the *Godfather* movies. And résumés, not that I was such an expert. The first job I'd ever had was waitressing at D'Amico's Pizza in Asbury Park. The getups they'd made us wear were inspired by Olivia Newton-John in *Grease*, when she finally hooked up with John Travolta in the last scene. I hadn't needed a résumé to get hired, just big hair and spandex pants. I fell asleep remembering how badly I'd wanted to be blond that year. And Australian.

I was awakened the next morning by my cat, who stared me down across the quilt. I could feel her warm breath on my face. The little yowls were about to begin. It was sort of a ritual.

I had a morning ritual, too, only it in-volved the *L.A. Times*, the *N.Y. Times*, and a pot of Hawaiian hazelnut coffee. On Sundays, I sometimes threw in a cheese Danish from the bakery at Gelson's, the most overpriced market in the Los Angeles metropolitan area, which just happened to be located around the corner. I sat up and looked at the clock. Five forty-five. I flopped back down and pulled the quilt over my head. The papers hadn't even been delivered. The coffeemaker was set for nine. Mimi burrowed under the covers and started nipping at my feet. It was hopeless now. Oh, well. It was a good thing to rise before the sun. One could accomplish many things.

I hurled the covers onto the floor, put on my slippers, and padded out to the office. I would work on my index, a hideous, thankless task of epic proportions. If I started now, perhaps I'd be done by the turn of the next millennium.

I put the heat on low, settled myself at my desk, and started composing a list of key names, words, and phrases.

Carolyn Keene. Nancy Drew. Stratemeyer Syndicate. Harriet Stratemeyer Adams. Mildred Wirt Benson. This wasn't so bad. All I had to do was come up with maybe a thousand of these. Russell H. Tandy. Ned Nickerson. George Fayne. Bess Marvin. Hannah Gruen. It was a piece of cake, really. Missing will. Lost inheritance. Misplaced manuscript. Stolen jewels. Roadster. Country club. Clothing allowance.

Spoiled rotten. Pudding. Nancy and her friends never missed a pudding. Bess had weight issues, George was the athletic type, and Nancy wouldn't know a diet if it hit her over the head. Pot roast. Creamed spinach. Lemon meringue pie. Anorexia. Bulimia. Self-loathing. Adolescence. Woman's intuition. Feminine identity. Liberation. Servitude. Double bind. No exit. Man, was I tired.

Four hours later, I woke up at my desk with a crease running down my left cheek. It was from a second edition of *Honey Bunch: Her First Little Treasure Hunt,* one of Mildred Wirt Benson's lesser efforts. It made a very bad pillow.

I turned off the heat and went inside to brush my teeth, which usually woke me right up, but I had a scare before I could squeeze the toothpaste onto the brush. It consisted of seeing my face in the mirror. My eyes were puffy, my hair was a mess, and there was a red stripe extending from my forehead to my chin. I looked ghastly. Working on my index had not been good for my feminine identity. I could've been a painting by Salvador Dalí.

Which gave me pause.

I had been neglecting my index cards.

One of them in particular seemed to be calling out to me. That would be the pink one that read "Salvador Dalí/Too many nipples/Too many coincidences." I was listening now. Why the hell not?

Woman's intuition beats reverse chronological order on average three to one.

"Watch it!" A girl in a UCLA sweatshirt sped past me on her bike, her long blond hair slapping me in the face.

"You watch it!"

Late for a chemistry lab, or an astronomy lecture, or maybe a Chaucer reading group. I hated her. Only because I'd once wanted to be her. But I'd made the mistake of taking that job at D'Amico's when I was sixteen instead of prepping for the SATs.

And yet, if I hadn't still been working at D'Amico's a year later, I never would've met Roger, the handsome Princeton grad student from Newport, Rhode Island. And if Roger hadn't had a father he wanted to punish (turned out I was the punishment), he wouldn't have come down to Asbury Park for the weekend. And if he hadn't been hungry for pizza (it seems obvious, doesn't it?), I wouldn't have had Annie. And if I hadn't altered my master plan to raise her and help Roger get started in his career, who knows where I'd be? I certainly wouldn't be writing biographies of dead mystery authors. That, ironically, only came about because of Roger's chief character defect. He was a shirker.

I could've said ass, but I'm a lady.

Early in his battle for tenure at the University of Chicago, Roger — currently the world's second leading authority on James Fenimore Cooper, much to his chagrin — was assigned a course in American popular literature, fondly known as "Shit Lit." Since I was the one who regularly cleaned up his shit, he'd doled out the research to me. Let's just say he lived to regret it. I spent weeks digging into police procedurals. I was so thorough I surprised even myself — not to mention one of Roger's colleagues with her own imprint at a small press. My first book contract about killed him. He liked me a lot better when I was hostessing at the faculty club.

Anyway, some things still made me feel young and dumb. Being at UCLA, for example. Getting slapped around by a coed. But here I was, just the same.

The art library was nearly empty. Maybe college students didn't use libraries anymore. Maybe they did everything online. I found the section on surrealism, borrowed an available trolley, and loaded it up with books on Salvador Dalí.

I loved research. I'd learned by watching Roger, then doing everything the opposite way. It was a lot like shopping. Your senses are on high alert. Your pupils shrink to pinpricks. Nothing escapes your notice. You are searching for the clever juxtaposition. The creative solution to the recalcitrant problem. Take Adrian's emphasis, during World War II, on pockets, plackets, and goring to create interest in lieu of techniques that would have cost rationed fabric. There's a creative solution. If you stumble upon a piece by Adrian, consider yourself lucky. Or a peplum jacket from the fifties, maybe in a nice mohair and cashmere. Lilli Ann, a California label, did some gorgeous ones. Nothing, and I mean nothing, camouflages childbearing hips better than a peplum.

I sat down at the nearest open carrel and pulled a heavy book from the stack on the trolley. It must've weighed ten pounds. I shook my head in disapproval. Good research involves culling the telling detail, not accumulating them willy-nilly. I heaved the book onto the table and it fell open to a double-page spread of a painting from 1938.

It was lovely, a sepia-toned image of a young woman, almost Vermeer-like in its stillness. The woman's head was bent reverently over a letter. Not what you'd expect from Salvador Dalí. I stared at it awhile. Then, suddenly, it dissolved into an image of a man with a heavy mustache and beard, sort of Sigmund Freud crossed with William Shakespeare. The big daddies. The title of the painting was *The Image Disappears*. There was a quote from the artist: "We see what we have reason to see, especially what we believe we are going to see."

I flipped back to the front and started reading. Dalí was born May 11, 1904, in Figueras, a small town in Spain, though he liked to claim he was born not once but twice. This was because he was not the first Salvador Dalí his parents had. The first died as a baby. The second arrived exactly nine months and ten days later. Creepy. That was Dalí's life in a nutshell.

He was a teenage prodigy known for his bizarre outfits as well as his uncanny ability to fake any style: impressionism, pointilism, purism, cubism, futurism. It was when he began experimenting with surrealism in the late 1920s that he finally came into his own.

His dreams became raw material. He made paintings of angelic babies eating bloody rats, disembodied heads being attacked by ants, flaccid limbs, melting watches, drooping tigers, and gelatinous everything. Everywhere were double images and concealed self-portraits. Favorite fetishes included keys, nails, zippers, and teeth. And his audience couldn't get enough.

Pale as a cadaver, his mustache waxed to perfection, he became a master of self-promotion. He designed shirts, fabrics, ties, calendars, ashtrays, oyster knives. André Breton, the leader of the surrealists, eventually turned on him, calling him by an anagram of his proper name, "Avida Dollars."

His phobias multiplied as fast as his successes. He was afraid of everything. He couldn't buy shoes because he feared exposing his feet in public. On his first crossing to the United States, he never took off his life vest. He was so shy that he once addressed the public in a diving suit and almost suffocated when he couldn't remove the helmet.

I was riveted. I wanted to keep reading. But personal edification wasn't the goal. I had to maintain focus, a key axiom of shopping and scholarship alike. What did any of this have to do with anything? Nothing. I was looking for some esoteric clue that wasn't there. After all, there was one perfectly plausible, perfectly logical answer to the question of why Salvador Dalí's name kept cropping up. Edgar Edwards was an art collector. He had an interest in buying work by Salvador Dalí. Asher Farrell and Mitchell Honey were art professionals. They had an interest in making that possible. They were doing their homework, that was all. That had to be it. And it made perfect sense, Edgar's attraction to this particular artist. Dalí was strange; Edgar was strange. Dalí loved practical jokes; Edgar did, too.

I walked back to my car swinging my purse around and around in circles. Okay. So Dalí was a dead end. Back to square one. Shit. Too bad Lois hadn't panned out. But how could I have expected anything from her? She and Marlene were hopeless.

I pulled out of the parking garage and turned onto Sunset Boulevard, going east.

Avida Dollars. That was really good. I wondered if you could come up with any good anagrams for Edgar Edwards.

"Rage" was in there. "Dada," too. Also "sad."

Poor dead Edgar. None of this should have happened.

If Edgar's name had had an *l* in it, you could've spelled out "raw deal."

22

It was almost eight p.m. Gambino would be here any second.

I shimmied into a pair of black leggings and a pink off-the-shoulder sweater. The mirror was behind me. I turned around and studied my reflection.

All ready for the remake of *Flashdance.*

Next I tried a Halston ivory cashmere tunic and matching palazzo pants.

I looked like a milkman.

A striped shirtdress from the forties made me look like a USO volunteer. The addition of stiletto ankle boots made me look like a demented USO volunteer. But maybe that was okay. I was getting bored.

Tut, tut. A girl cannot afford to be complacent. There was always my fuchsia sari dress; the matching stole was big enough to use as a tent if we decided to camp out. Or my sheer metallic cowl-neck ensemble, a must for the shy girl coming out of her shell. But since I wasn't shy, it seemed redundant. Then it came to me. You can never go wrong with Azzedine Alaïa.

I pulled the long-sleeved black dress off the hanger. I remembered the afternoon I bought it, after catching Roger in bed with one of his grad students. It was a thick, semigloss knit with a low square neckline and a seam running up the center of the back that gave new meaning to the phrase "lift and separate." And separate we did. He had an excuse, like always, but that was the day I finally gave him the boot.

I wriggled into the dress and twisted my neck to get the rear view. I could live with it. The sixties were difficult for me to pull off, with all those straight up-and-down lines, but the eighties, now those were good years for shapely women like myself.

A car door slammed. I slipped a lipstick into my purse, and opened the front door.

Gambino, freshly shaven and in a dark sports jacket and jeans, was standing there with a bouquet of red roses.

"Did the guys tell you to do that?" I asked.

"If I did everything the guys told me to do, I'd be in a lot of trouble by now."

"I think you're already in trouble."

"I am?"

"You're looking more and more like husband material." Shit. I didn't say that. "I didn't say that." Shit.

247

"Say what?" He was grinning from ear to ear.

"Stay here while I stick these in a vase."

"Am I taking orders from you now?"

"Any complaints?"

"Nope."

I found a black lacquered vase under the sink, but it had several chips. It was over. Ditto the wildflowers Lael had picked for me. I pulled them out of my tall crystal vase, dumped the brackish water, filled the thing with clean water from the tap, and arranged the roses. Impulsive. Unrestrained. Rash. Only a fool says everything that's on her mind.

We drove to Nancy Olsen's cabaret show in silence.

Finally, Gambino said, "Do you want to talk about it?"

"About what?" I asked, opening my window.

"About what you said before."

"No. The light's green."

He hit the gas. "Do you want to talk about anything?"

"The weather."

"It's cold out. Why'd you open the window?"

I closed the window. The traffic got bad around Hyperion. We were stalled for a while behind an old yellow Pontiac.

"Why don't you put the siren on? Isn't that one of the perks of your job?"

"Cece."

"Okay."

"Can we talk about it soon?"

"It what?"

"Us. The future. We need to talk."

"Okay."

"When?" he asked.

"In one week."

"Seven days?"

"Seven days."

"Make it six, and you have a deal."

"Deal."

He pulled into the driveway of the Witching Hour, which was located in a former body shop on a back alley in Silver Lake.

"You take me to all the best places," I said.

"I thought you were taking me."

"Does it matter?"

"Nope."

Inside, the walls and ceilings were painted black. It was Sunday night, but Saturday night had evidently lived on. There was broken glass on the floor, dirty cups on empty tables, and a hostess with matted platinum-blond hair who seemed to have just emerged from a coma. With great effort of will, she seated us at a small table near the

249

stage. An Asian girl who looked about twelve took our drink order. As she walked away, I caught a glimpse of her tattoo poking up over the back of her leather shorts. It was a royal flush.

"Do I need a tattoo like that?" I asked, still pouting a little.

"You, babe, have everything you need."

I rewarded him with a lip lock.

"So what happened to our drinks?" he asked after a while.

The room was starting to fill up. Maybe the waitress was overwhelmed. She should've probably been home, practicing her multiplication tables or something.

"I'll check."

I walked over to the bar and waited. There were two guys in lumberjack shirts standing next to me. I thought I heard them talking about Nancy Olsen.

"Do you know what time she comes on?" I asked.

"Why? You in a hurry to get out of here?" asked the taller one. The shorter one just leered into his beer.

"No," I said. "I'm with the gentleman over there." I pointed toward Gambino.

"The cop?" asked the tall one.

I nodded. They made themselves scarce. With our drinks in hand, I returned to the table. Gambino was deep in conversation with the hostess. When she saw me coming, she disappeared.

"What's with her?"

"She wanted to know how to get rid of the hookers that hang out in the back of the parking lot."

"How do all these people know you're a cop?"

"People know."

The lights dimmed as the musicians came out. A guy on keyboards, another on drums, and a third with an electric guitar. They sat down and the stage went black. Then a white spotlight shone on somebody's teeny-tiny form. Nancy Olsen. What a piece of work. She was wearing her tartan minikilt, her tank top, and a spiked dog collar with a chain that circled around her body several times and hooked onto one of her motorcycle boots. She scowled at the audience, which I think meant hello. Then the guitar started screeching and she started wailing.

What followed was the weirdest performance I've ever seen. And I don't mean Nancy howling "Some days it don't pay to get out of your crypt," because on occasion I've felt the very same way. No, things got weird when she wrapped up the vampire number, and "I Wanna Be Sedated," and disappeared backstage only to emerge as Dolly Parton — I mean with boobs spilling out of a peach sequined halter dress, foot-tall blond hair, and foot-long peach fingernails, belting out what sounded like "My Tennessee Mountain Ham." The twang was dead-on.

"Who is this girl?" Gambino whispered.

"I have no idea."

"Do you want another drink?"

"Good idea."

After warbling her way through "9 to 5," Nancy went backstage again. A Betty Boop cartoon came on. When it was done, she returned in a mauve cocktail dress with padded shoulders and a come-hither look in her eyes. She blew a few kisses around the room, then draped herself across the top of a baby grand piano the keyboard player had wheeled in. He put a wineglass out with a couple of dollars already in it, sat down, and played a few bars. She introduced him as "Bobby," then did a credible job with "Stormy Weather," though she positively burned through "I Got It Bad (and That Ain't Good)." She was still a kid, but to sing like that you had to have survived some messy affairs of the heart.

"Would you call her versatile?" Gambino asked.

I tapped my fingers on the table. "Schizo-phrenic."

The hostess came over again and whis-pered something in Gambino's ear. He nodded and got up.

"I'm going to go help this woman for a second."

"I thought you were off duty."

"I'll be right back." He leaned down to kiss me.

"Be careful."

"I think I can handle a couple of hookers."

Nancy left the stage and the guitar player announced it would be a few minutes until the grand finale. They started projecting footage of Marilyn Monroe singing "Happy Birthday, Mr. President" to JFK. You couldn't hear Marilyn, though, because the room was so loud. I checked my watch. It was eleven forty-five. Almost the witching hour. I got up and headed to the ladies' room.

It hit me as I stood in front of the bath-room's grimy mirror. Gambino and I were having a normal evening. An actual date. Okay, maybe I'd jumped the gun a little with my comment, but he'd taken it well. I reap-plied my lipstick. Very well, in fact, consid-ering that marriage was one of his sore spots, too, thanks to his own cheating ex-spouse. That was part of the problem the first time we got together four years ago. It was too soon for both of us. Maybe this was finally the right moment. We were learning to trust each other.

Earth to Cece.

This was not a normal evening. This was not an actual date. I was doing surveillance on Nancy Olsen. I had to tell Gambino because we had no chance whatsoever of making it if I kept having all these agendas he knew nothing about. I regarded my mouth dispassionately. An error. I would be throwing away all my heavy lipsticks. Heavy lipstick was yet another defense mechanism I was done with.

"Sorry to bother you," came a voice from one of the stalls, "but there's no bathroom tissue in here. . . ."

I checked in the other stall, but there wasn't any in there either, so I grabbed some paper towels from the dispenser and bent down to shove them under the door. I found myself face-to-face with a pair of high-heeled red slingbacks and some expensive-looking stockings.

"Clarissa?"

There was a flush and the door opened, almost knocking me over.

"Cece, dear, watch yourself. What a lovely surprise."

"Clarissa. All the way from Phoenix. What are you doing here?"

"I wanted to surprise my daughter, of course."

She washed her hands ferociously, like she did everything else. "Nancy doesn't know I'm here, though. I don't want to make her nervous."

I was nervous just standing next to her.

She yanked down some paper towels and dried her hands until they were almost as red as her shoes and her dress. Red was her signature color, I guess.

"How's the book coming?" I asked.

"Spectacularly. And yours?"

"I finished it." A white lie. White was my signature color.

"I can't wait to read it."

"Thanks for the support."

"We don't want to miss the finale."

"We certainly don't," I said, heading for the door. She didn't move. I paused. "Would you like to join me? There's room at the table."

"No," she said, smiling furiously. "I'm fine here."

I supposed she'd come out when she was ready.

By the time I returned to my seat, Nancy was back, clad in a white lace skirt and bustier, a tangle of crucifixes, and masses of bleached blond hair. Behind her, a slide show was in progress. Every few seconds, the image changed.

A marble statue of Aphrodite.

A Raggedy Ann doll.

"Gambino. I have a confession to make." I fidgeted in my seat. The dress was not good for sitting. "Gambino?"

He was mesmerized by an image of a kinky Helmut Newton model, naked except for a pair of thigh-high boots.

"I have a confession, too," he said. "I love performance art."

I kicked him under the table.

A geisha girl holding a flower.

A female nude curled up like a seashell.

It couldn't be.

Nancy writhed across the stage moaning "Like a Virgin" and doing distinctly unvirginal things with her microphone stand.

A little girl from the Victorian era sitting on a riverbank.

These were the slides I'd found in her car.

A headless mannequin draped in fur.

They were part of her act.

I was glad I couldn't see Clarissa's face,

because I knew what was coming next. Indeed, at the precise moment Nancy screamed "Like a vir-ir-ir-ir-gin," it materialized on the wall: the painting of naked Nancy Drew, in all her fleshly glory. It was like the return of the repressed, only in stereo-surround sound.

Was Grace Horton turning in her grave? Or proud of her feisty granddaughter, who was doing it on her own terms? And Clarissa? I turned to see if I could catch a glimpse of her, but all I saw was a blur of red moving out the door.

I sighed deeply.

"What did you want to confess?" Gambino asked.

"Nothing," I said, adjusting his collar. "How'd it go with the hookers?"

23

The phone rang at 2:11 a.m. Startled, I reached over Gambino to pick it up, but there was no one on the other end. Must've been a bad dream. I put the phone down and he pulled me into his arms.

"Everything okay?" he mumbled, still half asleep.

"Fine."

"Good."

"Go back to sleep."

The phone rang again at 2:13 a.m. There was still nobody there.

"Damn," I said out loud.

"What is it?" Gambino sat up and rubbed his eyes.

"Wrong number, I guess. I don't know." I rearranged the blankets a little. My feet were cold.

"You look sexy in that thing."

"It's called a sweatshirt," I said, smiling.

We were back asleep by about 3:00 a.m.

The phone rang again at 4:10 a.m.

"Who the hell is this?"

"Cece?"

I lowered my voice. "Andrew?"

"Listen, I'm sorry to bother you."

"Did you call before?"

"When?"

"Never mind. What's going on? It's the middle of the night." I glanced over at Gambino.

"It's Jake. He's all riled up. He wants to see you. He says he's got to get something off his chest."

"I'm not a priest."

"I realize that."

"Can't it wait until morning?"

"I don't think so. Jake insists on talking to you."

"It'll be light in a couple hours. I can come over then."

"Please."

"Andrew, this is crazy. I'm sleeping."

"You don't understand. I have to be at the store at seven this morning. We're doing inventory before we open. The only time is now."

I groaned.

"You're a good person."

"I'm an idiot."

"Oh," he added as an afterthought, "Jake said to bring what Edgar gave you. He'll explain."

And what exactly did either of them know about what Edgar had given me? And while we were on the subject of explaining, it was about time Andrew explained how he happened to have my missing key in his desk.

I hung up the phone and looked at Gambino again. He was out cold. I'd be back before he woke up. And I didn't need to bother him. He'd been working so hard, it was the last thing he needed. He had the morning off. Maybe I'd bring back a guava and cheese pie from Café Tropical in Silver Lake, and we'd eat the whole thing in bed.

My sweatshirt was lying on the floor inside out. I pulled it on and tiptoed over to the closet, where my sweatpants were hanging on a hook. I put them on, stuck the black-and-white photograph Edgar had mailed me into the front pocket, jammed my feet into an old pair of fleece-lined boots, and walked as quietly as I could to the front door. Buster appeared out of nowhere, thrilled at the prospect of an impromptu stroll.

"No, boy. Later. I promise."

I shut the door behind me.

Traffic was light. I made it in fifteen minutes. There was an open spot across the street from Andrew's. It was permit only, but I doubted any cop cars would be patrolling the area at this hour. Plus, the sign was so covered with graffiti you'd have a hard time making the ticket stick. I got out and locked the car. The air smelled like rotten meat. I sidestepped some Styrofoam packing crates that seemed to have been dismembered right there on the sidewalk. There was a baby crying in the distance. Then the sound of a car backfiring. Then someone kicking a can. There were people all around. Businessmen.

"Smoke?"

"No."

"Smoke?"

"No."

"Smoke?"

"No."

"Where you going?"

I kept my head down.

"Need company?"

"No."

"Whore."

Echo Park Lake in the wee hours of the morning was not the happiest place on earth.

I started up to Andrew's apartment. I was almost at his door when I heard some scuffling at the top of the stairs. Probably rats. Spooked, I looked up, prepared for anything. Anything except someone running past me faster than the speed of light.

It looked like Andrew.

I turned around and watched him disappear.

There was no answer when I knocked at his door. What was going on?

"Jake? Open up, Jake!"

Silence.

"Andrew? Please open the door!"

That was when I felt a hand grasp my shoulder and spin me around.

"You think I'm going to let you wander around the street in the middle of the fucking night?"

"Gambino! You scared me."

"You scared me."

"I was going to get you a guava and cheese pie."

"We're a long way from the Tropical."

"On my way home, I meant."

"From where exactly?"

"Bridget's boyfriend's. He's with Edgar's boyfriend. They're in trouble."

"Please tell me you're not talking about the one the cops are looking for."

"Okay, I'm not."

"Damn it, Cece."

"I have to go inside. They need my help." I tried the door. It was unlocked. Before he could stop me, I swung it open and started inside.

"What are you doing? Do not take another step!" Gambino pushed me behind him and drew his gun. "I mean it."

I nodded, knowing he meant it. But I'd made a promise, and when I make a promise, I mean it, too.

He headed back into the bedroom. I waited for what seemed like hours, not moving, barely breathing. The living room looked as small and shabby as it had the other day. The wallpaper was grimy, the couch was threadbare, the plants needed watering.

"Jesus Christ!"

"What is it?" I yelled.

"Don't touch anything. Just come in here."

I walked into Andrew's bedroom. My legs felt like water. Gambino was standing there, looking down at the floor.

"You know this poor bastard?"

"It's Jake Waite," I said softly.

Gambino knelt down. With a white handkerchief he'd taken out of his pocket, he picked up a small gun lying next to Jake. Then he took Jake's hand. It looked small in his large one.

"Holy shit!"

"What?"

He laid his head on Jake's chest. "He's not dead."

"He's alive?"

Gambino pulled out his phone and called an ambulance. "For the time being."

"Jake, Jake, it's Cece." I fell to my knees and stroked his cheek. "You're going to be okay. Who did this to you?"

"He did it to himself," Gambino said. "Some fucking suicide."

"Suicide? What are you talking about?"

"Read this," he said, holding up a small piece of paper.

I'm sorry for the people I hurt. I'm sorry for who I've become.

Jake

That was it. Short and not sweet. "This isn't right, Peter."

"I know."

"No, this note isn't right. Jake isn't sorry about who he is. He doesn't have any regrets. He wanted to tell me something. That's why I'm here."

"This guy is wanted for questioning. What the hell are you doing running over here when he calls?"

"It was important. He had something to say to me."

"I think he said it."

"Jake loved Edgar. I know he didn't kill

him. And I know he didn't try to kill himself."

"How do you know?"

"He isn't the type. Plus, he of all people had everything to live for."

"What are you saying?"

"I'm saying that somebody faked this." But who? Andrew? Mitchell?

"That's a serious accusation you're making."

"I realize that."

The paramedics arrived, put Jake on a gurney, and slipped an oxygen mask over his mouth and nose. Then they hooked him up to an IV.

"Is he going to make it?" I asked.

"Not if you don't get out of our way."

I squeezed Jake's hand as they wheeled him out. "Don't worry," I whispered. "Just get better. I'll be by the hospital later."

"That remains to be seen," Gambino said with an unpleasant undertone to his voice.

He walked into the kitchen and rummaged around in the drawers until he found a box of Ziploc bags. He put the gun in one baggie and the note in another.

"What kind of gun is it?"

"Looks like a twenty-two." The same as the gun that killed Edgar. "Since when do you care about guns?"

"Is this your case?"

"For now. I'll have a better idea of what we're dealing with soon. And where you will or won't be going."

"News flash. You're not my father. I'll go where I want to go."

"Not if you don't want to get arrested for obstruction of justice you won't."

"You wouldn't do that to me."

"Watch me."

"You can forget all about your guava and cheese pie," I said.

"I'll call you. I've got work to do here. The crime scene guys are on their way."

"Are you dismissing me?"

He walked me back out to the living room and pushed me out the door. "Don't turn this into something personal. This is business. I've got to take care of things here, then go to the hospital. Just pray he wakes up and can tell us what the fuck's going on."

"I don't pray. Not anymore."

"I don't have time for this, Cece."

"Neither do I." I had to find Andrew.

24

"What are you doing here at this ungodly hour?" asked Bridget as she unlocked the front door to her shop. "And in sweatpants?"

I think it was safe to say she usually slept through this part of the day. "I was in the neighborhood and figured I'd say hello."

"Well, come on in, then," she said, rubbing her eyes. "Though I'm not exactly ready to face my public."

"I'm not your public."

Helmut, nobody's fool, smelled cinnamon rolls and leapt for the white paper bag I was carrying.

"Helmut, down! Stop that nonsense right now!" Bridget turned to me. "His vet has him on a low-carb diet."

"We'll eat his, then." I opened the bag and pulled out the rolls and two lattes. "So where's Andrew?" I asked, handing her the one with two sugars. "I brought one for him, too."

"He's late."

She sat down at Andrew's desk, took a sip of her latte, and made a face. She opened the top drawer, grabbed two sugar packets, ripped them open, poured the contents in, and took another sip. "Now this is what I call coffee."

"How can you drink it like that?"

"It's delicious." I watched her, waiting for the right moment. But there wasn't going to be a right moment.

"I've got to tell you something, and you're not going to like it."

She slammed down her cup. Coffee went everywhere. "I do not want to hear another word about Andrew! That's what this is about, isn't it? Leave it alone, will you?"

"I can't."

"You *won't*."

"Andrew called me last night."

"What?"

"You know Edgar's boyfriend, Jake Waite? The one who's been missing?"

She pushed the top drawer closed. It made an unearthly sound, like a death rattle. "I keep telling Andrew to oil this drawer," she said.

"Bridget. Listen to me. Jake's been hiding at Andrew's. They're old friends."

"I'm not listening."

"They thought I could help them figure

out who killed Edgar, and clear Jake's name."

"I said I'm not listening."

"Yes, you are."

"Well, what you're saying is insane."

She stood up, then sat back down.

"I realize it sounds that way. Jake remembered something in the middle of the night, something he thought I should hear about right away. So I headed over to Andrew's. It was a disaster. I saw Andrew, at least I think it was Andrew, bolt out of there without a word to me, and when we went inside —"

"We?"

"Gambino and me. When we went inside, we found Jake. He'd been shot. They took him to the hospital. I don't even know if he made it."

I stopped.

"You think Andrew had something to do with it, don't you?"

"I need to talk to him," I said gently.

"Well, you can forget about that." She stood up again. "He's not coming."

"How do you know?"

"He phoned just before you got here. He said he'd been called away on a family emergency. He didn't know when he'd be back."

"Why didn't you tell me?"

"I knew it sounded like a lie." She tossed what was left of her coffee into the trash. "The police must be looking for him, too."

"They will be."

"Jesus," she said. "I really thought he was special."

"We don't know anything yet. It may all be perfectly innocent."

"You don't believe that."

"No."

She turned to look at the racks of beautiful clothes filling the hallway. Sheer net blouses. Spangled sweaters. Cocktail dresses. Dinner suits. Princess coats. "Fuck."

"Do you need my help with all this, Bridget?"

She scratched her short curly hair. "I'm fine."

"Really?"

"Really." She gave me a sorry attempt at a smile. "It's funny. You peel off the top layer of skin and sometimes you find a stranger underneath."

"I'll call you later," I said, hugging her good-bye. She didn't hug me back.

I got home around eight-thirty in the morning, realizing only then that I'd forgotten to check Andrew's drawer for the key. Was it still there? Unlikely.

It'd been a long night. The instant the

door closed behind me, I kicked off my boots, put Edgar's photograph back in my drawer next to the Lanvin cape, and yanked off my sweats. I needed a shower. It took exactly three and a half minutes for the hot water to warm up, during which time I think I sat on my bed staring vacantly into space, though I can't be sure. Following the monumental task of washing my hair, I collapsed at the kitchen table, then got up briefly to put on a pot of coffee. The phone machine was blinking. There were two messages. The first was from Lael.

BEEP. *You're up and at 'em awfully early this morning. Good for you! I guess we haven't talked all weekend. Asher's a fox, I'll give him that, but there's no there there, if you know what I mean. That's all I'm going to say on the subject. He has a good orange juicer, the kind that costs a hundred and thirty dollars at Williams-Sonoma. And there's a Jackson Pollock painting over his bed. But that's absolutely all I'm going to say on the subject. There's a huge stack of that particular issue of* People *in the bathroom, by the way.*

There would be.

The second message was from Gambino.

BEEP. *I hope you got some sleep. I've*

been with the guys in the lab. You were right. Most suicide notes don't have two different sets of fingerprints on them.

Because nobody had tried to commit suicide. Somebody had tried to commit murder.

I called him back immediately, but he was unavailable. I spent the next half an hour trying to get an actual human being on the phone, anyone who could tell me about Jake's condition. But the Cedars-Sinai automated phone system outmaneuvered me at every turn. I don't know why I expected otherwise. Clearly, I was going to have to do this in person.

I hated hospitals. In my experience people go to hospitals and they don't get better. They die. My father, for instance. One minute he's walking around, mean as all get-out, the baddest cop in town. The next minute he's dying in a hospital bed, with silent nurses padding about silently.

I took a last sip of coffee. That was so long ago.

I got dressed quickly, grabbed my car keys off the table, and headed out the door. Halfway down the path, I swung back around. I'd forgotten to turn off the lights. My father used to be a real stickler about things like that.

★ ★ ★

Jake was alive, but barely. They'd removed two bullets from his brain, but there was still too much swelling to know exactly what kind of damage had been sustained. He was in recovery. He'd been in surgery for almost four hours. He'd be on a respirator for at least a few more days.

I wanted to see him. He was an artist, a sculptor. I didn't even know what kind of work he made. I wanted to hear about it. I wanted to talk to him, to tell him not to give up. But there are no visitors permitted in the intensive care unit except immediate family, and I just didn't have it in me to pretend to be Jake's sister or aunt or cousin. I wasn't even sure I was his friend.

Not that the armed guards would've fallen for a scam like that anyway. I smiled at them, a pair of big guys in uniform, dispatched by Gambino, no doubt, in case somebody should happen to show up wanting to finish what he — or she — had started back at Andrew's.

One of the two smiled back.

"What's your name, Officer?"

"Jimenez, ma'am."

"Officer Jimenez, let me ask you something."

"All right." He was a baby, fresh out of the

academy, I'd bet. This wasn't exactly the most challenging assignment.

"Has Mr. Waite had any visitors this morning?"

"No visitors, ma'am." He was trying to keep a straight face.

"Thank you."

"You're a visitor," said the other one.

I ignored him. "Keep up the good work, Officer Jimenez."

Somebody didn't like that. "Lady, this isn't a playground." He patted his holster menacingly.

"That isn't necessary, Officer. Really."

Jimenez shrugged his shoulders.

I went and sat down on a bench across from the nurses' station.

"Can I help you, dear?" asked an older woman. She looked like she'd been helping people her whole life.

"No, not really. But thank you."

She smiled. "I'm Hattie, if I can do anything for you."

So I got to thinking, sitting there on that bench. And the thing was, Jimenez and the other guy, they didn't know who they were looking for. But I did. I knew the whole motley crew. They wouldn't let me see Jake. Fine. But there was no law against hanging around, maybe seeing who the cat dragged in. Or who dragged in the cat. Or whatever. Hattie didn't seem to mind.

I glanced at my watch. It was only nine o'clock. It definitely wouldn't kill me to stick around for a while.

25

I sat there for almost two hours. Back and forth went the nurses with their tubes and vials and jars. In and out went the orderlies with their stacks of white linen. Administrators patrolled the hallways with their clipboards and false smiles. Entire families wandered about like zombies. Jimenez closed his eyes a couple of times. His burly colleague fiddled with a silver console that looked like a PalmPilot but was actually a Game Boy, and who could blame him? Police work can be profoundly uneventful.

I gave up. Jake's would-be murderer was probably not dumb enough to make a reappearance this early in the game anyhow. If he knew what he was doing, he'd lie low for a while. And maybe if he were really lucky, Jake would die anyway.

As I was leaving, I asked Hattie if I could call her later for an update. She said yes. Then I pushed open the swinging door and crashed directly into Mitchell Honey. He was carrying white roses.

"Ms. Caruso. Why am I not surprised?"

"White roses are for funerals, Mitchell."

"What are you doing here?"

"I could ask you the same thing."

"I'm here for Jake, of course. Have you seen him? How is he?"

"Still among the living. How'd you find out what happened?"

"It's all over the news."

That was fast. Too fast. I wished I could run out to my car and turn on the radio to see if he was full of it.

He pulled a tissue out of his pocket and blew his nose. "I can't process all of this. It's too much."

"It must be a nightmare for you, Mitchell."

"It is, yes. First Edgar, and now Jake. I was too hard on him. He had to have loved Edgar more than I ever knew to pull a stunt like this."

"Like what?"

"Trying to kill himself, of course. He was despondent over Edgar's murder. That's what they said."

"What radio station?"

"I don't know. I don't care. I'm cursed." He slumped onto the bench, then looked up at me. "Actually, you're cursed."

"Me?"

"Everything was perfect before you came into our lives."

"Oh, perfect. I saw it that day at the house. One big happy family."

"Look. Why don't you just go, Ms. Caruso? I'm sure you have a wonderful, fulfilling life of your very own. Go live it."

"Answer one question for me. What do I have that everybody wants?"

"I don't know what you're talking about."

"Yes, you do," I said, my voice shaking. I was angry and confused and tired of all the lies.

"Please keep it down," said Hattie. "This is intensive care. There are very sick people here." She looked at the roses. "No flowers allowed, sir."

Mitchell went over to the trash can. "We're finished, Ms. Caruso." He tried to stuff the whole bouquet in, but it was too big, so he shoved it in one flower at a time.

"No, we aren't. All of you keep asking me about what Edgar gave me. Why do you care? What could it possibly matter?"

"Stay out of it. Ouch." He sucked on one of his fingers.

"I'd love to stay out of it, but I keep getting dragged back in."

"No one is dragging you anywhere. I don't know you very well, but I sincerely doubt you've ever gone anywhere you haven't wanted to go."

"You don't know me at all."

He started to walk away. Then he turned around. "Look in a mirror sometime. Maybe you don't see yourself the way other people do."

Why did everyone want me to look in the mirror all of a sudden? "And how is that?"

"Edgar thought you were tough. *Tenacious* was the word he used. But I don't think he understood you at all."

"You don't think I'm tenacious?"

"I think you've got some strange sense of mission. But not everyone wants to be a part of it. Not everyone wants help. You may even find that they resent it."

"That sounds like a threat."

"It's not a threat. It's not anything," he said wearily. "I don't know why I'm talking to you at all. I want to see Jake."

"Two police officers are watching him."

"Why?"

"Figure it out," I said. "And by the way, you're bleeding."

He looked down at his hand.

"Damn thorns."

"At least you're in the right place. To get help."

He stared at me.

"Don't worry, Mitchell. Not from me. Despite my sense of mission, I'm done with you. All of you."

At least I thought I was. Until I saw Nancy Olsen pulling her green Prelude into the visitors' lot as I was pulling my silver Camry out.

I was sitting on the slate steps outside the Holly View Apartments when Nancy came back, sometime around three. I saw her see me from a distance and expected her to turn and run, but she didn't. She kept on walking until she was standing right in front of me.

"I'm glad you're here, Cece."

No, she wasn't what you'd call the predictable sort. Today she was dressed like a management trainee, in a navy blue wool suit with matching navy blue high heels. Her hair was pulled into a low ponytail and her face was stripped of makeup.

"Who are you supposed to be now?" I asked.

"A person who works at a car rental agency."

"I don't get it."

"I was at an interview earlier today. I need a job."

"Did your mother cut you off?"

"I cut myself off. I need discipline. I'm a mess."

"At least you're honest."

"So are you, which is why I think I can talk to you. Anyway, I'm out of options. Will you come in?" she asked, unlocking the gate.

"All right."

We walked up the stairs to her apartment. Outside the door was a small urn filled with calla lilies.

"What happened to the jasmine?"

"It was dead. You've got to whack it back, you know."

"Yeah, I know."

She opened the door and we went inside.

"Sit down." She pointed to an overstuffed easy chair adrift in the middle of the floor. "My mother bought it for me."

I sank down into what felt like an upholstered marshmallow and looked around. Books were stacked into skinny little towers against one wall. Clothes and shoes and jewelry and makeup were jumbled together in a cardboard refrigerator box lying open on its side. There was a TV set, a CD player, and that was it as far as furniture went. It felt like a rec room in a halfway house.

"Where do you eat?" I asked. There was a cheap cut-glass chandelier hanging over an empty space where the dining room table should have been.

"Out."

I should've seen that one coming.

"I don't really know where to begin," she said, pacing.

"Why don't you stop that, for starters? You're making me crazy."

She went into the bedroom and came back with a milk crate. She dragged it over to my chair and sat down.

"Tell me why you went to see Jake."

"I didn't go to see Jake."

"Then what were you doing at the hospital this morning?"

"How do you know I was there?"

"I saw you," I said. "Listen, I thought you wanted to talk to me. What's the point if you're going to lie?"

"I'm not lying. I don't even know Jake."

"Then why were you there?"

She closed her eyes, then rubbed them with the heels of her hands. "I was looking for my mother."

"I can't hear you."

She lifted her head. "I said I was looking for my mother."

"Your mother? Why would she be there? What does she have to do with Jake?"

She sprang up, avoiding my glance. "Are

you thirsty? I have bottled water in the kitchen. It's not cold, though."

I grabbed her arm as she brushed past me. "Nancy, are you trying to tell me you think your mother had something to do with what happened to Jake?"

She pursed her lips. "I didn't say that."

"But you think that."

"I don't know what I think."

I extricated myself from the chair and followed her into the kitchen. "Did you see your mother last night at the Witching Hour?"

"As she was leaving. It wasn't like you could miss her, making the usual commotion." There was hurt in her voice. I knew that kind of hurt inside out and backward. "She wasn't supposed to be there. I didn't want her there. She just showed up."

"She wanted to surprise you."

"Why does she always try to surprise me when she knows I hate surprises?"

I guess it ran in the family. "I don't know."

"It was a mistake."

"Everybody makes mistakes."

"My mother's been making big mistakes. The kind you can't just fix."

I thought about Grace Horton's body, a swath of flesh glowing white in the dark, sticky room. How angry Clarissa must've been.

"I have to find her," Nancy said.

"Maybe she's gone home."

"Home?" She mulled that one over. "I hadn't really thought of that."

"Well, why would she stay here? Your show was over."

"Maybe you're right." She paused, then a grin spread slowly across her face. "I'll bet she went straight to the airport from the club. She was probably on the very next flight out, furious at me. I can picture her up on her high horse, telling the whole ugly story to her friends. Once again, Nancy embarrasses the entire family." That scenario made her happy, maybe because it was so familiar. "Here, take this." She handed me a bottle of water.

I put it down on the counter. "Back up a little. You aren't sure that's the way it went, are you?"

She looked down at her hands. Her nails were red today, as slick as her mother's.

"You're worried. You're worried that after your mother left the club she tried to kill Jake. And then when she found out he was still alive, she raced to the hospital to finish the job."

"She'd never do that."

But how would Clarissa have known Jake was at Andrew's? That's what I didn't understand. Had she followed them? Had she followed me? And why Jake? What did Jake have on Clarissa? Oh, god.

"Jake saw your mother that day in Palm Springs, didn't he?"

"No." She shook her head.

"The day that Edgar died. You're afraid it was your mother who killed Edgar."

"No. I don't know."

"But she couldn't have killed him," I said, thinking it through. "Because that was the day of the scavenger hunt. She was at the hotel, planting clues. She was there all morning."

"Not all morning." Her voice was barely audible.

"What are you saying?"

"She left. Just for a little while."

"How long?"

"Maybe an hour, that's all."

"That's impossible. What could have dragged her away from her precious Nancy Drew?"

"She was on the phone, upset. I don't know exactly what it was about. She was stomping around the Oak Salon. Everyone saw her. Then she pulled herself together and said she had a quick errand to run."

"Have you explained all this to the detectives in Palm Springs, Dunphy and Lasarow?"

"They talked to her at the hotel. They seemed satisfied with what they heard. I'm hardly about to implicate her, and neither are you," she said, flashing me a warning glance.

"The last thing I want to do is implicate your mother if she hasn't done anything. But the truth is going to come out one way or another, and I'd prefer it to come out before anyone else is hurt."

"Look, I just needed to talk to someone. I thought I could trust you. I thought maybe you could help me figure out what I'm supposed to do."

The painting. Blue Nancy Drew.

"What does Edgar's painting of your grandmother have to do with all of this?"

"I wish it had never seen the light of day."

"When did your mother find out about it, Nancy?"

She was crying now. "I didn't want her to find out about it, not ever."

I looked at her, perplexed now. "When did *you* find out about it?"

"Me?" she asked, wiping her eyes with the sleeve of her jacket. "I've known about that damn painting my entire life."

26

"You've got freckles."

"Yeah," said Nancy.

"I didn't notice them with all that make-up."

The waitress came by with our second round of sodas. I ran my hands up and down the frosty glass. Nancy watched me silently.

"Eat your hamburger. It's getting cold."

"Okay." She took a big bite, then wiped ketchup off her chin.

It's hard to repress your maternal instincts even when you have reason to suspect you're being had, and I had reason to spare. She was doing an excellent job — but then again she was a professional. All I knew for sure was that she'd managed to blow whatever alibi Clarissa might've had for Edgar's murder without looking like she was even trying.

"You're good."

"Excuse me?"

"Last night. At the club."

"Oh. Thanks." She had another bite of her hamburger. "This is delicious. It was nice of you to take me out."

"Your Dolly Parton was amazing."

"My father was a big Dolly Parton fan. I grew up listening to her. Have you ever heard of Dollywood?"

"I don't think so."

"It's Dolly's theme park in the Smoky Mountains. Pigeon Forge, Tennessee. My dad took me when I was eight. I got to try on one of Dolly's very own wigs."

"I would've loved to have seen your mother in a Dolly Parton wig."

"She wasn't there. They were already divorced. Then he died, when I was thirteen. He left me the pictures."

"So. Are you ready to show them to me now?"

She wiped her hands on her napkin and reached into her purse, pulling out a small stack of black-and-white photographs. She sat there for a minute, then closed her eyes.

"I'm ready." She pushed the pictures across the table.

They were worn at the edges. They reminded me of a rabbit's foot I'd once had. I'd rubbed it so many times the pink fur had come off, leaving only a misshapen piece of cartilage on a rusted chain. But it had gotten me a bike I'd wished for. I wondered if these pictures had gotten anybody anything.

I picked up the first one.

A young woman is seated on a man's lap. His face is in shadow. She is radiant, her head tossed back in laughter. She's wearing rolled-up dungarees and a man's white shirt.

I had to catch my breath.

Grace Horton.

Now Grace is standing with one arm draped across the shoulder of a good-looking man. Russell Tandy. I recognized the mustache and long, serious face. This Grace I'd know in my sleep. Her features are carefully composed. They reveal nothing but suggest everything. This is the Grace who poses for a living. For Tandy. For others, too. This is the Grace who wears the mask.

But sometimes the mask slips. That's what Asher Farrell said that day.

Now Grace and Tandy are clowning around. She's put on his hat and pulled it down low over her eyes. He is standing at the easel, pretending to paint her. They look happy.

"They didn't mean much to me at first," Nancy said. "Except that I thought it was cool to see my grandmother so young. She looks a little like me, don't you think? I always thought so. My mother and I don't resemble each other at all."

"I wouldn't say that." Nancy had her mother's ferocity. She was ferocious to the bone.

"When I started kindergarten I was really scared. I thought at the end of the day they wouldn't give me back to my mother because my hair was so curly and hers was so straight. I thought no one would believe I belonged to her." She gave a little laugh. "Wishful thinking."

I picked up another picture. Tandy and Grace are standing on either side of an easel. They are in a studio, with spilled paint on the floor and dozens of drawings pinned to the walls. The drawings are too small, too faint to make out. The painting on the easel is not. It is Edgar's missing painting. Blue Nancy Drew.

"I had this one blown up and cropped," Nancy explained. "For my show. But my mother wasn't supposed to see it, not ever."

My gaze moved from Nancy back to Grace, standing there next to Tandy, but I couldn't see anything there — nothing in her eyes, nothing in her smile. She had to have loved the painting. Who wouldn't want to be seen as that kind of beautiful? But why, then, had she let the painting slip away? Had she sold it long ago, needing money? Had she given it to an admirer? Had she tossed it in the garbage, thrown it out the window, or just walked away from it, sick to death of looking at herself?

The last picture is of Grace in the studio, with the painting on the easel in front of her. But this time there are two men there. The first has his arm around her slim waist. Tandy again. The second is standing behind her, his hands covering her eyes, his chin resting on her shoulder. He is wearing what looks like a crown of laurel leaves. He is smiling, and his mustache seems like it is smiling, too. It is long and curled at the ends, as thin and spindly as if it had been drawn on with a pencil.

"It can't be," I said in disbelief.

"What can't be?" God, I wish I could smoke in here.

But it is. The second man is Salvador Dalí.

When I got home I went straight out to the office and started pawing through the mess on my desk. Notes and scraps and abandoned outlines and cryptic messages to myself I'd jotted down upon waking and crumpled photocopies and balled-up mistakes, and there it was. The very piece of paper.

"Here you go," read the memo scrawled on top. "No charge. Just keep me updated on your project." It was from the publisher of an obscure journal called *Yellowback Library*. It'd taken me weeks to locate him. A librarian at the Society of Illustrators in New York had tipped me off to an article she thought he'd run back in the early eighties on Russell Haviland Tandy. She'd had a good memory.

The article was very useful. There was lots of personal information. Though he'd become almost totally deaf at the age of fifteen as a result of double pneumonia, Tandy had been a fine musician — a trumpet soloist and band director. Fond of alcohol and tobacco, he was known to have visited relatives carrying a suitcase filled only with handkerchiefs and bottles of gin. Prior to his work on children's books, he'd worked as a commercial artist out of his studio in New York City. His first regular employment was in 1917 as cover artist for packages containing Butterick sewing patterns. He was soon doing catalog ads for Sears, Montgomery Ward, and JCPenney, all during the twenties. His sons remember visits paid to their father by Edward Stratemeyer. Their friendship, plus Tandy's reputation, led to his being hired as staff artist for the publishing firms Grosset & Dunlap and Cupples & Leon. His work for those and other companies publishing works supplied by Stratemeyer, most memorable among them the Nancy Drew mysteries, lasted from 1929 to 1949.

And here was the good part. It had slipped my mind until now. Tandy was always up to something. The incorrigible type. Obstreperous. Loved a challenge. During the thirties he'd taken part in an art competition to see which artist could produce the best piece of work within a four-hour period. Among the contestants were himself, Norman Rockwell — *the* Norman Rockwell — and a favorite drinking buddy of theirs, an eccentric Spaniard enjoying great success in his adopted hometown of New York.

Salvador Dalí.

Salvador Dalí was Russell Tandy's drinking buddy, his sidekick, his partner in crime.

27

The thing about mind-bombs is they generate an awful lot of noise. I needed quiet. I needed caffeine. And I needed to find out about Jake. Salvador Dalí had been dead for a long time. Russell Tandy, too. They could wait a little longer.

I called Hattie. She was sweet, but there was nothing to report.

"Well, no news is good news, right?"

"I'm afraid that isn't the case here, dear."

"What do you mean?"

"We would have liked to have seen some progress by now."

"There's been no progress?"

"No. But we mustn't give up. Things can change at any moment."

Even she didn't sound like she believed it. Not a good sign. Neither was the sound of the doorbell, which normally buoyed my spirits even when it was only Javier needing me to move my car so he could bring the trash forward on pickup day. Today there was a nasty, tinny undertone in there I'd never heard before. Another thing that needed fixing. And that wasn't the half of it.

Standing on my doorstep were four people, only one of whom I was happy to see. And in the company of the other three, he didn't look all that appealing.

"Peter."

"Hi, Cece. Sorry to bother you at this hour."

"It's only six. Not exactly my bedtime."

The look he gave me was so pained I almost regretted my smart mouth.

"You remember Detectives Dunphy and Lasarow, from Palm Springs, don't you?"

It was an ambush. "Of course. Come in." I swept the myriad items on the couch over to one corner, along with several fur coats' worth of cat and dog hair. It still wasn't very inviting, but it was the best I could do on short notice.

"Sit down, please." Nobody did. "Would anyone like a Diet Coke?" They stared at me like I was an alien from Mars. "I could make coffee. I have wine, too, but you probably don't drink on duty. And you're on duty, aren't you?" I looked right at Gambino. "All of you."

"Nobody's thirsty," said Dunphy, ever the diplomat.

"Cece, I don't think you know Detective

King." Gambino indicated a short but powerfully built man in his midfifties. He was mean, and I'm not talking the kind of person who wouldn't tell you there was a piece of lettuce stuck between your teeth. I'm talking big mean. Bad mean. I looked at Gambino, who was shaking his head ever so slightly. I wasn't sure what he was trying to tell me, but "Don't mess with this guy" was a distinct possibility.

"Ms. Caruso, let's get something straight right away." King gave me a hollow smile. "The Jake Waite case is mine now. And insofar as it ties in to the Edgar Edwards investigation, I will be working with the detectives from Palm Springs."

"Okay."

"This is a courtesy call. Playtime is over. Am I making myself understood? Because if I'm not, I'll be glad to go over anything you might be unclear about back at the station."

"I think Ms. Caruso understands the gravity of the situation," Gambino said, walking over to me.

"You don't need to protect her, Gambino."

"I don't need you telling me what to do."

"I think we're done now," I said, heading to the door.

"You're not the one who decides when the

interview is over," said King, who sat down on the couch and started jiggling his leg. Why do people do that? It had to be a caveman thing. But maybe he was just trying to shake off the pet hairs.

"While we're here, maybe you can clear up a couple of things."

"You said this was a courtesy call," I said, holding my ground.

"We've just been to see your friend Bridget Sugarhill."

Shit.

"We were looking for some information about Andrew Damiani. You know Andrew Damiani. You and Detective Gambino found Jake Waite at his apartment last night."

Damiani. I hadn't known his last name until now. I wouldn't have guessed he was Italian, but you never can tell. Mary Lou Retton, the Olympic gymnast, is also Italian.

"Ms. Sugarhill was expecting him at work today, but he never showed up."

"Oh."

"You don't seem very surprised."

"I'm not."

"Why not?"

"I don't know. Look, Andrew has nothing to do with me."

x

"What did he say to you to get you to come over to his house in the middle of the night, Ms. Caruso?"

I paused a beat. "It was Jake." Why did I say that? I shouldn't have said that. But I wanted them to leave Andrew alone, for Bridget's sake. And it was clear they didn't plan on leaving him alone. He was their number one suspect.

"Jake Waite called you?"

"Yes."

"Not Andrew Damiani."

"No." What was I doing?

"You and Andrew have no special relationship?"

"No." What was he insinuating?

"No business relationship?"

"No relationship of any kind."

"Fine. We're getting off track here. Was Andrew Damiani there when Jake called you last night?"

"I don't know."

"Did Jake sound as if he were speaking under duress?"

"No."

"What did he say exactly?"

"That he'd remembered something. Something I should know."

"Fuck!"

Everyone turned to look at Lasarow.

"Sorry. I broke a nail."

King looked disgusted. Misogynist. "Was anybody else there when you arrived at the Echo Park address?"

"No. Well, Detective Gambino."

"Lucky for you."

What he meant was that if Gambino hadn't been there it would've been me, not Andrew, who was on the top of their list.

"Detective, don't you think a more fruitful line of inquiry would involve the gun? Or maybe the fake suicide note? Detective Gambino said there were two sets of prints on it. One was obviously Jake's. So who does the other set belong to?"

"We don't have any matches at this time."

"Sounds like you have your work cut out for you."

"Show some respect," said Dunphy, back from the dead.

"I can take care of myself, thank you very much," King shot back.

"Of course." Dunphy turned red. This jerk was making me feel sorry for two women I didn't even like.

"I suppose we're done," he said, getting up. "For the time being."

Lasarow took Dunphy's arm and pulled her toward the door, desperate to get away.

"I have something to add here," Dunphy

said, disengaging herself from her partner. "Something Ms. Caruso will find interesting."

"Yes?"

"It's about that painting. The one that belonged to Edgar Edwards."

I bit my lower lip. "Uh-huh."

"You asked us about it at the memorial service. Do you remember?"

"I remember."

"Well, we found it."

Finally. Finally, I was going to get somewhere.

"Aren't you going to ask where?"

"Where?"

Lasarow jumped in. "At the bottom of a trash can at Mr. Edwards's place in Palm Springs. The one in the service porch, near the washing machine. Destroyed. Totally ripped up. Thought you'd want to know."

"I'm going to walk them out. I'll be right back," Gambino whispered to me. "Don't move."

I wasn't even sure I could breathe.

28

A minute later there was a soft knock at the door.

I opened it.

"What the hell just happened here?" I asked Gambino as I headed into the kitchen.

How could that painting have been destroyed? Who would have done such a thing?

"I'll take that wine now," he called.

Clarissa's name sprang to mind. She was upset that morning. Or maybe Nancy did it, to make her mother look bad. I didn't know.

"Do you have red?"

"Bad Chianti."

"Sounds good."

I came back out with two glasses. "I ordered a large pepperoni and olives. It'll be here in half an hour." Breathe. Edgar's painting of Grace Horton is in shreds and you just lied to the police, but you still have to breathe.

"King's a good detective, I have to give

him that," Gambino said, unbuckling his holster.

"Can you put that thing in the closet? I don't want to look at it."

"No problem," he said, taking off his jacket as he walked down the hall. "But he treats everybody like shit." I heard the water running in the bathroom. Then Gambino came out wiping his face with a towel and sat down next to me. "What King was really pissed off about was me. I should've called him that night. It should've been his case from the beginning."

"When did Lasarow and Dunphy show up in L.A.?" And why did Dunphy choose that particular moment to mention the painting?

"I don't know. But when I realized the three of them were headed over here, I thought I'd better come along."

"Thank you." I leaned over and kissed him. I had to pull myself together here. "Your five o'clock shadow becomes you."

"I'm not ready to go there yet, Cece. What about this painting? When Lasarow told you it'd been trashed, you looked ready to jump out of your skin."

I took a sip of wine. "I did?"

"Yup."

"Time marches on, but his powers of observation are undimmed."

"Let's hear it, Cece."

I took another sip. "That painting meant a lot to a lot of people."

"Like who?"

"Well, Edgar, for one."

"What did it mean to Edgar?"

"I don't know exactly. Give me that towel." He handed it to me and I folded it up and put it on the coffee table.

"Who else?"

"That girl we saw perform last night. Nancy Olsen. The painting was a portrait of her grandmother, the original model for the Nancy Drew covers. For her, it meant family history."

"And?"

"And then there's me. It mattered to me."

"Why?"

"I wanted to understand the woman in it. Now I don't think I ever will." I shook my head. "Can we change the subject?"

"Sure."

It was quiet for a few seconds.

"So. Tell me how your case is going."

"It's going nowhere fast."

"Can you be more explicit?"

"You really want to hear this?"

"Yeah."

"Really?"

"Yeah." I moved closer to him.

"Two good-looking young men, no criminal records, no mob ties, nothing. Solid citizens. They're found pumped full of bullets inside a burning car on a quiet side street in a residential area. No gangs, no drugs."

"What, then?"

"The one thing these poor suckers have in common is Tiffani Lowrie."

"Who?"

"Tiffani Lowrie. She and her identical twin sister, Brandi, were Playboy models in the early nineties."

I rolled my eyes. "What do people expect when they name their children Tiffani and Brandi?"

"Those aren't their real names, Cece."

"Whatever."

"Playboy models attract stupid men. Like this bogus Wall Street trader, came from a family of Iowa pig farmers. He was behind a major hedge fund scam. While he was riding high, he fell for Tiffani. Gave her houses, cars, millions of dollars' worth of jewelry. The feds caught up with him eventually, and when they found out where the money went, they wanted it back so they could reimburse the poor fools this pig farmer had conned. Tiffani informed them she had no knowledge of any fraudulent business dealings and they could go screw themselves."

"Poor girl earned her keep the hard way."

"No doubt, but legally she had no claim to it. Eventually, she handed over the items she said she still had, but there were a few key omissions."

"Is that where the dead guys come into it? The solid citizens?"

"Yup. They'd fallen under her spell, too. An out-of-work actor and a doorman at a nightclub. Not exactly a brain trust."

God, they sounded like Jake and Andrew, poor fools. Was Bridget really in love with Andrew? Why would Andrew have hurt Jake? Could Jake have been blackmailing Andrew about the old days? Was Andrew hiding him so he could keep tabs on him?

"They were trying to sell seven hundred thousand dollars' worth of jewelry for Tiffani that night."

"So the buyers killed them and kept the money and the jewels?"

"And torched the car to cover up their tracks. That's how it's looking, at least."

"What about the Wall Street guy?"

"In federal prison in Pensacola, Florida."

"And Tiffani?"

"Rock-solid alibi."

"You sleep with the right person and you've got a rock-solid alibi."

"She was at a church dance."

"Please."

"I'm not kidding," he said, laughing. "There were close to a hundred people there. A little Unitarian church in Yucaipa. She made the punch."

"The Nancy Drew books are full of twins and look-alikes pulling fast ones. Maybe it wasn't Tiffani that night. Maybe it was Brandi."

He slapped his forehead. "Now why didn't I think of that?"

"Are you kidding me?"

"Yes, I'm kidding you. She was out of town."

I was reaching for a pillow to hit him with when the doorbell rang.

"Saved by a pizza."

Out of town. Who knows what that means? Was someone with this out-of-town twin every second? You can go from out of town to in town pretty quickly. This was the age of flight, after all. Had anybody checked the punch bowl for fingerprints?

Fingerprints. How could I have forgotten about fingerprints?

I was going to get Andrew's fingerprints.

How hard could that be? And then they could be checked against the second set on Jake's suicide note, and when they didn't match, well, then Bridget could have her boy toy back.

Unfortunately, Andrew was AWOL. How was I going to find him? Maybe I didn't actually have to find him. Maybe I could get his prints off some personal possession of his, like a toothbrush or a piece of clothing. But then I'd have to get into his apartment, which was a designated crime scene, and that was a big no-no. Maybe Bridget had some of his stuff at her place. Oh, she was not going to like this.

"Here you go, babe."

"That's some lethal dose of pepperoni."

"At least you're going to die happy."

I looked up at him, dizzy with the heady scent of rendered pig. If it weren't for a few unsolved crimes, yeah, I could die happy right now. But I'd die happy later. First, I had to make sure Bridget was going to die happy, too. All I had to do was exonerate her Peter Frampton look-alike lover — with or without her help.

29

Turned out I got Mitchell's fingerprints instead, which wasn't entirely beside the point if they could get Andrew off the hook. There was also Mitchell's generally unpleasant demeanor to consider. As per Nancy Drew, the culprit is invariably the one who racks up the most negative adjectives, and if you asked me, Mitchell Honey was nothing if not one big negative adjective.

The way it happened was a bit convoluted. I called Bridget first thing the next morning to discuss my plan, but she, too, had gone AWOL. No answer at home, no answer at work. But the fact that the store was closed on Tuesdays precluded the need to panic, at least for the moment.

Meanwhile, all that talk about the ex–pig farmer detained in a Pensacola, Florida, prison reminded me of a certain felon closer to home. I decided to pay another visit to Asher Farrell's gallery, to pump Melinda for some details about her boss.

By ten-thirty the place was already

crowded, meaning that there were three tat-
tooed hipsters in baggy shorts prowling
around. It must've been that rave review in
the *Times* that brought them in because it
sure wasn't Melinda's people skills.

"Good morning!" I said cheerily.

"Oh!" she exclaimed, leaping to her feet.
"Good morning!" Her hair was askew and
her cheeks were flushed. She stepped out
from behind the desk to greet me with three
catalogs in one hand and Asher Farrell's
leather folio in the other. She looked pan-
icked. "Back so soon?"

"The show really stuck with me. I wanted
to see it again."

"Did you enjoy the catalog? Oh, dear!"
The folio had slipped out of her hand.

"Are you all right?" I bent down to retrieve it for her. While I was down there, I
cast my eye over today's date. Asher Farrell
had back-to-back appointments until five,
starting with Mitchell Honey in (I looked
up at the clock) less than half an hour. Too
bad. I was not prepared for Mitchell Honey.

"Thanks," she said, taking back the folio.
"I'm fine. It's just so early for clients. Usually
I have a while to get things organized."

I glanced over at the three young men, all
of whom were wearing Von Dutch trucker
hats. "They're clients?"

"They run an alternative space in Holly-wood. Their dad is actually the client. They're kind of like scouts."

"I see."

She made her way over to them and passed out the catalogs. They shot out their hands without taking their eyes off a photo-graph of two prepubescent models having their makeup done. You wish.

"I did enjoy the catalog," I said. "Very provocative essay. But comparing Lari Uklanski to Rembrandt, isn't that a stretch?"

"The handling of shadows, that's all. Anyhow, you're doing great!"

"What do you mean?"

"The dyslexia."

"Thank you."

"Okay, then. Why don't you look around? I've got to take care of a few things."

"Can I ask you a quick question?"

"Of course." I followed her over to the front desk.

"I have a friend who's in the market for a Salvador Dalí print. Does Asher handle things like that?"

"It's interesting you should mention that."

"It is?"

"Yes. And no, I've never known him to handle anything by Dalí."

"Why is it interesting?"

"Dalí 's interesting, that's what I meant."

I wasn't so sure about that. "So you're saying no collectors have popped up lately looking for something by Dalí?"

"Not as long as I've been here."

So much for the theory that all Asher and Mitchell were doing was helping Edgar with his shopping needs.

"How long has that been?"

"Two years."

"And you would definitely know about it if someone had popped up?"

"I would definitely know about it."

"Of course you would. You run the show around here, I'm sure."

"That isn't true," she said, looking down demurely. "But Asher can find anything. Maybe you want to talk to him when he gets here. He's busy today, but I'm sure he can squeeze a good friend like you in."

Speaking of good friends, Mitchell Honey had arrived, twenty minutes early. I couldn't exactly hide.

"Hello there." I gave him a little wave.

"Ms. Caruso. Yet again."

"Do you two know each other?" Melinda asked brightly.

"We're ex-lovers," I said. "Just kidding." Just then I noticed the unopened bottle of

Perrier sitting on Melinda's desk, and — what can I say? — inspiration struck.

"Do you mind if I wait for him in his office?" Mitchell asked Melinda.

Before she could say yes, I swooped upon the small green bottle, wiped it down with the dangling sleeve of my sweater, and without letting it touch my skin, shoved it into Mitchell's left hand.

"You look really thirsty!" were the words I heard coming out of my mouth, on the tail end of which I snatched the bottle back and dropped it into my purse, directly on top of a wad of Kleenex. "Actually, I'm the one who's dying of thirst here! And I love Perrier! I'm going to guzzle it on the ride home, if that's okay with everyone!"

"Ms. Caruso," Mitchell said, inhaling deeply. "Oh, forget it."

He retreated to the back, fuming, no doubt.

"It is important to keep hydrated," Melinda said cautiously.

"Our bodies are mostly water," I said. I was going to walk out of Asher Farrell Fine Art with Mitchell's fingerprints. He already thought I was crazy, and Melinda was hardly about to pluck the bottle out of my purse. I was actually going to do this.

"Our next show is going to have a water element, speaking of water. The artist has been saving her tears for the last eleven months. She keeps them in glass beakers in her apartment in Brooklyn."

"How intriguing." I glanced toward the back, but Mitchell wasn't anywhere in sight. I had a minute. "While we're talking art, you haven't encountered a young sculptor named Jake Waite, have you?"

"The name doesn't sound familiar. Should I know him?"

"Well, he's a real up-and-comer, and I know Asher has the reputation of having an eye, so I figured you guys would be all over him."

"Wait." She turned beet-red. "Is he . . . good-looking?"

"He looks good in jeans."

"I know him. I'd just forgotten his name. But I could never forget *him*. I mean, the work."

She went to a shelf and pulled down a thick three-ring binder marked "Walk-Ins/ 2003." It was stuffed with page after page of artist's slides. I shuddered at the thought of all the wounded egos trapped in there.

"When did Jake drop those off?"

"He stopped in, must have been a couple

of months ago, with an older guy, a friend of Asher's."

Edgar.

"Look at this," she said, laying a sheet down on a small light table.

I'd expected tacky bronzes. Big, triumphant phallic things. What I saw startled me. Arranged on the floor and mounted on the wall were what looked like the craggy rocks and mountains of Japanese landscape scrolls, but rendered in shiny, rainbow-hued plastic. It was safe to say I'd never seen anything like it.

"Asher wasn't particularly taken with it."

"Not his cup of tea?"

"You could say that."

I smelled discontent brewing. "What's your opinion?"

She looked pleased to have been asked. "I think the work is amazing. It reconciles all sorts of oppositions: nature and culture, East and West, contemplation and consumerism. And it's luscious, absolutely luscious."

"Melinda, I think you're the one with the eye."

"Not at all," she said, smiling as wide as humanly possible.

30

Perhaps it was naive to expect Detective King to welcome me with open arms.

"I have new evidence!" I exclaimed. "We might be able to use it to nail Jake's attacker. The one who faked his suicide!"

King stared at me from the other side of a scuffed-up metal desk. It was covered with papers. Bulging file folders, ripped-open manila envelopes, newspaper clippings, reports to be filled out in triplicate.

"Detective?" asked a uniformed cop who had followed me over.

"It's okay, Brooks," King said, still staring at me. "You can go."

I noticed then that all the buttons on his phone were lit up.

"You must be busy," I said.

"Now why would I be busy, Ms. Caruso?"

He indicated a chair, then interlaced his thick fingers so tightly they turned bright red. All the veins in his hands were popping out.

I sat down and pulled the bottle of Perrier

out of my purse with one of the Kleenex tissues.

"You must be parched. Shall I send out for finger sandwiches?"

"No, you don't understand," I said. "This is evidence."

"What's evidence?"

"This bottle. It's got Mitchell Honey's fingerprints on it. He lived with Edgar and Jake, and he hated Jake. I think there's a distinct possibility that he —"

"He who?"

"Mitchell! That he, Mitchell, set this all up to make it look like Jake killed Edgar for his money and then decided to kill himself out of remorse. All you have to do is check these fingerprints against the ones on the suicide note. Then we'll know for sure."

He looked distinctly underwhelmed. "Jake Waite and Mitchell Honey lived in the same house, is that correct?"

"Yes."

"There were communal spaces in that house."

"Yes."

"Living room, dining room, kitchen, library, den."

"Yes."

"Do people in general keep paper in any

of those rooms? Say pads of paper for market lists, or scraps for phone messages or games of tic-tac-toe, or letter paper for letters?"

"Yes."

"Can we say, then, with any degree of certainty that a piece of paper Jake Waite may have taken from his house could not at some point in time prior to the writing of the suicide note have been touched by someone else living in that house, say, Mitchell Honey?"

Asshole.

"Your evidence is shit."

"Aren't you going to dust it for prints anyway? Just to see?"

"Just to see what? How you muddied the prints with your grimy tissue paper, with dust from your purse, with —"

"All right already!"

"Excuse me?"

A secretary had appeared holding a stack of While You Were Out slips.

"Toss them on top," he said. "And I'll take a refill. Black this time." He handed her a chipped Lakers mug, then turned back to me. "Was there anything else?"

"Now that you mention it, yes." I was here. I might as well ask.

"I knew there would be."

"That painting that Lasarow and Dunphy say they found all ripped up at Edgar's house in Palm Springs. I'm really curious. I want to see it."

He stood up abruptly. "If it's evidence, it's in an evidence locker, where it can be maintained until such time as it becomes necessary. Nobody's going to break the chain of custody to satisfy your curiosity."

"It pertains to my research. And it's not evidence, it's trash. That's why it wound up in the trash."

"I suggest you take up its status with the lady detectives."

"Where are they? Are they still in L.A.?"

"I believe they are still here, yes."

I certainly hoped so. Because a plan of action had just popped into my head, and I didn't want them interfering.

As I climbed back into my Camry, I cracked open the ill-fated bottle of Perrier and took a swig.

Assuming traffic wasn't too heavy, I'd be in Palm Springs in no time.

You know how it is in classic Westerns. The sheriff and his trusty six-shooter are at the city limits, waiting for the guy in the black hat to come riding up. That's kind of how it was when I pulled onto Palm Canyon

Drive and saw the flashing lights in my rear-view mirror.

When Lasarow and Dunphy stepped out of the cop car, I understood this was no routine traffic stop.

"Welcome to Palm Springs, Ms. Caruso," said Lasarow, whipping off her sunglasses. Dunphy was wearing the kind senior citizens wear. Big old blinders. She left them on.

"Well, thank you. Lovely weather you're having." The sun felt warm. The air smelled like Creamsicles. I had a sudden desire to take the aerial tramway up to the top of Mount San Jacinto and stick my nose in a Jeffrey pine. They're supposed to smell like butterscotch. But I went on the offensive instead. "Let's not waste time with small talk. I'm concerned about how the case is going. I have to say I'm disappointed an arrest hasn't been made."

Dunphy started to sputter a response, but Lasarow interrupted. "You think you're awfully clever, Ms. Caruso. But you aren't half as clever as you think. Listen to me very carefully. Whatever you think you're looking for, forget about it. You are to stay away from Edgar Edwards's house. Far, far away. Do you understand? You will be arrested for trespassing if we find you there."

"Who said anything about going to Edgar Edwards's house?"

"Why are you here in Palm Springs?"

"Body scrubs, herbal pedicures. Rest and relaxation. Dry air."

Dunphy snorted.

"Where are you staying?" asked Lasarow.

My mind raced. "The Wyndham. They really take care of you at the Wyndham."

"We'd be happy to escort you."

"No need."

"We insist."

They got back into their car, pulled out in front of me, and put on the siren. I followed them the quarter mile or so there. I felt like I was part of a presidential motorcade, sort of.

Despite the crowd we attracted at the entrance — gawker types with nothing better to do — things were more sedate than they were last time I was in town. No visors.

The valet — not Norman, unfortunately — handed me my ticket stub. "Don't forget to get a validation. It's good for three hours."

"Oh, she'll be busy with beauty treatments much longer than that," Lasarow interrupted. "You can park her car way, way, way in the back. Ms. Caruso here won't be needing it." She handed him her business card. "Are you on duty for a while?"

"Yes, ma'am. Until midnight."

"Excellent. Please give me a call if Ms. Caruso comes looking for her car. And inform whoever comes on duty after you to do the same. She's a VIP — that's Very Important Person — and we want to be extra sure she gets the protection she needs if she leaves the premises."

"I'm on it."

"And can you get someone out here to help the lady get checked in and settled in her room?"

"I'll call Randy. He's the head bellman. He'll get her all squared away, make sure the climate control in her room is up to snuff, show her the entertainment options, the works!"

Yeah, they really take care of you at the Wyndham.

31

With the midweek discount, the room only cost me $159 that I didn't have.

I hated Detective King.

I hated Detectives Dunphy and Lasarow.

There was nothing good in the minibar.

There was, however, a shower that didn't take precisely three and a half minutes to warm up (not that I particularly needed a shower, but what else was I going to do?) and a sign on the bathroom counter that read "If you have forgotten any essentials, please call housekeeping and you will be provided with those items free of charge." Within minutes, a woman in a neatly pressed uniform had brought up a blow dryer, brush, comb, toothbrush, toothpaste, razor, and honey-mint body lotion for dry, sensitive skin.

I was down but not defeated.

One hour later, smelling like a cough drop, I slipped back into my Jean Paul Gaultier tribal tattoo dress, which over the years had proven an exemplary purchase. Stretch mesh doesn't wrinkle.

I had revised my plan of action.

I took the elevator down to the lobby and exited by way of the swimming pool, bypassing Lasarow and Dunphy's stool pigeon at the valet station. It couldn't have been easier. I walked up East Tahquitz Canyon Way, kitten heels clicking, toward Palm Canyon Drive, the town's main drag.

It was hard to imagine that two thousand years ago, Palm Springs's first residents, the ancestors of today's Agua Caliente band of Cahuilla Indians, had enjoyed a rich ceremonial life in the absence of thirty-four places to purchase a smoothie. Former Palm Springs mayor Sonny Bono was responsible for encouraging economic development in the late nineteen eighties and nineties (and outlawing thong bikinis), but it was actually the advent of air-conditioning in the postwar era that did Palm Springs in. It meant that visitors and residents alike could stay year-round.

Desert Communities Realty was located between a Nike store and a gallery of southwestern tribal art.

I opened the door and three people descended upon me.

"Hello!"

"Over here!"

"At your service!"

And they say warm climates kill initiative.

I picked the one with the extraordinary hair. It was yellow and had been sprayed within an inch of its life.

"I'm Rick Gould," he said, extending his hand. "And you are?"

"Patricia Canarski." My pep squad coach for the years 1981 to 1983.

"Patricia, a pleasure," he said, pumping my arm energetically. "Have a seat. What can I get you? Coffee? A soda? I need a Red Bull right around now."

I tried not to stare at the hair. It reminded me of a hood ornament, something to do with aerodynamic efficiency. "I'm fine."

"Everyone has a secret desire," he said with a twinkle in his eye.

"All right," I said. "You caught me, Rick."

"What do you want?"

"The perfect midcentury modern house."

He rolled up his sleeves, revealing powerful forearms. "I see you, Patricia, serving cocktails poolside, at dusk, spotlights illuminating three kinds of fruit trees and a dwarf oleander." Without missing a beat, he slipped me a color setup with a picture of a house for sale at the reduced price of $5.3 million. "I see a trapezoidal redwood trellis connecting the master bedroom to the semi-circular dining room. I see the subtle desert coloring, the scents, the sounds — but not a peep out of your Miele dishwashers. Oh, yes," he said, nodding, "there are two of them. State-of-the-art kitchen. Granite counters, brand-new Wolf dual-fuel range, Sub-Zero fridge, Viking freestanding refrigerated wine storage unit. The best! Been on the market for less than a week. I think I might have an offer coming in tomorrow morning, but if you're serious, we can make a quick move and preempt these people. It's a vision thing. I don't know if I see them there the way I see you." He stopped, exhausted.

"Actually, Rick, I have a house in mind already."

"You've been checking the listings yourself?" he asked, appalled.

"The house isn't actually listed yet. A friend of mine has this friend who is about to inherit the house. It's amazing. I was there several years ago for a cocktail party and I said to my husband, 'Lazlo, I was meant to live here,' and Lazlo being Lazlo agreed. So when my friend said his friend was planning to sell in the very near future, I thought I'd better jump on it."

Rick was hanging on to my every word. It was a real estate broker's fever dream. "Let me see if I have this right. Your friend's friend isn't working with anyone."

"No," I said, shaking my head.

"And you're not working with anyone."

"No."

He couldn't speak.

"That's right, Rick. I see a big fat double commission in your future."

He tried to control himself, but I swear he was shaking. "So how shall we proceed, Patricia? And shall we get your husband on the phone?"

"He's at the hospital."

"Is he ill?"

"Oh, no. Dr. Canarski's a brain surgeon."

"Wow. Yes. Okay. My feeling is that if we approach your friend's friend with an attractive offer — short escrow period, good terms, forgo the inspection — it's in the bag. Termites are not much of a problem around here, which is why I say that about the inspection."

"The thing is —"

"Yes?"

"It's been a while since I've been there, and there's one thing I'm a little hazy on."

"Cold feet," he said, smiling knowingly. "Happens to the best of us. But not to worry. You can always make cosmetic changes once you're in. There are excellent service people in the area. I'd be happy to make recommendations."

"It's nothing like that. It's the approach to the house. I can't remember how isolated it is. I don't want something that's smack in the middle of a bunch of people. Lazlo and I like privacy. So I was thinking —"

"Yes?"

"I was thinking we could take a drive up there, say, right now, so I could have a quick peek. It's only about five minutes from here."

"I'm game, Pat."

"It's Patricia."

"Patricia."

"Okay, then."

"Do you remember the name of the street?"

"Cypress."

"Ooh, baby. Cypress." He approved of Cypress.

I followed Rick out to his immaculate black Lexus. I slid into the back, which was equipped with a box of tissues and this month's *Town and Country*.

"I have mints, if you'd like one," he said as he turned off Palm Canyon and headed up into the hills.

"No, thanks."

"So who is this friend's friend?"

"His name is Jake," I replied, closing my window. The sun was starting to go down and there was a chill in the air.

"No matter how hot it gets during the day, the evenings are cool," Rick said. "That's the high desert for you."

We passed the house with the golf ball–shaped mailbox. Then the one with the Rolls-Royce golf cart parked out front. "I think you turn left here."

"Right you are."

So far, so good. I didn't see any police officers cruising around, and if there were any at the top of the hill, they'd be looking for a woman in a weather-beaten Camry, not a Realtor and his client in a Lexus.

Rick closed his window suddenly. "Patricia," he said in a low voice.

"Yes?"

"We're not headed where I think we're headed, are we?"

"I don't know," I said. "I'll take that mint now."

"Are we going to the Edgar Edwards house?"

"You can pull over right here. This is fine." I could see up the pebbled drive. It looked like an ordinary house — not ordinary ordinary, but untainted. Stainless. A person would never know that a week and a half ago it had been the scene of a crime. The yellow tape was gone.

Rick turned around to confront me. "I

don't know what to say here, Patricia. I feel somewhat misled. We're talking the disposition of Edgar Edwards's estate." He shook his head. "The man's a murder victim. The house is going to be tied up for some time. I think my involvement may be a bit premature."

"Sorry to interrupt, Rick, but I have to go to the bathroom."

"What?"

"You wait right here, okay? I'm just going to run up to the house for a second."

"Absolutely not. We'll be back at the office in five minutes." He started up the engine.

I swung open the door.

"What are you doing?" he shouted. "Are you crazy?"

"I can't wait five minutes."

"Oh, my god. I'm going to lose my license. I don't think you should go in there. It isn't legal!"

"I'll be out in a second. I promise."

I ran up the driveway. My heart was thumping in my chest. The blood was pounding in my ears. I tried not to dwell upon what I was doing. I racked my brain for the useful information I'd gleaned from the complimentary copy of *Palm Springs Life* on my dresser at the Wyndham.

In the nineteenth century a smallpox epidemic killed thousands of the Agua Caliente Indians.

Their ancestral homeland was the training ground for General Patton's troops as they prepared to invade North Africa.

There is a life-size bronze statue of Sonny Bono at the end of Palm Canyon Drive and you can sit on Sonny's lap if you want to.

Is it considered breaking and entering if you were originally given a key, which I was?

The front door was locked so I went around to the back gate, past the swimming pool, glittering in the dying light, and to the glass doors that led into Edgar's bedroom.

They slid right open.

I walked in and looked around. The mirrored closets were empty. The shelves vacant. The bed still looked like it had been carved out of rock. Had anyone slept in it since that night?

I'll bet Lasarow and Dunphy set this whole thing up, I suddenly thought. Dropped a hint about the painting knowing I'd run over here to find it. I slunk toward the front window. Pressing my body flat against the paneled wall, I peered out at the street. Rick was still there, all alone, no police car in sight. I sighed. Another paranoiac delusion. They had no reason to try and trip me up. They didn't like me and I can't say I blamed them. Not that I was unlikable, but I did keep turning up like a bad penny. I was probably the one making *them* paranoid.

Now what exactly had they said? They'd found the painting all ripped up in the trash can in the service porch.

I had to hurry. I really didn't want Rick to lose his license.

I raced down the breezeway toward the kitchen. Ouch. There were pebbles in my shoe. But I couldn't think about comfort at this particular moment. I smelled something bitter in the air. Ammonia. Had there been a cleaning crew here? Who would've authorized that? Not Lasarow. Not Jake, obviously. Mitchell would have been the one. Shit. The first thing a cleaning crew would have done was take the trash out.

Sure enough, when I lifted the lid off the can in the service porch it was empty. Not a single ball of dryer lint. Back in the kitchen, I opened the doors of the cabinet under the sink. Empty, too. Scrubbed clean.

I was too late.

If only I had known earlier. If only I had thought to call Dunphy and Lasarow. If I had just come out and asked them. They didn't consider it evidence. They would have told me. But I hadn't even thought of doing that. I was too busy with Peter Frampton and fingerprints and art history and other idiot pursuits. Why couldn't I ever be logical? Flying by the seat of your pants isn't always the best course.

Then something dawned on me. The trash doesn't get picked up every day, or even every other day. Javier only takes the cans forward on Wednesdays. Once a week. It could be the same story in Palm Springs. And depending on which day the cleanup people had shown up, I might still be in luck.

I ran out the same way I came in, heading for the storage shed at the rear of the garden, behind the garage. It seemed the logical place to stow the big cans. And there they were. My last chance. Blue is for recyclables. Green is for grass. Black is for destroyed paintings. I threw back the top of the black can.

There, at the very bottom, sprawling and oozing like sea urchins or some other slimy underwater creatures, were three medium-size Hefty bags.

So far, so good.

I thought everyone knew you had to twist-tie them. It stunk to high heaven. I tipped the can over on its side to jostle things around a little, hoping the garbage would sort of make itself visible for my perusal, but when are things ever easy? I got down on my knees. Maybe I could find some gloves back in the kitchen? No time. Maybe I could poke around with a broom handle? No broom handle. The hell with it. I pushed up my sleeves and thrust my hands way down into the soupy dregs: paper towels, coffee grounds, stained filters, orange peels, watermelon rinds, sticky clumps of seeds, candy wrappers, paper, tiny bits of glass (thanks, Bridget). Rick would be long gone by now, which was probably for the best. I'd call him from L.A. and apologize. I tossed several cans of cat food to the side. I didn't know Edgar had a cat. Please, god, no cat litter. Some empty rolls of toilet paper. The smell was really getting to me now. Some larger cardboard rolls, for gift wrap. I never threw those things out. You can affix tape to one end and fish out things that fall behind your headboard.

Then something bright caught my eye. I reached down, past some disgusting table scrapings, and pulled it out. A longish piece of wood, painted gold, with something red hanging off the end of it, like a flag.

This was it.

This was what was left.

The gold was the gold of the frame. The

red was the red of the drapery Grace Horton had sprawled across, on that long-ago day she was painted nude by Russell Tandy.

What a shame. What a waste. Edgar would've been devastated to have seen his painting end up like this.

But something was wrong. I wiped my hands on my dress and then rubbed the fluttery piece of canvas between my fingers.

This wasn't a painting.

When I looked at it closely, I could see the tiny pixels that made up the image.

This was a digital reproduction.

What had been shredded was not the original, but a copy.

I slumped on the floor, at a loss. Was this another one of Edwards's practical jokes? Had there ever been a painting of Grace Horton? I knew there had been. I knew what I had seen that day in the blue bedroom.

But had I seen what was there, or what I thought I was going to see?

32

I was on my way out when I noticed a black van pull up behind Rick's Lexus. I was hoping it would be somebody's pool cleaner or a plumber with one of those long metal snakes. The cable company would've been fine, too, but no such luck. Painted in white letters on the back of the van were the words "Hi-Tek Protective Svc, Palm Desert, CA."

This wasn't necessarily cause for alarm, I said to myself as I dove for cover behind a large boulder. In fact, it looked like business as usual. This was a wealthy neighborhood, and wealthy people like to know who's in the general vicinity of their stuff. These private security guys get paid to make their hourly rounds and ask questions if somebody's not where he's supposed to be. Then they move on.

I poked my head out a little so I could see what was happening. Rick and the driver of the van, a good-looking fellow in khaki bermudas, were deep in conversation. Actually, they seemed to be striking up a friendship.

There was more talking, some laughing, a few meaningful glances, then they swapped cards. Well, good for Rick. But bad for me.

After a fifteen-minute farewell scene, the security guy hopped back into his van and pulled in front of Rick, signaling out the window for him to follow, which he did. I emerged from my hiding place nonplussed. What had happened to Rick's professionalism? He was never going to advance in his career like this. What about that double commission looming on the distant horizon? Not that there was one, but he didn't know that.

I guess money is money and love is love. It kind of warmed the heart. I might have even choked up a little if the walk back down to the Wyndham hadn't been quite so long.

I had planned on sleeping like a baby in my $159 hotel room, but I was interrupted by a four a.m. phone call from Lael, who was bubbling over with news of her new veterinarian. Apparently a late-afternoon appointment to remedy her dog Flea's eczema had turned into a night of passion.

"In the office?" I asked. My vet's office, with its pee-stained linoleum, was about the least romantic spot on earth.

"Of course not. He actually lives near you. In a nice duplex on Croft. It's got Moroccan decor."

"What about Asher Farrell?"

"What about him? That's ancient history."

"What about the dog?"

"He came with. He played with Dr. Dan's beagle, Moo."

Was it me or was that sort of unappetizing? Lael, being the earthy sort, wouldn't have thought so. I fluffed my pillow and went back to sleep, dreaming about frolicking — puppies. Frolicking puppies.

The drive home later that morning was uneventful. And things in L.A. were pretty much as I'd left them.

There was no change in Jake's condition.

Andrew was still missing.

Bridget didn't want to talk to me.

Gambino was back in Yucaipa, trying to figure out who killed Tiffani Lowrie's boyfriends.

And the painting of Grace Horton was still out there, which meant I still had to find it if I still wanted to know why any of this was going on, and I did.

I'm happy to report that Buster and Mimi harbored no ill will about my spur-of-the-moment trip. Less happy that another tofu dish had been left on the doorstep, along with some gritty oatmeal raisin cookies — at least I hoped they were oatmeal raisin. God knows what those little black things were if they weren't raisins. I called my daughter to thank her, but she was out.

I spent the next day organizing my closet, which is what I do when I'm at a loss about how to organize my life. Sometimes it helps, sometimes it doesn't. I came to the realization that I own five full-length evening gowns, which is comical given the fact that I have no use whatsoever for even one. I also have too many scarves. And silky pajamas, the kind you'd wear in your stateroom on a luxury liner, not that I had any experience with staterooms or luxury liners.

At two in the afternoon, Victoria called from the bookstore to say hello and to let me know that they'd received a shipment of some children's series books. They were getting ready to send them off to a colleague who handled such things when it occurred to her that I might want to take a look. There were some Nancy Drews in the lot.

I changed out of my sweats and into a white blouse, thick raffia belt, and printed cotton circle skirt that evoked Portofino circa 1956, probably to no one but me. I think I was still fantasizing about luxury liners and day-tripping in glamorous ports of call.

"You look like our mother on her honeymoon!" said Victoria when she saw me. "Look, Dena!"

Dena grunted, her mouth full of jelly beans. She had no imagination, that woman.

"The box is in the back room," she finally managed to get out. "I would say take your time, but the UPS guy is supposed to pick it up by five, so don't take your time. Victoria and I are keeping a few things. They're stacked on the table. Don't touch those!"

I wandered back through a maze of dark and dusty rooms lined floor to ceiling with leather-bound volumes embossed with gold. In the center of one room were old maps of California from the mission days, curling at the edges. Yellowed photographs of railroad depots and cowboys in chaps covered the walls of another. The Dalthorp sisters specialized in California history and Western Americana. They owned multiple pairs of cast-iron spurs.

I found the box sitting on the floor between the bathroom and the water cooler.

I sat down on a step stool and opened the lid. Perched right on top was *Ruth Fielding at Cameron Hall*, which I recognized right away as a Stratemeyer book from the twenties.

Ruth Fielding was a plucky orphan who became an internationally celebrated screenwriter, actress, director, and studio head. She was a typical Stratemeyer heroine, embodying the get-up-and-go spirit of the new era of women's rights. Before her — before the Motor Girls, the Moving Picture Girls, the Radio Girls, and eventually Nancy Drew — all that girls had to read was nineteenth-century sentimental rot, equal parts linen-sorting and tears. No wonder they had to satisfy their desire for adventure with books written for boys.

I put down *Ruth Fielding* and picked up *Dan Carter and the Great Carved Face* by Mildred A. Wirt. This was one of the books Mildred had written under her own name. At least she finally got her due, poor woman, stuck all those years with that vow of secrecy. And, ironically, it was the doing of her great nemesis, Harriet Stratemeyer Adams.

After a seventy-five-year relationship between Grosset & Dunlap and the Stratemeyer Syndicate, Harriet was looking for a more creative approach to marketing, and a bigger share of her series' royalties. Grosset & Dunlap sued, claiming exclusive rights and charging the publishing house Harriet wanted to bring in with meddling into their contract negotiations with the Stratemeyers.

The trial took place in 1980. Mildred was subpoenaed, and lo and behold, it turned out that oaths of silence were irrelevant to district court judges. Everything came out — every last bit of correspondence and every last release form, which pretty much made clear the true identity of Carolyn Keene.

You had to feel a little sorry for Harriet. She must've gotten pretty used to being celebrated as the beloved authoress. "I thought you were dead," she was said to have stammered when she saw Mildred take the stand.

But Mildred wasn't dead, just a ghost.

I grabbed a cup of water, then dug deeper into the stack, past some well-worn Frank L. Baum books, *Ozma of Oz* and *Glinda of Oz*. Harriet died while watching *The Wizard of Oz*, as Edgar had reminded me the day we met. Some people made a big deal out of the fact that Nancy's dog was named Togo, and that her fictional hometown, River Heights, was as fantastic a fairyland as Oz, but I wasn't sure. River Heights must've had one of the highest crime rates in the country. Car bombs, home invasions, heists, kidnappings, dognappings. But I suppose there was a lot of crime in Oz, too.

More Oz books. A Vicki Barr book (flight stewardess). A Cherry Ames (war nurse). A Beverly Gray (newspaper reporter). Two Trixie Beldens in excellent condition (a farm girl bored with the usual chores). Finally, I saw the only one of these plucky girls to survive, way down at the bottom of the stack.

Number 32, *The Scarlet Slipper Mystery*, 1954. In poor condition. Tape on the obverse side, stains on the spine.

Number 34, *The Hidden Window Mystery*, 1955. Very good condition. Like many of the late ones, actually written by Harriet. Nancy, Bess, and George search for a missing stained-glass window and encounter a mysterious ghost. It, by the way, had a fantastic cover image: Nancy shining a flashlight on an enormous peacock, straight out of Mogul India. I'd loved anything even vaguely Indian from the time I'd learned that Diana Vreeland, legendary editor of *Harper's Bazaar*, had said that pink was the navy blue of India. I didn't know if that was true (it sounded vaguely colonialist), but I liked the sound of it. Maybe Victoria would sell the book to me. I could frame the dust jacket. Look at the peacock for inspiration.

Peacocks are so beautiful. Only the males, however.

Suddenly, I had a feeling of déjà vu. The dust jacket reminded me of something. Not the peacock.

The girl.

The high beam of light.

The burst of white.

I knew.

It reminded me of the black-and-white photograph Edgar Edwards had sent me from beyond the grave.

33

I drove home too fast and threw open the front door, which crashed against the wall of the entryway, leaving a knob-shaped dent. Now I could add replastering to the list.

I headed straight back to the bedroom, yanked open the chest of drawers, pushed aside my Lanvin cape, and pulled out the photograph.

Buster started to bark and Mimi started to whimper. They hated being ignored. I tossed them both into the hall and closed the door, gently this time.

I sat down on the edge of my bed with the picture in my hand. What was it trying to tell me?

The woman in the picture was holding a flashlight, pointing it straight out in front of her, hoping it would illuminate something. Her path. An object. She was alert, attuned to sounds, smells. She may have been frightened. Her head was turned slightly, as if she might have heard someone coming up behind her, looking for her, or maybe looking for the very thing she couldn't find.

The woman could've been my double. Edgar saw the resemblance, no doubt. What I couldn't figure out, though, was how he could have known that the picture looked exactly the way my life felt. I was looking for something and I wasn't even sure what. All I knew was why.

For him. And for Jake.

I turned the photograph over. L. Sands. L. Sands. Who was L. Sands? If I could just figure that out. I'd searched the Internet for the name half a dozen times, but maybe I'd missed something. I exited the French doors in the bedroom and walked through the soggy grass to my desk. I shoved everything in my way into the top of a cardboard box from Office Depot containing five thousand sheets of white paper, typed in "google.com" and then "L. Sands."

I waited.

A real-estate broker named Boris L. Sands. A physicist named Eunice L. Sands. The Lost Sands of Kuwait, a French video game. No, no, no.

I checked my e-mail.

The usual garbage. Mortgage refinances. Wrinkle creams. A snippy note from my editor, Sally, telling me she'd be out of the office for two weeks and was expecting the completed manuscript upon her return. Sally needed downtime. She was very tightly wound. Burn fat while you sleep. Enlarge your penis. Another posting from the Society of Chums. Bette from Cleveland had been given a Newfoundland puppy. Joe from East Aurora, NY, warned her that puppies are attracted to the glue in the spines of books. A heads-up: Turner Classic Movies was screening *Nancy Drew — Detective* from the 1930s, which I'd never seen, on July 17. A big kerfuffle: an English edition of *The Clue in the Crumbling Wall*, misprinted as *The Glue in the Crumbling Wall*, was for sale on eBay. Edgar would've loved that. Another curiosity for his memorabilia category.

Memorabilia. I looked away from the screen. Edgar was a collector of Nancy Drew memorabilia. And it was a Nancy Drew dust jacket that had reminded me of the photograph he'd sent me. Was that yet another coincidence — or was there no such thing? Then something occurred to me. I could take the question directly to the source.

Because I owned a scanner.

I'd gotten it last year as part of a package deal on my new printer. They'd thrown it in for almost nothing, which I'd always assumed meant it wouldn't work. I'd stuck the thing in the corner, thinking I'd get Vincent, a computer whiz, to hook it up for me one day, only I kept forgetting to ask him. Uncharacteristically, I'd saved the instructions. How hard could it be to hook up?

Two hours, two calls to the Hewlett-Packard helpline, and the rest of the bad Chianti later, I put the photograph on the glass, hit the button, and attached the image to a query to the Chums' Listserv. It read:

I was given this by a Nancy Drew collector and I'm baffled. If there's anyone out there who can decipher it, or who knows who L. Sands is, I'd be eternally grateful.

Yours in sleuthing, Cece Caruso

It was worth a shot.

I went back inside and checked my phone messages. Annie had returned my call. They were raisins, thank god. Gambino had called, too, from Yucaipa. I plopped down on the couch and called Annie back first.

She sounded good. Things were going well on *Testament*, the *Star Trek*-esque TV show for which she was head set designer. She'd blown everyone away with her new idea for a podule for the ecologically minded Commander Gow, which she described as a 100 percent recyclable holographic cocoon. Her garden was thriving. She'd bought a set of bamboo chairs at the Rose Bowl flea market. And on Friday, she and Vincent and Vincent's three-year-old little boy, Alexander, were driving up to Big Sur for the weekend. Annie wanted to know what I used to do to amuse her on long car trips, but to be honest, I couldn't remember any long car trips.

Then it was my turn. I told her in long and gory detail how I'd set up the scanner. She was impressed. Then I gave her the *Reader's Digest* version of the rest of my life, not particularly eager to get into my recent encounters with myriad officers of the law. She knew me well enough to know I was dodging something or other, but Vincent took that moment to sneak up on her and scare her half to death, or so she said between giggles, and she had to go.

I called Gambino next.

"You were right," he said. "I hate to admit it."

"Right about what?"

"Tiffani and Brandi. They would've gotten away with it, too, if Brandi hadn't turned on her sister. You should've seen them going at each other at Brandi's apart-

ment. They were throwing things, screaming."

I swallowed hard.

"Gambino?"

"Yes?"

"I'm really glad you solved the case."

"Thanks. You helped."

"Gambino?"

"Yes?"

"I haven't been completely honest with
you."

"About what?"

"About this Jake thing. And the related
Edgar thing."

He waited.

"I've sort of been poking around where I
shouldn't be."

"Cece —"

"The thing is, I'm finally getting somewhere. I'm really close."

"Stop for a minute. I want to say something. You were right when you blew up at
me the other day."

"I was?"

"I'm not your father. I can't tell you who
to be. I don't want to tell you who to be. I
love you just the way you are." He stopped
short. "Not a word."

"Not a word." Billy Joel. How embarrassing.

"But I also don't want to be the person who rescues you. Do you understand what I mean by that?"

"I think so. And I don't want to be a person who needs to be rescued."

"I know that. So I'm going to say one thing, and then I'm done. I trust you."

"Is that the one thing?"

"No."

"What is it?"

"Watch yourself."

I promised him I would. And I truly meant to.

For dinner, I made myself a nice sticky pasta carbonara. I ate slowly, stalling for time.

At nine, I checked on the Chums.

Nothing.

I came back inside and ate two Tofutti Cuties while watching a Lifetime movie about a woman who sleeps with her best friend's husband.

I went back outside at eleven.

I had an answer.

In fact, I had maybe a hundred answers.

Those Chums were something, all right.

Tabby Cat was the most succinct:

You ought to come to more conventions, Cece. Then you'd know that

"L. Sands" refers to Rudy Nappi's oldest daughter, Lynn, whose married name was Sands.

We all know about Russell Tandy, of course. But Rudy Nappi was the illustrator of most of the second and third covers of the Nancy Drew Mystery Series. Lynn was the model for many of those covers. Your picture is a trial cover of #21, *The Secret in the Old Attic*. It's reproduced in the eleventh printing of *Farah's Guide*. You really should have a copy of *Farah's Guide*. I know it's expensive, but worth every penny. Anyway, how thrilling for you to own something so rare and wonderful!

Best, Tabby Cat

P.S. I had my baby. It was a girl!! :)

We see what we believe we are going to see, not what is there.

I was such a fool.

I could've saved so much time.

And Jake. I could've saved him from so much suffering. What had thrown me was the fact that Rudy Nappi's daughter, Lynn Sands, was a brunette while Nancy Drew is blond — mythically, symbolically so. Blond as in fair, good, true. Blond as in one who shines light into the darkness, brilliant like the sun.

But anybody can have blond hair. All you need is a bottle of bleach. Or a wig.

Or an artist, to transform you from ordinary girl into icon.

I could've saved so much time.

If only I hadn't forgotten that art and life are not the same thing.

34

It was early Thursday morning, around eight. I was parked kitty-corner from Edgar Edwards's house with a pair of binoculars on my lap. I took a sip of my vanilla latte, then opened the window and tossed it out. Splat. Not all experiments are successful.

Carroll Avenue was more dead to the world than usual. The sky was dark and the clouds so menacing even the neighborhood dogs had forfeited their morning walks. And quiet. It was so quiet the only sound you could hear was the wind whistling through the half-naked trees.

It felt like the dead of winter.

A door slammed. I grabbed the binoculars and peered through the scratched lenses, more for effect than anything else because I could see perfectly well from where I was parked. It was a paunchy guy in his boxers, getting the morning paper. The wind had swept the door shut behind him. Shivering, he rang the bell and waited. His wife opened the door and handed him a steaming mug of something. These people had a great house, a crazy Victorian with purple trim and what looked like a baby grand in the living room.

The car window went up with a muffled whoosh. According to my calculations, Mitchell Honey would appear any second. Thursday was one of his two yoga days with Guru Chakravorty, whose studio was on Larchmont Avenue. Master class began at nine, and with so many asanas to work on, Mitchell would be wrapped up until at least noon.

The night before, I'd spent a while at the guru's Web site. It was a model of information design. I learned about yoga styles, yoga postures, yoga facials. That yoga is good not only for the muscles and ligaments but the nerves and glands as well. Then there was the cornucopia of yoga-related products available for online purchase: mats, mat covers, straps, blocks, yogatards, personalized yoga software, copper tongue scrapers, stainless-steel neti pots for nasal irrigation.

It's very important to dry the nose properly after nasal irrigation.

I heard another door slam. I picked up the binoculars. It was Mitchell Honey, skipping down the moss-covered steps, his yoga mat under his arm. He looked up at the sky with concern. Please tell me a little rain wasn't going to scare him. He pulled his keys out of his jacket pocket. No, rain didn't scare him. I'll bet the guru scared him. The guru scared me. Mitchell clicked the car alarm with his thumb. Two beeps later he was seated in his blue Jaguar, and then he was gone.

I waited five minutes before getting out of my car. Then I walked up to the front door and rang the bell. The pretty young Latina I'd seen at the memorial service answered.

"Yes?" she asked in heavily accented English.

"I'm Cece Woodbury from the Office of Historic Preservation." I flashed my expired gym membership. "It's a city agency. Is Mr. Edwards at home?"

She shifted uncomfortably. "I'm sorry. He is now dead."

"How awful!"

"Yes. Everybody feels very sad."

"Is there someone else I could speak to?"

"Mr. Honey goes to exercise. He comes back later."

"Oh. That's a pity."

"Have a nice day."

She started to shut the door.

"The thing is, Miss . . . ?"

"Vasquez."

"Miss Vasquez. Mr. Edwards inquired at our office regarding his attic. This was some time ago." I opened my briefcase and pulled out a clipboard with the one-year no-parts guarantee for my washing machine affixed to it. "Yes, here it is." I patted the guarantee. "Mr. Edwards wanted to build out the attic and we rejected his application for a permit. He was very upset about it. He had big plans. But in going over the documents, I realize there may have been an error made." I shook my head regretfully. "It happens. So I'm here to perform a reinspection."

"What?"

"I need to take a look at the attic."

"Please, you must come back when Mr. Honey is here."

"That's the problem. I was in the neighborhood, down the block at the Josephsons. Nice people. Anyway, I had a free hour, so I thought I'd squeeze you in. Otherwise, it's a minimum eighteen-month wait on re-inspections."

"I do not know the Josephsons," she said skeptically.

"Listen, I'm just going to run up there for a minute, do my thing, and get out of your way. It would be a huge help to me. Clear some paperwork off my desk."

"I am now going out." She waved her purse at me for proof.

Shit.

"Home Depot," she explained.

"The one on Sunset and Willoughby?"

"Yes."

My heart soared. "The one with the long lines?"

She laughed. "One mop is three hours in line."

"I've got news for you! You can forget about ever waiting in line at Home Depot again!"

It was more than she could fathom.

"Yup. All you have to do is ask for the manager, Raoul Ortiz, and tell him Cece sent you. He'll treat you like a queen." Raoul Ortiz was the brother of Tomas Ortiz, who was practically a part of Lael's family. Tomas was the default architect of Lael's ramshackle spread in Beachwood Canyon. They liked to keep it casual, Tomas and Lael. Nails and two-by-fours. Tomas was the king of two-by-fours. He could've built Versailles out of two-by-fours.

"I do not know."

"Look. All I have to do is go up to the attic, take a quick peek around, make sure

357

it's safe for wiring, check out the ducting, stuff like that, then I'm gone."

"It is not safe."

"I do this kind of thing every day. It's routine. I don't take chances."

"It is raining soon. The roof is bad."

"I'll be gone before it starts raining."

She looked down at my delicate slingbacks. "Your little shoes."

"This will save your employer a long wait. I know Mr. Honey will be grateful."

"Mr. Honey is very kind to me. He has been so sad." She grabbed her sweatshirt off the entryway table. "I am going to tell Mrs. Ramirez you are okay. She makes pies."

Mrs. Ramirez wasn't going to be a problem for me. Only Mitchell would have been a problem for me.

Miss Vasquez came back, smiling. "Okay. But do not bother Mrs. Ramirez. The door locks behind you when you go."

"Thank you so much."

"Raoul Ortiz."

"He'll change your life."

After she left, I realized I'd forgotten to ask her how you got up to the attic.

In the kitchen Mrs. Ramirez was up to her elbows in flour.

"Hola, señora," I said, tapping her gently on the back.

"Aiyeee!" she screamed, knocking over a bowl of egg whites.

"Oh! I'm so sorry." I grabbed a roll of paper towels off the counter. "Can I help you clean up?"

She snatched the paper towels away from me and started wiping up the sticky mess.

"Qúe muchacha más estupida! ¡Fuera de mi cocina! ¿No puedes ver que tengo que trabajar?"

I got that she didn't want to be friends. Still, it never hurt to be polite.

"¿Cómo estás?" That was about it for my Spanish.

"Cuál es tu problema?" She washed her hands and walked over to the refrigerator, pulling out a fresh carton of eggs. *"Estoy haciendo un merengue y está en un punto muy delicado. ¿No debes estar en el ático?"*

"Did you say *'el ático'*?"

"Sí."

She cracked one egg, separating the white from the yolk. The white went into a plastic mixing bowl, the shell with the yolk into the sink.

"Señora."

She was ignoring me.

"Señora. ¿Por favor, dónde está el ático?"

Mrs. Ramirez had moved on to the second egg. She said, without looking up, *"Hay una escalera raquitica cerca de los dormitories de atrás. Se queda cerca del dormitorio azul."*

Azul means "blue." The attic was somewhere near the blue bedroom.

"Muchas gracias." She said some other things to me as I left, but I didn't recognize a single word except *"interrumpiendo,"* which I think means if you don't get out of my hair, I'm going to hit you over the head with the frying pan.

Busy, busy. Everybody was so busy. The defunct mop, its handle broken in two, was lying on the floor at the bottom of the staircase, next to a bucket of soapy water. At the top of the stairs, there was a wooden ladder leading up to the stained-glass window, a bottle of Windex posed artfully on the top rung. Miss Vasquez had her hands full taking care of this house. And she was sweet, worrying about how sad Mitchell was. But if I was right, he was really going to be sad.

I walked down the hall, my briefcase whacking me in the calf with every step. It was that damn *Chicago Manual of Style*. I'd stuck it in there so the briefcase wouldn't look so empty, but the thing must've weighed ten pounds. On the bright side, it was the closest I'd gotten to exercise in months.

I jog, but only when I'm feeling fat or testy.

Now what I was feeling was edgy. And embarrassed. I'd taken advantage of Miss Vasquez. I wanted to run straight home to West Hollywood. But I couldn't do that. I couldn't leave this house. Not without what I came for.

Just past the blue bedroom I came upon a low door with a finely cut glass knob. I hadn't noticed it the other times I'd been in this house. It looked like something out of *Alice in Wonderland*. I turned the knob slowly, half expecting that when the door opened I'd go tumbling down a rabbit hole. But when the door opened there was no rabbit hole. Just a steep, curving staircase.

I ducked my head in and looked up, but it was hard to see anything despite the light flooding in from the hallway. I ran my hand against the wall, feeling for a switch. I couldn't find one. I opened my briefcase and pulled out the flashlight I'd put in there, just in case, and flicked it on. With the brief-case tucked awkwardly under my arm, I started up the rickety stairs, my free hand clutching the wall to steady myself.

There was no railing.

The staircase veered once to the right, once to the left, and from there it was straight up. I had a flash of a bad dream I'd once had, where I'd climbed a long flight of stairs to a diving board only to plunge into an empty pool.

I try to shake off my bad dreams, but they don't always want to go.

When I reached the top, I shone the flashlight around. The silvery beam illuminated a large, mostly empty space. Overhead were rafters draped with gauzy cobwebs. Below, wooden boards with sizable gaps between them, which seemed to be all that remained of the floor. I stuck out a foot and tested the nearest one. It felt sturdy, which was a good thing considering there was nothing on either side of me or beneath me (at least for ten feet, estimating conservatively) except dead air. If I walked straight across without losing my balance, I'd live — for starters. I'd also be able to see what was concealed beneath the sprawling canvas tarp opposite. It was long and low and lumpy.

Under the tarp.

It was the only place it could be.

Looking straight ahead, my briefcase slung around my neck, I put one foot in front of the other. That was the plan. I was almost there, everything was fine, until the heel of my left shoe got stuck on an exposed nail. I pulled and pulled but it wouldn't budge. I suppose I could have taken it off and kept going, but my general disinclination to abandon a Maud Frizon shoe, not to mention a long-standing phobia about splinters, prevented me from doing the sensible thing. Instead, I bent over to extricate myself, forgetting about the briefcase around my neck. As I yanked my heel free, it tumbled forward, and I lost my balance and went hurling into oblivion.

"Omigod!" I cried, throwing my arms out in front of me. Somebody must've been listening because I managed not to crash through the rotted-out floor into whatever room on the second floor I was currently suspended over, but to latch onto the floorboard with both hands.

Dangling there was extremely unpleasant.

My life flashed before my eyes. It was not a pretty sight. There was a particularly humiliating scene in gym class. The occasion was fitness testing. We had to do pull-ups and I couldn't manage even one. The physically challenged among us were given the option of performing the ignominious "flexed arm hang," which turned out to be merely an alternate form of torment. I could still hear the underarm ligaments of dear friends tearing all around me.

I snapped back to reality. I was not at Asbury Park High. I was in Edgar Edwards's attic. A flexed arm hang wasn't going to cut it right now. I needed to pull myself up. One pull-up, that was all. I was extremely motivated to succeed.

Unfortunately, however, my fingers were numb. And the sweat was spilling off my brow. I couldn't see. But there was no choice. I steeled myself. My legs flailed. I grunted like a wild boar. And I did it. I hauled all one hundred forty-four pounds of me back up onto the board, landing stomach-first.

I rested for a moment in that unlovely position, grabbed my briefcase and flashlight, then dragged myself the rest of the way across.

Once I was on safer ground, I struggled up to standing and adjusted my clothes, which weren't too much of a mess, considering. I still couldn't go home to West Hollywood. I checked my watch. It was already ten o'clock. Mitchell wasn't going to be gone forever. I had to hurry.

I looked around desperately.

No boxes, no crates, no piles, no parcels, no suitcases, no nothing, just that tarp. I stepped closer. It was cream-colored canvas, speckled with blackish mildew. I didn't relish the thought of touching it. But way over on the left side, it had been folded over neatly, like a dinner napkin. I ran my fingers over the creases. Dust-free. Exactly what I'd been hoping.

It meant someone else besides me had been here recently.

I lifted back the tarp, crazy with anticipation.

Hatboxes. Half a dozen hatboxes were under there, decorated with pictures of eagles and flowers and scenes from American history. A minuteman signaling the alarm. The standoff at the Alamo, I think. A simple country lass milking a Holstein.

Not to worry. What was *in* the hatboxes, that was the real question.

I lifted the delicate cardboard lids off, one by one.

Velvet bonnets. Plain velvet bonnets, velvet bonnets with feathered ornaments, velvet bonnets with striped sashes. Very nice, but I wasn't here for millinery.

I aimed the flashlight way in back, behind the hatboxes. Something shiny glinted in the light. It was a large leather trunk with tarnished gold fittings. I pushed the hatboxes away and dropped to my knees in front of it.

It was one of those old trunks, the kind people used to take on their travels, when they'd go someplace far away and stay awhile.

It was padlocked.

Now what was I supposed to do?

There was no choice but to remove the offending shoe and use it to whack the padlock open. It was leopard-skin, which really killed me.

I started banging and kept on banging even when it was obvious that banging wasn't going to do it. Then I dumped the contents of my briefcase onto the floor. The clipboard wasn't going to work any better than the shoe had, but maybe I'd have better luck with a ballpoint pen. It was a gift from Bank of America. New account. I unscrewed the back of it and pulled out the thin cylinder of ink. Just the thing to pick a lock. I inserted it slowly into the hole at the bottom of the padlock and started jiggling. I jiggled as if my life depended on it. I jiggled to make the Holsteins come home.

Lo and behold, the padlock sprang open.

It must've been really cheap.

The trunk opened with a creak.

It was full of junk. A pair of old-fashioned roller skates, some sheet music, a corn-husk doll, keys, change, a guidebook to California gold country, some kind of uniform, bells, a harmonica, some pastels and a sketchbook, a rotary-dial phone — and then I saw the bundle of red velvet way in the back.

The soft fabric was wrapped around something, as tight as swaddling.

I lifted it out and started unwrapping, and right away I saw the alabaster flesh. I kept unwrapping, and there it was, in its gold frame.

Russell Tandy's painting of the naked Grace Horton. Blue Nancy Drew.

But that wasn't what I was looking for.

I shook the painting.

I turned it upside down.

Then I flipped it around to the back. The reverse side of the canvas was covered by a thin wooden panel. I felt around, looking for an opening.

There was one at the top.

I stuck my fingernail into the small depression in the wood and carefully pried the panel off.

Inside was another canvas, folded flat.

You peel off the top layer of skin, Bridget had said the other day, and you just might find a stranger underneath.

I unfolded the canvas and laid it on the floor.

I saw a nude woman with lustrous blond hair and sapphire-blue eyes.

Grace Horton.

With bloodred gashes up and down her legs, and a colony of ants feasting on her milky stomach.

I checked the signature at the bottom.

It read "Salvador Dalí."

I suppose, if you were the type, it just might be worth killing for.

All of a sudden, the attic was flooded with light.

"You don't want to strain your eyes, Ms. Caruso, do you?" a familiar voice called out.

35

I froze in place.

"You missed the switch."

I didn't answer.

"Stupid mistake."

Yet another.

"You being so smart. I wasn't buying it, but you've proven me wrong, finding that painting — or should I say, paintings."

"How'd you know I'd be here?"

He twisted his mouth into an approximation of a smile. "You think you have an exclusive on those Nancy Drew obsessives? I just wished I'd taken care of things last night, after reading the answers they posted. Then we would've been spared this unpleasantness."

"You should go," I said in a thin voice I didn't recognize.

"I'm not going anywhere, Cece. You don't mind if I call you Cece, do you?"

"Not as long as I can call you Asher."

"Absolutely. I fucked your best friend. That makes us practically related."

Bastard. "If you're not leaving, I am. I am going to walk down those stairs and out of this house and you aren't going to stop me."

"Close." He seemed somehow unhurried, like he didn't want to spoil the fun by rushing things. "You're going to walk across the attic, right over to where I'm standing. Then you're going to walk down those stairs and out of this house and I'm going to be with you every step of the way."

He pointed a gun at me. It looked big. Bigger than the .22 he'd used the previous times.

"We have business to take care of, you and me. We need to find someplace more private."

"Why'd you have to kill Edgar? That's what I don't understand."

"I know you liked Edgar. He was a real sentimentalist, wasn't he? He fell in love with that painting. The moment I saw it, I knew he would. He didn't want to part with it."

"Why'd you sell it to him in the first place?"

"I sold him a Russell Tandy. I wouldn't have thrown in a Salvador Dalí for free."

"When did you realize what you'd done?"

He paused for a minute, then thought better of it. Why not tell me? He was going to kill me, after all. "Mitchell made that discovery when he was having the Tandy reframed."

I knew Mitchell was in on this. "So the two of you conspired to kill Edgar and get the painting back."

"It would've been so much easier if Mitchell hadn't been an idiot and left the Dalí where he'd found it. He thought it was the safest place."

"But Edgar was suspicious. Something wasn't right. So he hid the painting of Grace before the two of you could arrange a sale."

"You don't know Mitchell very well, do you?"

"No, I don't." If I kept him talking, maybe Mrs. Ramirez would come up here and save me. "I'm a terrible judge of character."

"Mitchell," he said, shaking his head, "is a jealous and resentful man. He thought he deserved something, working so hard for Edgar all these years. Hazard pay, he called it. Edgar didn't even know the Dalí existed, so no one was really getting hurt."

"Interesting logic."

"The ends justify the means."

Spoken like a true seducer. "But you can't sell a painting by Salvador Dalí without attracting attention, can you?"

"Someone like Mitchell can't."

"But someone like you can."

"Someone like me can."

"That's why Mitchell had to tell you what he'd discovered. He needed your help. And you took the ball and ran with it."

"So to speak," he said, laughing.

"It was you and Mitchell who broke into my house. You thought Edgar had given me the painting for safekeeping. And then you followed us to Palm Springs. You broke into my car. You slashed my tires."

"Mitchell didn't want to pursue things after that. I don't have to tell you what a coward he is."

"Does he know what you've done?"

"Mitchell thinks he knows everything."

He was going to kill Mitchell when he was finished with me.

"I'm waiting, Cece."

He cleared his throat. He shifted his weight. He was getting nervous, I could feel it.

I kept my voice steady. "You can wait until hell freezes over, but I'm not moving."

"I don't want to hurt you. All I want is the Dalí. You can keep that fucking Tandy monstrosity for all I care."

"I'm going to scream."

"I need that painting."

"Mrs. Ramirez is in the kitchen."

"The pies are done. Mrs. Ramirez is gone."

"Liar."

"Try me."

"Help!" I screamed at the top of my lungs. "Help! Somebody please help me!"

"Get moving, Cece."

"What about Miss Vasquez? She'll be back any minute."

"I drained her gas tank."

If I could just stall him long enough for Mitchell to get home. Good god. It had come to this: I needed Mitchell. We needed each other.

Then I saw my cell phone, which had fallen out of my briefcase when I'd dumped everything out. I could get Gambino on auto-dial. But he was going to kill me. Stand in line, buddy. Maybe I could call 911.

"Don't even think about it," Asher said.

"What?"

"I'll shoot you if you so much as touch that phone."

"Like you shot Jake."

"Jake shot himself."

"Of course. I forgot. Jake shot himself because he felt so awful about killing Edgar."

"And nobody's going to mourn him when he dies."

"He's not going to die."

"What a sorry fucking life he led. Waiting around for somebody to take notice. Always showing up at the wrong time."

"Like in Palm Springs?"

"Time is up, Cece," he said, his voice cold. He stepped onto the same board I had used to get across.

I tucked the Dalí back into its hiding place and lifted up the painting by its frame. "Stay away from me!" I shouted, waving it in the air. "Stay away from me or I'll destroy them both!"

"You wouldn't do that."

"Yes, I would," I said, bending down to pick up my mangled sling-back. "I'm going to slice through both paintings with the heel of my shoe. I'm going to shred them just like you shredded that copy Edgar made, the one you found in Palm Springs. You were furious, being duped like that, weren't you? Well, I'm furious, too."

He said nothing.

"I'm warning you, Asher."

He started walking toward me.

"Don't take another step."

There wasn't anyplace for me to go. There wasn't anyplace I could hide.

"Look at Grace Horton. How lovely she is," I said. "It will all have been for nothing if you let me do this."

He took another step.

It had cost Edgar his life, this painting of Grace Horton. Gambino had once asked me what it had meant to Edgar. He owned dozens of beautiful things: why did this one matter?

Grace posed as Nancy, who was brilliant like the sun. But Grace wasn't Nancy; she was Grace, and fickle like the moon. Quicksilver. What Edgar saw in the painting was a woman who didn't want to be true to type, all of a piece, constant. What he saw in Grace was his own restless spirit.

I looked at the painting one last time. Was I willing to destroy it? Them both? Then I noticed something. A speck of dirt clinging to Grace's ankle. I went to brush it off, but it wasn't dirt. It was something painted onto the canvas.

A zipper.

A tiny, curving zipper, perfectly placed to allow Grace to slither in and out of her own skin.

Jesus. This painting wasn't by Russell Tandy. It was by Salvador Dalí, too.

Salvador Dalí, the man who had understood Grace all too well.

I was so blind. I'd seen only part of it. Dalí had staged a painting contest, yes; but not against his old drinking buddy, Russell

Tandy. He'd staged a contest against him-self.

Dalí versus Dalí.

It was the only way he could be sure he'd win. The only way he'd know the crown of laurel leaves would be his.

Suddenly, there was a clatter from the staircase.

"Cece!"

"Stay where you are, hon, we're coming!"

"Careful!"

"They need Tomas in here to fix these steps."

Bridget and Lael.

"Who the fuck is that?" Asher asked, turning around. In that split second I could see him start to lose his balance.

"The cavalry, you asshole," I yelled as I bent down, dropped the paintings, picked up *The Chicago Manual of Style*, and hurled it at him with all my might.

Who knew I had perfect aim?

36

"Let's go over the whole thing again," Lael said.

"We like the part where we save the day," Bridget prompted. "Tell that part again."

"Okay," I said. "I'm getting us refills and then I'm going to tell that part again."

It was Friday morning, and we were at the Farmers Market on Third and Fairfax, an L.A. institution since the thirties. In the old days, farmers used to park their trucks on the undeveloped land and sell produce to the locals. These days, it was tourists who spilled out of state-of-the-art motor coaches to marvel at the monster strawberries. The regulars — sitcom writers, rock-and-rollers, aggressive retirees — liked to feign nonchalance, but it was obvious that even for them, breakfast at the Farmers Market was akin to a sacrament. We weren't regulars but knew enough to arrive early if we didn't want to duke it out with the old ladies for one of the good tables near Bob's Coffee and Doughnuts.

I returned to the table with three coffees and a pink box.

"We're celebrating," I said, handing around doughnuts. "There's three for each of us, two for the pigeons, and one for the memory of James Dean."

Legend has it that James Dean ate breakfast at Bob's the day of his fatal car crash.

"Delicious," said Lael, getting powdered sugar all over her blouse.

"All right," I said, sitting down. "He was about to kill me."

"Shoot you dead without mercy," Bridget interrupted. "It's the details that make the story."

"He was about to shoot me dead without mercy. He owed the government eight million dollars."

"Honey, that's really getting all over you," Bridget said. "Here." She handed Lael a napkin.

"You only get two hours free with a validation, ladies. Shall we get on with it?"

"Sorry," said Bridget.

"It was the money or the slammer. He needed that painting. I was a goner. I wouldn't be here today if my two best friends, my stouthearted chums, hadn't charged in like the cavalry."

Bridget beamed.

"It was a phone call that alerted you to my situation."

"A phone call from Mitchell," said Bridget.

"Go away, now! Shoo!" said Lael. A pigeon had landed on her green wooden shopping cart and was about to go after the loaf of rye she'd just bought at J and T Bread Bin.

"Excuse me," said a good-looking guy at the next table, looking deeply into Lael's eyes. "Do you need any help?" Another one bites the dust.

"No, thank you," she replied, but without her usual sparkle.

Bridget cleared her throat. "I thought we were focusing here."

"Right. So Mitchell remembered about your shop and called you there around ten in the morning. His housekeeper, Miss Vasquez, had gotten him on his cell at yoga class. The guru was probably apoplectic."

"You don't call them gurus," said Lael.

"As Cece was saying," Bridget interrupted, "the housekeeper told Mitchell she'd let a woman into the house, a very odd woman who'd wanted to take a look around the attic. The housekeeper was worried she'd made a mistake, but this very odd woman talked so fast and was so insistent, she couldn't think straight. Mitchell said that sounded exactly like you."

"It does," Lael said, nodding. "You misjudged him, but he didn't misjudge you."

I decided to let that one pass. She was in some mood.

"Anyway," Bridget continued, "he called me. He wanted to give me a chance to get you out of there before he called the police."

"I think he had a sense something might be wrong," I said. "That I might be in trouble."

"We rang the bell a few times, but there was no answer."

"Asher Farrell sent Mrs. Ramirez away," I said.

"So we let ourselves in."

"Bridget."

"Don't stop me now. I'm on a roll."

"No, I want to apologize about Andrew."

She let out a sigh. "All right."

"That night you had me look in Andrew's desk for your wallet? I saw the missing key from Palm Springs in there. I was worried you might be in over your head with Andrew."

"You found the what in where?"

"The gold key Edgar gave me. In Andrew's desk."

"There was a gold key in there all right, but it wasn't what you think it was."

"It wasn't?" I put down my doughnut.

"It was a key to my house. I had it made for Andrew. I left it in there as a surprise for him."

What kind of idiot thinks she can tell one key from another? Jeez. I wanted to slap myself. Luckily, I didn't have to. Bridget would tend to that. I knew what was coming next. She was going to get huffy. Imperious. Make me pay for leaping to conclusions. But there was none of that. She was actually squirming in her seat.

"What is it, Bridget?"

"I should tell you something, too."

"What?"

"Andrew was with me the whole time."

"What are you talking about?"

"Well, not the whole time. He showed up at my place Tuesday, after I saw you. He was in my bedroom while those miserable cops were grilling me."

How could that be?

"Andrew was hiding in the kitchen that night when Asher came to his place to kill Jake, only Andrew didn't know it was Asher. He had no idea who Asher even was. And it all happened so fast, by the time Andrew came out of the kitchen, Asher was gone.

Andrew thought Jake was dead. He didn't know what to do. He ran out of the apartment and just started driving. He wound up at a twenty-four-hour coffee shop on Ventura Boulevard. He sat there for hours, drinking coffee. That was when he called me to say he'd had an emergency and wasn't coming in to work."

"Then what happened?"

"After you left the store, he showed up. He didn't know what he was doing. He only knew he needed to see me." She took a deep breath. "I'm sorry, Cece. I should've told you right away. I should've had more faith in you."

Lael finally spoke up. "I slept with that man."

Bridget and I looked at each other.

"I don't have a lot of regrets, but I regret that." She looked down at her lap.

"Lael," I said, reaching for her hand.

"Forget it," she said, screwing up her face. "You didn't know."

"I didn't want to know."

"I wouldn't be here if it weren't for you, Lael."

"She's right," Bridget said. "It's just like in frigging Nancy Drew. Us girls against the world. What could be better?"

I laughed. "Life isn't exactly like that."

"Women do need men," said Lael, wiping her eyes.

"What I meant was, where's the happy ending?"

My cell phone started to ring. I reached down into my purse and pulled it out.

"Hello?"

It was Gambino.

"What?" I asked.

"What?" Lael asked.

I held up a finger for her to wait.

"Me, too. Bye."

"What?" Bridget asked.

I dropped the phone back into my purse and smiled. "Jake's up."

He was the only person I'd ever seen who looked good in a hospital gown.

An orderly was taking his pulse and a nurse was fluffing his pillow. It looked like a scene from a porno movie.

"People, I keep telling you I'm fine," he said with a grin. "Go take care of somebody sick."

"You're amazing," the orderly said.

"Thanks. Can you give us a minute?"

Reluctantly, they left.

I sat down on the edge of the bed.

"You saved my life, Cece."

"Jake," I said, shaking my head.

"No, I mean it. I don't know how to thank you."

"I'm glad you turned out to be such a fighter."

"I don't remember much about what happened."

"There's time for that later."

"Somebody came to the door."

"Jake, stop."

"I assumed it was you, so I opened it."

"You couldn't have known."

"I should have known."

"What do you mean?"

"It was me who let it slip where I was."

I stared hard at him.

"I left a message on the phone machine for Mitchell."

"You didn't."

"I needed money. Asher Farrell must've heard it."

Or twisted Mitchell's arm pretty hard. Mitchell was finally going to get back at him, though. Mitchell was going to escape prosecution by telling the cops everything. His testimony was going to be the nail in Asher's coffin.

"That piece of shit left me for dead. If you hadn't shown up, I'd never have made it."

"That's not important right now. What's important is that you get better."

"You can't keep a good man down."

"Rest up a little first, would you?"

He laughed. "Do you want some candy?"

"Always."

He held out a velvet-lined box and I took a cocoa truffle with a hazelnut on top.

"Since we're on the subject, there is something I want to know," I said. "Umm."

"A busy mouth is a happy mouth."

"Jake."

"Sorry. Sometimes I can't help myself. What?"

"What was so urgent that you had to get me to Andrew's in the middle of the night?"

"I couldn't sleep," he said, suddenly sheepish. "I was driving Andrew crazy, walking in circles, pacing around. He was exhausted. He couldn't keep his eyes open another minute."

"You were looking for company?" I asked incredulously.

"No, that wasn't it."

I looked into his blue eyes. There were circles under them the same color. Two matched sets.

"I remembered something Edgar kept talking about the last day we were together. And Edgar never said anything unless he had a very good reason."

I realized that now. I'd finally had a

chance to look up who gave Harpo Marx a harp with barbed-wire strings. It was Salvador Dalí. Edgar was trying to tell me something even then. That he knew. He knew about those paintings, that they were both Salvador Dalís, from the very beginning.

"Well, what was it?" I asked Jake.

"The attic. He kept talking about the attic."

Now he tells me.

"Edgar wasn't sure you'd realize our house had an attic. Good thing you read all those Nancy Drew books."

That was an understatement.

"Knock-knock. Am I interrupting?"

It was Melinda, from Asher Farrell's gallery, a mouse no more. She sauntered in wearing low-rider jeans, spike-heeled pumps, and a filmy chiffon blouse.

"Cece, meet my new dealer!" Jake said.

"That's right," Melinda said. "I'm opening my own gallery — thanks to something you said, I might add — and Jake is my first artist."

"I'm not really dyslexic," I burst out.

"Great," she said without blinking. "So how are you today, Jake? You look better."

"I feel better."

"Listen," I said, getting up. "I'm going to

386

leave the two of you alone. You probably have a lot to talk about."

"Cece." Jake took my hand. "Before you go, I have something for you."

"I don't need anything."

"Don't be so rash," Melinda said. "He inherited the entire kit and caboodle. And he's giving it all away."

"I'm keeping the house in Palm Springs."

"Okay, one thing. The art, all those fabulous collections — all going to the best museums. One of the Salvador Dalís is going to the Met — the creepy one, with the ants. They'll probably make him head of the board of trustees the way he's going!"

I could just see Jake seated in the boardroom of the Met in a tight silk shirt unbuttoned to the waist.

"Where's the other Dalí going?" I asked.

"To Nancy Olsen," Jake said. "It's only right she should have it."

I was floored. "Does she know?"

"I'm going to tell her," said Melinda. "I'm a fan of her work, you know. My gallery is also going to represent performers."

"She's an artist who sings," I said.

"Of course."

"You really are amazing, Jake," I said, rumpling his hair.

"Melinda," he asked, "did you bring it?"

"You're blushing, silly," she said. "Here, Cece." Melinda handed me a book.

It was a first printing of *The Secret in the Old Attic*.

"Jake, I can't accept this."

"Sure you can."

"I can't break up Edgar's collection. It meant so much to him."

"Edgar of all people understood that a complete collection is death. A collection is vital only insofar as it is marked by a void."

Even Melinda looked surprised.

Jake turned a deeper shade of red. "I think I read it someplace."

37

A registered package was waiting for me the next day at the post office on Santa Monica and San Vincente.

For a moment I wondered if Edgar had another surprise for me. But this surprise had come from Clarissa, of all people. I couldn't wait until I got home so I opened it right there in the parking lot. It contained a thick folder with the notes for her book on Grace Horton, which she'd decided to abandon, and a handwritten letter, on whisper-thin watermarked paper.

Nancy, it turned out, had flown out to Phoenix to see her mother after talking to me on Monday, frantic with worry about what Clarissa might or might not have done. Had I been a more sensible individual, Clarissa chided, I would have allayed the poor girl's fears immediately. But what, she wondered, could she possibly have expected from someone like me? In any case, she was certain her notes would prove helpful. Per- haps they would clear up my numerous misconceptions. As for her, she was on to a different project, a guide to child-rearing in the age of instant gratification. Since she'd done so well with Nancy, she was certain others would benefit from her sage advice.

In closing, Clarissa admonished me not to miss a small volume with a blue leather cover she had included with the notes.

I found it at the bottom of the stack.

It was Grace Horton's diary.

January 17, 1930. A job. It's what I've been waiting for. The illustrator is a wonder. He thinks I look the part, except for my hair, which is all wrong. He wants me to bleach it.

February 3, 1930. I don't know why I bothered. My hair, half of which fell out in the sink, wound up under a blue cloche hat. My back still aches a week later. I had to stand there, bent at the hip, for almost four hours. When I left, I took the hat.

April 27, 1934. I am the queen of the fifty-centers! Everyone teases me. My nieces are beside themselves. But I've had no work in months now. My parents sent money, again. I must say it's nice to be rich. Not all of us must suffer for our art.

February 2, 1936. Dentine, Pond's, Milky Way.

March 8, 1937. Jergens, Colgate.

August 20, 1940. Lux.

November 2, 1941. His studio is cold. There is a nasty draft that comes up between the floorboards. Goose bumps aren't sexy, he tells me. So take off your clothes and see how you like it, I say, laughing. He unbuttons his shirt and then, when he sees my face, he buttons it up again. He lays out a bolt of red velvet he found in a closet. Nonetheless, I spend the day shivering.

January 9, 1942. Nothing.

January 22, 1942. Ry-Krisp.

February 18, 1942. He shows me a collage he's just finished. He's cut a ridiculous picture of me out of an old magazine and surrounded me with a coterie of adoring sheep. The baby of the family has a drawer coming out of its stomach and a phone mounted on its little back. I am supposed to be delighted. I heard from the agency today. Nothing.

December 2, 1943. There is a character in the new Nancy Drew, an artist who is in fact a long-lost prince. His name is R. H. Ellington. R. H. Tandy — Russell — and I have a good laugh about it.

September 22, 1944. I'm going home.

September 23, 1944. What if I couldn't go home? What then? I'd have to stay. I will stay.

January 18, 1945. I get out a knife. I pry the picture out of the frame. I don't know if I hate it, but I know I can't bear seeing it. I contemplate throwing it away, but I wind up hiding it. I hope it never sees the light of day.

I looked up. The rain was falling onto my windshield in big fat drops. I watched it fall, watched each drop hit the glass, then splatter and trickle down.

Clarissa had had the diary all along. Nancy had been protecting her mother from something she had known about before Nancy had even been born. But Clarissa had made a mistake. She'd assumed that Grace had come to despise the portrait Edgar had purchased, the one Dalí painted in the style of Russell Tandy. She'd assumed that Grace had regretted posing in the nude. So when she discovered what Edgar's big surprise was, she'd canceled his appearance at the convention. She'd believed she was honoring Grace's wishes, her desire that the painting never again see the light of day. But of course what Grace could not bear wasn't the fact that she'd posed in the nude — hardly that — but rather, Salvador Dalí's horrific vision of her as a cadaver being eaten alive by ants.

The secret truth about Grace Horton was that she wanted to be seen not as a surreal fantasy but as a woman.

The secret truth about Carolyn Keene was that she was only ever a fantasy.

The secret truth about Nancy Drew was that she was only ever a fantasy of a fantasy. (Try saying that three times fast.)

The point is, fantasies are powerful things. They take you places you don't otherwise get to go. They are like airplanes, or boats. Or cars. It doesn't particularly matter if it's a blue roadster or a silver Camry, as long as the engine turns over when you put the key in the ignition.

On the way home, I called Gambino on his cell phone.

He picked up on the second ring.

"Where are you?" he asked.

"On Melrose near Crescent Heights. Where are you?"

"In your living room."

I started to laugh. "Do you have plans?"

"I plan to walk out your front door and watch you pull into your driveway."

"I'm only a couple blocks away now. I'm passing Gelsen's. I'm passing Melanie and her dog, Scarlett. They just went into the park."

"Do you know what day today is?"

I knew it like I knew my own name.

"Six days later, Cece. One week minus one day. We have a date. Remember?"

I turned onto Orlando Avenue. "A date. You and me. That definitely rings a bell."

Gambino was shutting my front door behind him as I pulled a left into the driveway.

"I put some champagne in an ice bucket."

"Aren't you jumping the gun?"

"I don't know. Am I?" He was walking toward me.

"Where'd you find an ice bucket? I don't have an ice bucket."

We were face-to-face now, still talking into our phones.

"I bought one."

"You hate shopping."

"Cece," he said, "answer the question."

"What question exactly are we talking about?"

He took the phone out of my hand and pulled me close. "Am I jumping the gun?"

"No," I said slowly. "You aren't jumping the gun."

"I don't think so either."

"You don't *think* so? Don't you *know* so?"

Poor guy. I gave him no choice. He had to shut me up with a kiss.

About the Author

Susan Kandel is a former art critic for the *Los Angeles Times*. She has taught at New York University and UCLA, and served as the director of the international journal *artext*. She lives in West Hollywood, California.